PRAISE FOR TRACY BROGAN

Crazy Little Thing

"So funny and sexy, I caught myself laughing out loud."
—Robin Covington, *USA Today*, Happy Ever After

"Witty one-liners and hilarious characters elevate this familiar story . . . Readers will love the heat between the leads and by the end they'll be clamoring for more."
—*RT Book Reviews*, 4 stars (HOT)

"Brogan . . . shows a real knack for creating believable yet quirky characters. Her contemporary romance has the usual misunderstandings and requisite happy ending, but the surprising emotional twists along the way make it a satisfying romp."
—*Booklist*

Highland Surrender

"Plenty of action, romance and sex with well-drawn individuals—a strong, yet young heroine and a delectable hero—who don't act out of character. The story imparts a nice feeling of 'you are there,' with a well-presented look at the turbulent life in 16th-century Scotland."
—*RT Book Reviews*, 4 stars (Scorcher)

"You know a historical romance is a keeper when you daydream about time traveling back to that setting and meeting the characters. I adored this lush, panoramic love story and didn't want it to end. Myles and Fiona and their sexy yet dangerous world of medieval Scotland kept me spellbound all the way to the heart-stopping, thoroughly satisfying conclusion. I want more from this fabulous author—the sooner the better!"
—Kieran Kramer, *USA Today* best-selling author of *Loving Lady Marcia*

hold on my HEART

ALSO BY TRACY BROGAN

Crazy Little Thing

Highland Surrender

TRACY BROGAN

hold on my HEART

The characters and events portrayed in this book are fictitious. Any similarity to real persons, living or dead, is coincidental and not intended by the author.

Published by Montlake Romance
P.O. Box 400818
Las Vegas, NV 89140

ISBN-10: 1611098882
ISBN-13: 9781611098884

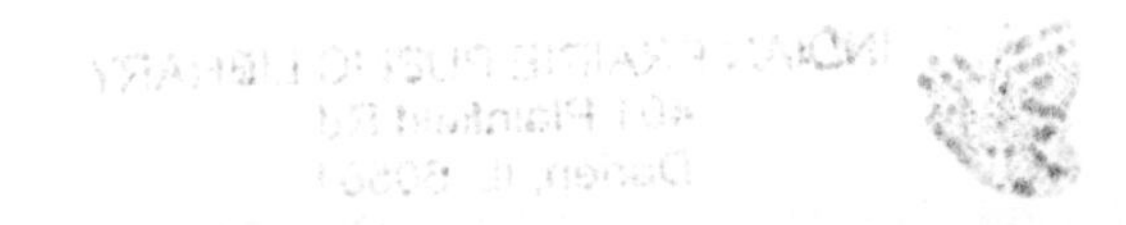

For my mother, who is probably wishing right now that I'd do something different with my hair.

CHAPTER *one*

"I don't mean to hurt your feelings, Dad, but this place looks like a crack house."

Libby Hamilton frowned at the dingy interior of the abandoned one-room schoolhouse and shook a possum-sized dust bunny from her running shoe. The aroma of funky dog tinged with faint undertones of broccoli having passed through a digestive system assaulted her nostrils. Her resulting sneeze echoed through the empty room, sending whorls of dust into the single shaft of light coming through a cracked windowpane.

She had been lured into this decrepit building under false pretenses. Her father had promised her a morning bike ride and a cup of coffee. She should have known he was up to some kind of shenanigans. Instead of exercise and caffeine, she was getting his visionary monologue about transforming this pile of historic scrap wood into a vintage ice-cream parlor.

At least this was one she hadn't heard before. Implausible schemes and Peter Hamilton went together like George Washington and the proverbial cherry tree, but this venture was grandiose, even for her dad.

Libby sneezed again and checked the time on her watch. She had an interview that afternoon for a job she'd be perfect for. A job she desperately wanted. One she desperately *needed,* too. But it was an hour-long drive into the city, so even if she wanted to indulge her father's latest whim, she didn't have the time.

"Seriously, Dad. I need to get moving. Let's go."

Her father stood with his hands on his hips, his pale, skinny legs protruding from khaki shorts. He smiled at one wall, then another, as if miraculous transformations were taking shape even as he gazed about. He looked younger than his sixty-seven years, with his hair just a hint more silver than dark brown, but a year of retirement had left him restless instead of relaxed.

"Sure, it's nothing to look at now, Liberty, but this place has real character. Scores of little pioneer children must have spent time here, reading their primers and practicing arithmetic on slates. There would have been rows of wooden desks and maybe a chalkboard over here. This place would make a delightful ice-cream shop. Can't you picture it?"

Libby was a corporate event planner in Chicago. At least she had been until a few months ago, when she'd been unceremoniously fired. She knew exactly how to size up an empty room and evaluate its potential, but whatever appeal her father saw in this shell of a building was beyond her comprehension.

Maybe losing her job had cost her more than her dignity and self-esteem. And possibly her boyfriend and her apartment. Maybe it had robbed her of her vision, too.

Libby had lost count of how many job rejections she'd gotten lately, but each one felt like a face-plant on rough cement. And all because she'd accidentally hit "reply all" and sent an email to every employee of Kendrew/Graham & Associates stating her boss possessed fewer brain cells than a potted geranium and possessed all the cuddly appeal of a cactus wrapped in barbed wire. It was a stupid, silly email, meant to be a joke for one person, yet it cost Libby more than just a job. It was costing her a career. Because apparently it's hard to get a good reference after suggesting your boss is a moron. Even if you apologize.

Libby plucked her damp T-shirt away from her skin. It was stuffy in here, in this dark hovel, the air pressing down like a wool blanket. But it wasn't the temperature making her skin prickle. It was regret.

Unemployment made her sweaty. And demoralized. She'd never realized how much her identity revolved around what she did for a living. Or that all her friends were work associates. Without projects to talk about, Libby didn't have much to offer.

She was good at her job, but now that she'd lost it, she suddenly didn't feel good at virtually anything at all.

"The soda fountain could go right along this wall." Her father gestured to one side. "And we could put some small tables over here. And more outside. Your mother will love it. She'll think it's a fabulous idea." His blue eyes glowed bright with a kind of desperate enthusiasm.

Libby's chuckle felt as hollow as it sounded. "Uh, I bet she won't. Has she been inside this place?"

If patience was an Olympic event, Libby's mother would have once been a gold medalist, but too many challenges had worn her down. Like the time Libby's dad decided to fence in their yard so they could become alpaca breeders. Or the time he bought two sheep from Craigslist so he wouldn't have to mow the lawn. But what had really extinguished his wife's enthusiasm was the time he brought Nana Hamilton home to live with them.

Her father shook his head. "No, I haven't brought your mother here. I want her to be surprised."

"Oh, she'll be surprised all right. Look, I hate to rain on your old-fashioned soda-fountain parade here, Dad, but you're a history teacher. You don't know anything about running an ice-cream parlor."

His caterpillar brows lifted at the challenge. "I don't know how to ride an elephant either, but I can learn." He pointed over the door. "That extraordinary trim work is from the original building. Do you know what it would cost to install hand-carved trim like that today?"

"No. Do you?"

Honestly, her father must be having some sort of post-retirement crisis to even consider buying this catastrophe with walls. It may have been a charming old schoolhouse in its day, but now it sat like an aging prom queen, forgotten and forlorn, knowing time had passed it by without a second glance.

Nudging dark-rimmed glasses up the bridge of his nose, her father eyed her squarely. "As a matter of fact, young lady, I do know what it would cost. I've done quite a bit of research, and this place has tremendous potential. The city commission just changed the zoning all along this side of the lake, and these wonderful old buildings are going to get snatched up by savvy guys like me. All we need is a little elbow grease and a good marketing strategy, and we could be the next big thing. Maybe we can even get a TV show out of it."

His tenacity was impressive, even if his logic was about as sturdy as the cracked foundation beneath her feet. Libby hadn't seen him this worked up since he won front-row tickets to see Lyle Lovett at the Monroe County Amphitheater. It was kind of adorable, but it was also a little sad, because this ice-cream parlor thing was never going to happen.

"Getting this place up and running would take a ton of work and a boatload of money, Dad. I'm sorry. I just don't think Mom is going to go for it."

His shoulders drooped. He turned away and scuffed at something on the floor with his old Top-Sider. "Well, that's where I was hoping you could help me out."

Libby crossed her arms, her skin prickling once more. "I doubt it. Mom's already on my case about finding a job. And she's been pestering me for details about why I moved out of Seth's apartment and came back home. I can't give her any more ammunition. Besides, do you really think I'd have better luck convincing her to let you buy it?"

He turned to face her again, jaw stiff and tilted upward. "No. But I want you on my side when I tell her I already did."

Libby's breath popped from her lungs in a painful burst. "You already bought it? With what money?"

His skin flushed. "We had some money set aside for . . . well, for whatever might come up, and I took out a tiny loan, but this is an investment for our future. The whole town's future, really. This building is a historic landmark." His hands landed on his hips again. "You know, Liberty, ever since I retired, your mother has been telling me to find a hobby, find something to do. Well, this is it. I'm turning this place into a turn-of-the-century ice-cream parlor with a soda fountain and waitresses in old-fashioned uniforms. And saltwater taffy!"

He said the word *taffy* as if that were the key ingredient to a successful business venture.

"What possessed you, Dad? Even if you had the money for the building, what about the other stuff? Contractors and permits and furniture and ice-cream paraphernalia? Just updating the wiring in this place alone is going to cost a fortune. Mom is going to have a heart attack."

This was much worse than his buying a couple of sheep.

Her father shuffled on his feet like a sixteen-year-old caught between guilt and defiance. "I am my own man, Liberty, and I make my own decisions. I don't need to clear everything through your mother. I'm not some kind of . . . some kind of anglerfish!"

She'd regret asking. She knew that before the words even formed in her mouth, but it was like watching a car crash. "What do anglerfish have to do with anything?"

He puckered his lips for a moment and squinted at her. "Do you know how the anglerfish mates?"

"Oh, geez, Dad." Her hands turned to lead and dropped to her sides.

Peter Hamilton was fascinated by reproductive anomalies of the animal kingdom, and because of that, Libby and her sisters had grown up hearing all about how the banana slug has a penis as long as its body, and that bonobo monkeys have a proclivity for face-to-face copulation. And that bedbugs engage in something called traumatic insemination, which is apparently every bit as unappealing to a lady bedbug as it sounds.

"Just hear me out. It's fascinating stuff," he said, stepping closer. "When the male anglerfish chooses his mate, he attaches himself to her. Then he stays there. Forever. His digestive system erodes since he can't get his own food, and then the rest of his body is slowly absorbed into hers. Even his heart and his brain get sucked in because he doesn't need them anymore. Eventually there is nothing left. He literally just . . . fades away. As if he'd never existed at all." Her father's hand flitted against the air, a feather on the wind.

"Dad, you're not going to fade away into nothingness just because you retired. And you're not too reliant on Mom, if that's what you're driving at."

He shook his head. "It's more than retiring, Liberty. A man wants to leave his mark in this world."

"You left a pretty big mark in the football field over at Monroe High School when you crash-landed that hot-air balloon. Wasn't that enough?"

He frowned. "They were going to lose that football game anyway. And you know that's not what I mean. That's not the kind of legacy I want to leave for future generations."

"And an ice-cream parlor is?" She wanted to be supportive, but this pile of rubble was not the solution to his anglerfish issue.

"This building is the legacy." His voice grew louder and more certain. "It's a piece of the past, a one-room schoolhouse. It's pre–Civil War, you know."

"I know my history, Dad."

"Then you should understand it's a travesty to let these old buildings crumble to the ground. I'm not the only one who thinks so. We talked about it on the town council, and everyone agrees we should invest in this whole area." He gestured to the street, his eyes bright, his cheeks flushed. "You could join me, you know."

A butterfly of eagle-sized proportion flapped in her stomach. Her father could be persuasive to the point of hypnotic, but she did not want to get drawn into one of his adventures. She had her own troubles to worry about. Namely, finding a new job and working things out with her boyfriend, Seth. Things between them had been strained ever since she'd lost her job, and she had to fix that. She did not have the time or energy to get sucked into some vortex of her father's.

"Join you in what way?"

"Be my business partner."

She might have laughed at that little bit of absurdity, but surprise squeezed every bit of air from her lungs, leaving her breathless.

Still, her father stared at her, nodding with encouragement. "Think of it, Liberty. You've got the time right now. You can keep looking for another job, of course. I know you want to get another corporate job and move back to Chicago, but until you find something, I could sure use your help and expertise." He gazed at her expectantly.

She found some breath and used it to laugh this time. "My expertise? Other than loving ice cream, I have no expertise that could help you."

"Sure you do. You're a details person. The perfect complement to my vision. You can help with getting permits and ordering supplies and keeping things on track. And when the place is ready, you can plan the big grand opening. It'll be glorious."

Rock. Libby. Hard place.

She was currently living at home, sponging off her parents like a deadbeat dropout. They wouldn't accept her money for rent or food because they pitied her. It was beyond humiliating. This was the first thing either of them had asked of her since she'd moved back. How could she say no? But how could she say yes?

"I just don't know, Dad. You have to let me think about it, okay?"

Her father's smile tightened. "Okay. I understand. But this could be really fun. Remember when we built the birdhouses together? We had a great time, didn't we?"

"We forgot to add holes, and the birds couldn't get in."

He shrugged. "Sure, but they enjoyed sitting on the roofs. And crapping all over them."

Why did she have a feeling that she was about to get crapped on herself? This was a lose-lose situation. Her mom was going to be mad, her dad was going to be disappointed, and adding carpentry skills to her current résumé was not going to help Libby find a job or fix things with Seth.

Her father reached over near her shoulder and caught a drifting cobweb with his fingertips, flicking it away. "It has a bell, you know."

"What?"

"A school bell, up on the roof. The rope is gone, but come upstairs with me, and I'll show you."

She didn't want to climb some rickety old steps to see an old bell. "What I need right now is functional plumbing. Does this place have a working bathroom?"

He shook his head. "Not currently. You'll have to go outside."

"Outside? It's broad daylight. Can't we just go home?"

Her father frowned. "Give me ten more minutes. I want to show you the bell tower. And the cellar. We have more exploring to do."

"Dad, I really need to pee."

"Well, there's a Dumpster out back. Just go cop a squat behind it. No one will see you."

Few things in life are more distasteful than urinating next to a Dumpster. Unless it's hearing your father tell you to cop a squat next to one. But nature was calling too loudly to ignore.

"If I get poison ivy I will never forgive you."

She stepped out the back door and spotted the Dumpster. A cluster of overgrown forsythia shaded most of it and might provide her a modicum of privacy. Plus her father was right. There were run-down old buildings on either side but certainly no people. Just the sounds of traffic rumbling in the distance.

Libby chose her spot and, with a final look to the right and left, shimmied her black shorts down her legs to assume a most undignified position. Nearly assaulted by a frisky weed, she shuffled forward to avoid its advances, her motion complicated by the restriction of the spandex bike shorts. Cop a squat, indeed. This was ridiculous. Her bladder thought so, too, and resisted—but at last, relief.

Except that she was peeing on her foot.

"Damn it!" She moved too abruptly, lost her balance, and fell back with a *whoosh*, whacking her arm against the side of the Dumpster. It was filthy and foul, and with nothing to grab on to, she fell to the ground with a *whoof* and a *thud*. Breathless, she lay sprawled out in the dirt and weeds, her shorts twisted at her knees. "Damn it!" she said again, louder this time.

"Hello?" A masculine voice floated around the corner of the old schoolhouse, followed by the six-foot-plus-something man who came with it.

Libby gasped and flopped like a fish on a hook as she tried to twist and stand up while simultaneously pulling up her resistant shorts.

He caught sight of her, his brown eyes going wide before he turned away and blocked his vision with his hand. "Holy— Oh, uh, sorry. Are you okay?"

Libby managed to scramble to her feet and yank up her shorts, but she could feel bits of gravel and weed fragments stuck to her ass. Her face burned with humiliation. Couldn't a girl get a moment to herself around here?

The man glanced through his splayed fingers. "Are you okay?" he asked again, his voice solicitous but edged with humor.

"I'm fine!" She smoothed the waistband of her shorts. "I just fell down. What are you doing back here? This is private property."

"Not that private," he murmured, a smile tugging at his mouth.

"Excuse me?"

"I, ah . . . nothing. I was just looking for Peter Hamilton. Is he here?" His cheeks flushed under tanned skin.

She slipped her hand inside the back of her shorts discreetly to dislodge a pebble ingrained in her skin. "That's my father. He's inside."

He looked at the door, then back at Libby. "Should I just go in?"

"Oh, come on," she said with more growl than she intended. "I'll show you."

It couldn't have been some sweet little old lady with bad eyesight who found Libby splayed out in the weeds without her pants. Oh, no. It had to be a guy like this. A macho type . . . with wavy chestnut hair and shoulders as wide as a doorframe.

A little smirk played around the corner of his mouth. She frowned. That smirk was at her expense.

"Dad," she barked as they stepped inside. "There's somebody here to see you."

Her father appeared from a doorway, wiping a cobweb from the front of his shirt. "Oh, hello there!" He extended his arm. "Are you Tom Murphy?"

Peeping Tom was more like it.

The man nodded and shook hands with her father. "You must be Mr. Hamilton."

"I am. Proprietor of this fine establishment. I see you've met my daughter."

The man nodded once, not meeting her eyes. "Sort of."

Libby sighed audibly. "Dad, you didn't mention you were expecting someone."

"I wasn't sure when he was coming. But how lucky that you caught us here," her father said.

Libby winced. She was the one who'd been caught.

Her father continued, the smile on his face bright. "Tom, this is my daughter, Liberty Belle Hamilton."

Insult, meet injury.

It wasn't bad enough this stranger had seen her floundering with her pants down next to the Dumpster, now he also knew the full extent of her ridiculous name, courtesy of her history-loving father.

"Just Libby," she corrected.

Another single nod and a fast flick of the man's big brown eyes completed the introductions.

"Tom is a builder. And a restoration specialist," her father said. "He's going to help us get this place back to her former glory, isn't that right?"

Tom tipped his head. "I'll try. Let's have a look around and see what we've got to work with."

The men started walking toward the other side of the room, leaving her behind.

"There's a lot to be done, but I'd love your ideas on where to start," Libby heard her father say.

The man chuckled as he answered, "I think I'd start with a Porta-John."

CHAPTER *two*

The Hamilton clan, minus one, was gathered in the sage green dining room for their once-a-month-you'd-better-not-miss-it Sunday dinner, the invitation for which was as binding as a subpoena. Beverly Hamilton, Libby's mother, sat at one end, presiding judiciously, her red-gold hair held back from her face by a brown barrette. A sturdy platter piled high with succulent roast beef surrounded by steaming vegetables was in the center of the table, smelling delicious and ready to be eaten, but as usual, they were waiting for Libby's youngest sister.

Libby shifted on her wooden chair and tried to sneak the corner from the dinner roll in front of her.

Her father glanced down at his watch, his forehead creased in annoyance. "Beverly, let's just start without her, or this will all be too cold to eat."

"Thank goodness. I'm starving." Libby's older sister, Ginny, reached for the mashed potatoes and plopped a huge mound onto her plate. "Doesn't she realize when she makes us wait, she's making the baby wait, too?"

Ginny was older than Libby by thirteen months and four days, and wore the crown of that achievement regally on her strawberry blond hair. Libby was forever trying to catch up. It wasn't a race, of course, but thanks to the recent setbacks in Libby's personal and professional life,

Ginny was a career, a husband, and a pregnancy ahead of her. Libby needed to get her life in order soon, or she'd be lapped by a sweet-smelling newborn baby.

Ginny smoothed a hand over her expanded belly, the fabric of her pink-striped shirt taut and nearly giving up at the seams, before she reached for the gravy. She was round and plump and serene, one half of a picture-perfect couple. Her husband, Ben, sat next to her, his arm draped around her chair and his sandy-blond head tipped close, just in case Ginny should need to whisper some sweet little something into his ear.

Looking at them, Libby felt the twinge of missing . . . all of that.

She hadn't confided in anyone about the status of her relationship with Seth. How could she, when she wasn't entirely certain of it herself? They'd lived together for a year and a half and dated for two before that. And not once in all that time had they talked about any future beyond the next weekend. They'd never discussed getting married or having children, except in the most abstract way. And she hadn't minded. Much.

Libby wasn't pining away for a diamond ring or a white picket fence in the suburbs. She didn't need a proposal from Seth. But she did need the promise of a future, something to be certain of and to cling to when everything else seemed unstable and out of reach. But once she'd lost her job, her fair-weather boyfriend became decidedly vague about their relationship. And then he asked for her half of the rent.

It was Seth's idea for her to leave Chicago and stay with her parents until she found a new job. He was traveling all the time for work anyway, and so it made sense. Sort of. But she'd been home a month now, and he didn't seem to be missing her all that much.

"Mother, can I get you some roast?" Libby's father asked Nana, nudging Libby back to the moment.

Nana Hamilton spread her dark green napkin across her tiny lap. "If you could find a bit that's not too overcooked, that would be nice. Beverly's roasts are a little tough."

Libby's grandmother was hard of hearing, or at least pretended to be so she could say whatever she wanted to in a dramatic stage whisper and then feign embarrassment when she was overheard. Not that she was any gentler when speaking directly to someone. "Ginny, that extra weight you've put on won't come off the same day the baby is born, you know. Maybe you should put back some of those potatoes."

"Thank you for your concern, Nana." Ginny put another scoop of potatoes on her plate, clanking the spoon against the side.

"Ginny has been taking great care of herself, Nana," Ben said dutifully. "And I hope our baby girl looks just like her."

Libby's father passed the platter laden with beef. "So, the baby is a she? I thought it was a boy."

"We thought so last week." Ben nodded. "But this morning, Ginny decided he was a girl."

"I had a dream she was a girl," Ginny explained.

"Can't you get a picture taken so you know what it is?" Nana asked.

"I want to be surprised," Ginny answered.

"She'll be surprised, all right," Nana fake-whispered to Libby. "That baby's going to weigh seven pounds, and she's gained fifty."

"I dreamt all three of you were boys," said Libby's mother, talking over Nana. "Except for the one time I dreamt Marti was a baby ostrich. *That* was disturbing."

Her comment was interrupted by a crash, a bang, and a clatter as the third Hamilton daughter burst through the front door. She wore cargo pants and a gray T-shirt. She was flushed and giggling and dragging a scruffy young man behind her.

Libby turned to Ginny and rolled her eyes.

Ginny nodded in silent agreement.

Marti's boy toys were like snowflakes. No two were exactly alike, and they seemed to drift away just as silently as they arrived. This soul mate du jour was mangier than most, with long black hair, ripped jeans, and a vivid green dragon tattoo clawing its way up his left forearm.

"Oh, Mom! I'm so sorry we're late!" Marti said, her multiple necklaces swaying as she bent over to kiss her father's cheek. "Hi, Daddy. Hi, everybody. This is Dante."

The newcomer raised his tattooed arm in greeting and smiled a lopsided smile. "Hello, family."

Marti nudged him into the chair next to Libby. "Here, baby. Sit in this one." She grabbed an extra chair from the corner and plopped down next to him, her auburn hair swirling around her face. Marti was twenty-two, looked twelve, and acted somewhere in between. "So, did we miss anything?"

"Did you lose your phone again? You might have called," Libby's mother said. "I was getting worried."

"I'm sorry. I meant to call, but . . ." Marti stole a glance at Dante and giggled again. "We lost track of time."

Ginny let out a faint grunt of distaste. Ben patted her hand.

Libby's mother pursed her lips for a minute, and her shoulders lifted a fraction before she said, "Well, we're all here now. Welcome to our home . . . Dante, is it?"

He nodded.

"Well, Dante, help yourself to some roast beef."

Marti shook her head. "Oh, no thanks. We'll just have the salad. Dante is vegan."

A hush fell over Libby's meat-and-potato-loving family.

"Did she say he's a heathen?" Nana said. She didn't even pretend to whisper that.

"He's also a locavore, but we'll make do with what's here," Marti added.

"He's a loca—what?" Libby's father asked, shaking his head as if it might rattle.

"A locavore, Daddy. It's someone who only eats foods that are grown locally."

"That's . . . interesting," Ben said.

Libby exchanged another eye roll with Ginny. This guy wouldn't last through an entire meal at this house.

Her father waved around an inordinately large bite of meat before stuffing it into his mouth. After chewing and swallowing he asked, "So, Dante, did you two meet at school?"

The dragon guy grinned. "Hardly."

"We met at that medieval banquet I went to a couple of weeks ago." Marti turned toward her mother. "I told you about it. Remember? Dante was my jousting champion. I tied a scarf on his lance, just like in the movies. It was so romantic." Her delicate cheeks blushed rosy pink, and she looked back at him like he was a fluffy kitten, a yummy donut, and a million bucks all rolled into one.

He leaned over and kissed her with a loud, juicy smack.

Ginny let out another huff of dismay as Libby just stared.

Her father cleared his throat. "Well, Dante, that's . . . also very interesting. So where do you go to college?"

Dante took a bite of salad and talked around it. "Life is my education. I don't need college."

Three of Libby's family members simultaneously choked on their food. To almost anyone with Hamilton DNA, there was no higher calling than academia. Libby's father had taught history for thirty years at Monroe High School, and her mother and Ginny both taught there now. Libby was decidedly the black sheep for choosing corporate America over the blackboard jungle.

"Everyone needs college," her mother said, aghast.

"Could we hold off on the inquisition for a bit and just enjoy this dinner, please?" Marti said.

Dante glanced around and finally seemed to realize his mistake. "I don't have anything against college. I tried it for a while, but it wasn't a good fit for me."

"Dante is a jousting instructor," Marti said. "And he's studying filmmaking, just not in a formal program."

Libby knew if Seth was there, he'd bet ten bucks that meant the kid sat around all day watching movies and talking about how he could make them better. She took a bite of roast beef and was glad to not be a locavore.

"So, Ginny," Marti said, clearly intent on redirecting the conversation, "are you sure there's only one baby in there? You're looking kind of wide."

Ginny wiped a bit of gravy off the front of her shirt with a napkin. "I have *not* gained too much weight. Someday you and Libby will be pregnant, and you'll see—"

"All right. All right. Let's not start bickering." Their father tapped his fingers against the tabletop, drumroll style. "Now that you're all here, I have an announcement to make."

Libby glanced at her mother, taking a mental "before the homicidal breakdown" snapshot. She'd hoped her father might hold off on this grand proclamation until after dessert. There was strawberry shortcake in the kitchen, and she really wanted some, but she could hardly sit there eating it while her mother wept. Could she?

Her father cleared his throat again. "Since my retirement last year, it's no secret I've been floundering a bit. There's only so much golf a man can play, especially since I don't particularly like golf."

He seemed to be waiting for them to chuckle. Open with a joke and all that. Only no one laughed, even his own mother, so he plowed forward, making eye contact with each of them to ensure their rapt attention. "I have found myself a project. A pretty big one, and you are all invited to help me with it, if you'd like to. Or not. It's your choice."

"What are you talking about, Peter?" Beverly prompted.

He took a sip of water. Libby saw the liquid quaking in the glass as he set it back on the table.

"Beverly, kids, Mom, I bought the old Mason schoolhouse, and I'm going to turn it into a vintage, turn-of-the-century ice-cream parlor."

A *whoosh* of stunned silence swept through the room. The air around Libby felt thick with their disbelief. She looked at their stunned faces, her gaze finally landing on her mother.

Beverly's expression blanked even as a telltale flush crept up her peach-hued skin. She touched her throat with one hand. "You did . . . what?"

"I bought the old Mason schoolhouse, and I'm turning it into an ice-cream parlor." He said it with a hint of defiance this time, as if saying it louder and faster made it seem like a better idea. "I have all the details worked out. Well, most of them. And I've asked Libby to help me," he added with far too much enthusiasm.

"I haven't said yes." Libby shook her head.

Her father frowned at her lack of solidarity.

She couldn't help him. She really wanted that shortcake.

Beverly blinked rapidly. "I see." Her voice was honey-soft, but her skin was turning a mottled sort of fire-ant red.

"Which place?" Nana asked.

"The Mason schoolhouse, over near the lake." He smiled tentatively at his wife. "I didn't want to tell you beforehand, Bev, because I wanted it to be a surprise. So . . . surprise!" His voice was strained with painfully false glee.

Libby shook her head at his simplicity. He was playing the dense card, pretending it had never occurred to him that her mother would be upset. Then he could act wounded and victimized when she got angry. It was textbook passive-aggressive. Nana had taught him that.

"That's amazing, Daddy," Marti said. "What a fabulous idea. Everybody loves ice cream."

"It's a crazy idea, Marti," Ginny scoffed. "Daddy's not a businessman. And the economy right now is terrible." She turned to her father. "Do you mean that old dump on Arbor Drive? There's nothing down there but empty buildings. No one will go down there for ice cream."

"Ah, that's where you're wrong, Virginia." Her father pointed at her with one hand while gripping the arm of his chair with the other. "The city council wants to renovate the entire area. They're adding a bike path and a new boat launch. That whole stretch along the lake will become just like the old Atlantic City boardwalk."

Like the fish that got away, every time her father told this story, it grew in size. There was just no telling where actual fact stopped and his optimistic vision began.

"The first businesses in, like mine, will anchor the whole development. There is even talk of bringing back the old merry-go-round that was there in the forties."

Yep, that was a new twist.

Her father smiled more broadly now. "Isn't it exciting, Bev?"

A thin white line had appeared around the edge of her mother's lips. Her eyes were like a doll's, round and unseeing. "Exciting? Peter, what do you mean you bought it?"

He rolled his shoulders. "I used some of our savings, and I bought it."

Her fingers fluttered around her throat again, and Libby felt real sympathy for her mother.

"How much of our savings?" Her voice was as thin as smoke.

"Not all of it. Just a little, and well . . . Libby's wedding fund."

A sizable boulder fell off a cliff and landed smack on the top of Libby's head. "My wedding fund? That's what you used?"

She hadn't even known her parents had a "Libby's wedding fund," but the fact that her father just spent it on that fossil of a building showed a distinct lack of his confidence in her ability to find a husband. She was only twenty-eight. There was still time.

"Her wedding fund?" Marti gasped. "What about my wedding fund? Is there still one for me?"

Libby's father waved his hand in her sister's direction. "You're only twenty-two years old, Marti. We'll have plenty of time later to save up for your wedding fund."

"Um, not really."

Everyone's gaze swung to Marti, and that *whoosh* of silence came back for another pass.

Marti flushed a shiny pink and glanced at Dante. He nodded and smiled, still eating his salad as if this were normal dinner conversation.

With a girlish giggle, she held up her left hand, showing off a chunky, green stone set on a thick, tarnished band. Somewhere a Cracker Jack box was missing its prize. "Dante and I are getting married."

"Your family is losing it," Ben murmured to Ginny.

"That's not funny, Martha," Beverly said. "We're discussing your father and this building he bought."

"It's not supposed to be funny," Marti said. "It's supposed to be awesome."

Dante leaned in and hugged her to his side. "It *is* awesome, babe."

Libby's father drew in a long, labored breath and pointed his finger at the interloper at his table. "This Dante? This college dropout with the ink all over his arms? I don't think so. No offense, kid."

Ginny reached over and grabbed Marti's hand, tugging it closer for examination. "That's not an engagement ring. Engagement rings are diamonds. I don't know what that is."

Marti snatched her hand back. "Geez, Ginny. It's an engagement ring if we say it is. Does everything have to be your way?"

"What do you mean you're getting married?" Libby's mother's voice cracked. The mottled splotches on her face went from red to purple. This was just not her night.

"Just like what it sounds like. We're getting married in two months, and we are going to live happily ever after. That is so awesome about the ice-cream parlor, by the way, Daddy. I am totally with you on this one."

Libby hiccupped. Two months? Marti and this derelict had known each other for three weeks and were already engaged, and she couldn't wrangle a proposal out of Seth after more than a year of cohabitation? Not that she'd really tried, but still—Marti was taking cuts in line. Libby should get married first.

"You're twenty-two years old, Martha," her father said again. "You are not getting married." His hands thumped down hard on the arms of his chair.

"In two months? What kind of wedding can you plan in two months?" Ginny said.

"I don't really think that's the issue here, Gin," Libby interrupted. "How about the fact that they don't actually know each other?"

Marti frowned. "We *do* know each other, all the important stuff anyway, and we can plan a perfect wedding. Libby can help us make the arrangements, and it will be amazing because we love each other."

"We do." Dante nodded and took another bite of lettuce.

Help them make the arrangements? Libby was a business event planner, not a wedding planner.

"Marti, this is nonsense. You can't possibly expect your father and me to blindly endorse your marrying someone we just met. And someone you barely know. This is all very abrupt." Libby's mother took a gulp from the wineglass in front of her.

Dante nodded sagely. "I totally understand you feeling that way, Mother Hamilton. Marti is precious, and you want what's best for her. So do I, and I'm it."

Jaws dropped, but none so far or so fast as her mother's.

Her father's fist thumped down on the table, his voice low in his throat. "Young man, don't you presume to tell us what's best for our daughter. Getting married at her age is not . . ." Suddenly his face blanched. "Oh, God. Martha. You're not . . ."

Beverly's intake of breath was a strangled sort of whimper, but Marti's eye roll was teen-queen dramatic. "Geez, Daddy! No, I'm not pregnant." She looked over at Dante, not the least bit chagrined. "At least, if I am, it's too early to tell."

CHAPTER *three*

"This area used to be quite the posh place to visit." Libby's father stood out front, gazing at his newly purchased yet very old schoolhouse. Marti was with them, too, but he wasn't really speaking to her since she refused to undo her engagement, and Libby wasn't really speaking to him since he had spent her previously unbeknownst-to-her wedding money.

Still, being with each other was better than staying at home and listening to her mother sniffle and sigh. The one-two punch of the ice-cream parlor and Dante the shaggy bridegroom had been too much for her. She was lying on the sofa at home with a cold washcloth on her forehead.

Libby's father shielded his eyes from the sun. "In the 1880s, the trolley line from downtown Monroe ended right over there. And over on that side, that building was a coach stop. The Mason Bridge Inn. Folks used to stop in there for a spirituous libation."

"You mean a beer?" Libby asked.

Her father nodded. "Or a julep. Maybe I should try to get a liquor license."

Libby shook her head. "Whoa. Slow down there, cowboy. You're getting ahead of yourself again. So far we have twenty-seven things written on this to-do list, and we haven't even gone inside yet."

In spite of being annoyed by her father's haphazard choices, Libby had agreed to help with his schoolhouse-to-ice-cream-parlor transformation.

She had the skills necessary to keep even him on track. And she sure didn't have anything else to occupy her time. No interviews lined up, and the last one in Chicago had gone so epically bad she was certain there would be no offer.

She'd been so ready for it, too. All dressed up in her best sexy but professional suit, with a portfolio of event photos arranged on her iPad to share with her future employer. She'd rehearsed answers for every possible question as she drove from Monroe to the city, even the most obvious one.

Chicago was a big town, but the event-planning community was tight, and her poster-child-for-bad-judgment email had made the rounds. So Libby memorized a carefully crafted response, specific enough to be honest but ambiguous enough to avoid discussing the mishap concerning her old boss if at all possible. But then the inevitable moment came. *Why did you leave your last job?*

Her mind went shockingly, brilliantly blank. All her years as an event planner had given her catlike reflexes. There she was, a problem-solving, out-of-the-box-thinking, fire-dousing ninja. But she just sat there, dazed as if waiting for a Magic 8 Ball to answer for her.

ALL SIGNS POINT TO NO.

What the hell? Libby Hamilton had lost her mojo.

She fumbled her way through the rest of the interview, babbling something innocuous about professional growth and her quest for a challenging career, but afterward she wasn't even certain what she'd said.

She'd had dinner in Chicago that night with work friends who caught her up on the latest office gossip, but it just made her feel worse. She wasn't in that loop anymore. All her knowledge and skills were evaporating like the polar ice caps. Seth was in San Diego for his own job, so she hadn't even bothered stopping by her old apartment. She just drove back to Monroe, feeling useless and wondering if he'd call as promised.

He didn't. He'd sent a text instead that said *MISS U. WILL CALL TOMORROW.*

Nothing was the way it had been. And nothing was the way it was supposed to be.

Libby heard the click of a camera and turned to see Marti pointing a sizable lens in her direction.

"Why did you do that?"

Marti smiled. "Dante and I are going to make a documentary of the building renovation. I told him I'd get some still shots today *since Daddy won't let him on the property*." She said the last bit extra loud and glared at their father.

"Don't start with me, young lady." He waved a finger in Marti's direction.

Marti shrugged and snapped another picture. "Stand up on the porch, you guys. Let me get a couple of shots of you up there."

Her father hesitated, but for only a moment. Libby sensed his internal struggle. He wanted to stay mad at Marti, but none of them ever could, and besides that, she knew he was grudgingly thrilled at the prospect of filming this adventure.

They climbed the few steps, and her dad leaned against a sagging railing.

"That's not going to hold you," Libby warned, as the wood creaked under his weight.

"Yes it will." He bounced against it, and the wood splintered in defeat. "Well, shit," he muttered.

Libby's laugh was cut short by the loud rumble of an aging truck turning into the drive. Tom Murphy had arrived, in a faded blue pickup. A flutter of residual embarrassment tickled low in Libby's body. Maybe he'd forgotten their inauspicious first meeting. Because most guys wouldn't think twice about seeing a woman with her pants down, right?

She swallowed the dull pain in her throat as Tom parked next to her father's sedan and climbed down from the cab. He gave them all a quick nod before leaning in to pull some long, rolled blueprints and a manila folder from inside.

"Good morning!" Libby's father hopped back off the porch and greeted Tom brightly.

"Good morning, Mr. Hamilton," Tom replied.

"Please, call me Peter. And you remember my daughter Liberty."

Tom nodded, one corner of his mouth lifted in a lazy half-smile, and he gave her a look that said he very much remembered seeing her with her pants down.

Libby straightened her shoulders and felt heat stealing over her cheeks.

Her father gestured toward Marti. "And this is my youngest daughter, Martha."

Marti bounded forward, smiling wide. Her auburn hair was plaited into two thick braids. With a dusting of freckles and flip-flop sandals, she looked more high school freshman than college senior.

"Hey, Tom. Nice to meet you."

"Martha is making a documentary of our progress here. I hope you don't mind if she takes a few pictures."

"I don't mind. Just remember it's a work site." Tom pulled a pencil from behind his ear and pointed it at Libby's feet. "You girls can't run around here in those flimsy things."

Libby bristled. She wasn't some mindless child, skipping around land mines. She had sturdier shoes in her dad's car, but it was hot today. Sandal weather. She opened her mouth to explain that, but Tom was already walking toward the building.

"I've ordered an industrial Dumpster," he said to her father. "That one out back is too small. We can salvage some things, but we'll have plenty to throw out. I've got some old photos from the historical society, but the original blueprints are long gone. Best I could find were these from about 1960, when this place was used as an insurance office."

Libby scampered after them. "I have better shoes with me," she said, when they paused by the front step.

Tom looked at her as if he'd already forgotten she was there. "That's good. Maybe you should put them on." He turned and went inside with her father.

Libby clenched her teeth, feeling as foolish as she had with her ass exposed next to the Dumpster. She heard the click of Marti's camera.

"Did you just take my picture again?" she demanded.

"Yes."

"Why?"

Marti shrugged, and smiled innocently. "I don't know. You had an interesting look on your face."

Libby scowled and stomped toward her dad's car to get her sensible shoes. "Well, warn me before you do that."

Marti trotted along next to her. "I probably won't. It's part of my creative process. But hey, you didn't tell me that restoration guy was so smoldery."

Libby stole a fast glance over her shoulder to make sure they couldn't be overheard. "Is he? I hadn't noticed." That was a lie. She'd noticed all right, but Tom Murphy was not her type, and even if he was, she was in love with Seth.

Marti turned around and walked backward so she might stare at him through the doorway, her green eyes bright. "Are you kidding? He's smokin' hot. If I wasn't engaged, I'd be going for a little humpty-hump with that. Hey, maybe *you* should." She flicked Libby lightly on the arm.

Libby flicked her back, not as lightly. "I'm not looking for a humpty-hump, Farti. Remember Seth?"

Marti flicked, harder. "Don't call me that. And anyway, Seth is, like, ten thousand miles away."

"He's in San Diego this week. It's barely two thousand miles from here." Although he may as well be on the moon for all the luck she'd had getting in touch with him lately. Libby reached out and opened the door to her father's car to get her shoes.

"Two thousand or ten thousand, it's still too far to keep a relationship going. Dante and I have vowed to never go more than two days without seeing each other."

Libby bent down to unbuckle her sandal. "Well, that's very charming and cute and romantic, Marti, but it's completely impractical. Are you really serious about this wedding thing? You've had more boyfriends than I've had dates, and yet suddenly you think Dante is The One?"

"I know he is." Marti's eyes glowed with illogical reverence.

Libby tossed one sandal in the car and pulled on her shoe. "Listen, I'll support you, whatever you decide. But you're talking about a serious commitment. This isn't some crazy whim like the stuff Dad gets himself into. Marriage is real life."

"I know that. But true love is spontaneous and powerful and impossible to ignore. If you and Seth had that, you'd never be able to live apart like this. I'm just saying."

The fairy princess bound and gagged and residing down deep inside of Libby's subconscious wanted to agree that love meant being impetuous and wild and all that silly, rainbow-bright gibberish, but Libby knew better. Practicality trumped passion. That's the only reason she'd moved home when Seth suggested it.

"Spontaneous and impossible to ignore? Seriously, Marti, life isn't a cartoon. Seth and I are grown-ups, and sometimes you have to be logical and focus on the big picture. He's traveling all the time, and I'm saving a lot of money by living in Monroe instead of Chicago. As soon as I get a job, I'll move back, and we'll pick up right where we left off."

Libby tugged off her other sandal and chucked it in the car.

"That is the stupidest thing I've ever heard. He's just being a coward," Marti said.

Libby lost her balance and fell against the side of the car with a grunt. "What's that supposed to mean?"

"It means his M.O. is benign neglect."

"And again, what's *that* supposed to mean?" Libby finally got into her other shoe and planted both feet on the ground, but this conversation was still making her dizzy.

"It means that Seth is too much of a coward to break up with you face-to-face, so he's going to neglect you until you finally get so frustrated that *you* break up with *him*. That way he doesn't have to feel guilty for dumping you. Trust me. I have been broken up with by every method ever invented. This is benign neglect."

Libby sensed a cloud passing over, dimming the light as if the ghost of relationships past hovered near her head.

Marti gripped her shoulder. "Did he say he wants to see other people yet? Because when he does, it means he wants to see them naked."

Libby shrugged her shoulder away from Marti's grip. "No, he hasn't asked to see other people! God, Marti."

Then again, how could he ask when they hadn't actually spoken in days? Seth blamed the time difference between Illinois and California for his lack of communication, but Libby could read between the lines of all those emails he *wasn't* sending. Marti was right. Seth's behavior felt very much like neglect, but there was nothing benign about it.

Irritation buzzed in her head like a fly—a fly in a happily committed relationship that wanted to mock her. Whether her relationship with Seth was over, or they were just taking a detour, Libby wasn't certain, and until she had all her facts, she didn't want to talk about it. Certainly not to her baby sister who thought love was so easy.

Libby pushed away from the car and stomped toward the schoolhouse with Marti on her heels.

"I'm sorry, Libby. I know it sucks, but I hate to see you waiting for him. You should find a better guy."

Libby halted in her tracks as if a railroad crossing bar had just dropped in front of her. "Find a better guy? Marti, Seth and I have been together for almost four years. I'm not just going to toss that away because things are a little rocky for us right now. You treat commitment like it's a game of Candy Land, and that's just irresponsible."

Marti eyes went round and puddled with tears. "You don't have to be mean just because you're jealous of me and Dante."

"Jealous? Of you and the boy with the dragon tattoo? Oh, yeah, that's what this is," Libby said, circling a finger around her own face. "This is me. Being jealous."

But Marti's gaze was so earnest, Libby flushed with remorse. There was no point in snapping at her sister just for being naïve. After a pause, she tugged Marti's braid and sighed. "I'm sorry, Marti," she said quietly. "I'm not jealous. I'm glad you're happy. I just think you should wait before jumping into marriage. If he's the right one now, he'll still be the right one in six months when you know him better. Or next year, even, after you've finished college. Don't do this spontaneously just to prove it's the real thing."

Marti blinked and let a tear come down her cheek. "I can't explain it, Libby. I just know I'm right about Dante. Okay?"

This was everyone's fault. Marti had been coddled and snuggled and indulged her entire life. By all of them. That little smattering of freckles across her nose made her impossible to resist.

Libby swallowed down another sigh. "Okay. If you say so. At least your wedding announcement got Dad off the hook with Mom."

Marti smiled, her mood lightening in an instant. She hugged Libby around the waist.

"Thanks for trusting me. Now let's go inside so I can take some pictures of Hottie McHandyman."

Tom Murphy tightened his grip around the blueprints and tried to shake off his unease. This job was going to be a challenge. Not because the building was in such sad shape, although it was, but because Tom could already sense Peter Hamilton was a talker—a good-natured but bored retiree with too much time on his hands and not a lick of common sense about construction. One who was eager and invested and wanted to learn. But Tom wasn't there to show some old schoolteacher how to build. He was there to get the job completed. Get in, get done, get out. That was his philosophy.

And then there were the two Hamilton daughters in their short shorts and flip-flops, who looked very much like they intended to hang around. They'd call it helping, of course, but they'd just be in the way. That was a complication Tom didn't need. He had enough feminine drama in his life already.

Still, he needed the income. He didn't have another big project lined up, and this renovation would carry him all the way to Christmas, maybe longer. Plus the building itself had plenty of charm, with wide crown moldings, high ceilings, even a bell tower atop the high-peaked roof. Restoring old places like this felt good. It was tangible. He could see the improvements as they came, see how he had fixed it with his own hands. So right now he'd smile, and nod, and try to keep Mr. Hamilton and his flimsy-shoed daughters away from the power tools. Especially that Dumpster-diving one.

Liberty Belle Hamilton. What a name.

She sure was pretty, though.

The thought caught him like a bee sting, surprising and painful, lingering no matter how hard he tried to ignore it. She had the darkest blue eyes he'd ever seen and the kind of thick blond hair that turned to pure gold in sunlight. She didn't look half bad in those shorts, either. Or the ones from the other day, once she'd brushed off all the dirt. She seemed like the serious sort, not bouncy like her sister with the camera. Tom liked serious women. His wife had been a serious woman.

"Let's take a look at those blueprints," Mr. Hamilton said, moving toward the window.

"Sure. Here we go." Tom spread the papers out on top of an old cabinet left behind by the previous owners. "These are the oldest I've been able to track down, but honestly, pictures from the Monroe Historical Society will give you better ideas for restoration. Then you'll have to decide how historically accurate you want to go. The truth is, you can find new materials and fixtures to make this place appear historic for a lot less time and money than it'll take to actually locate period-accurate materials. And obviously safety and building codes come first."

"Of course." Peter nodded and pushed his glasses up. "This shop has to function efficiently as a business, too. I've been watching plenty of television shows on the Learning Channel lately to sharpen my knowledge of the food service industry. I've got a strategy in place."

Television shows? Tom hoped Peter Hamilton had a better grasp of what opening an ice-cream parlor entailed than whatever superfluous sound bites he'd picked up from staged interventions on a TV show. Like having an actual business plan, or knowing what the health codes for a commercial kitchen were. But in the end, that wasn't really his problem. Tom's job was to refurbish the building, make it structurally sound and visually appealing. Whatever happened after he handed the keys over to the Hamiltons was completely up to them.

Libby and her sister joined him and Peter a few minutes later, nudging in next to the cabinet to get a closer look. Tom noticed that at least Libby had the good sense to put on tennis shoes. Not exactly regulation, steel-toed work boots, but it was a start. Her shirt was turquoise blue with some sort of saying on it, but he couldn't quite make out the words without staring at her breasts. That curiosity would have to go unsatisfied.

Then she leaned forward, and her long, silky hair brushed over his forearm like a caress. An innocent thing, bound to happen in such close quarters, but it sent a jolt of electricity through him. He knew right then—Liberty Belle Hamilton was going to be a hazard.

CHAPTER *four*

Tom's old truck shimmied as he shifted to idle. He was late. Rachel would be annoyed. Then again, when *wasn't* she? His fifteen-year-old daughter was in a perpetual state of exasperation, at least around him.

Sure enough, her pink-cheeked face was marred by a scowl as she pushed through the double doors of Monroe High School and made her way toward him. She dipped her head, hiding behind a swish of wavy blond hair, and climbed into the cab. She was dressed in various shades of gray and black, like a dismal little sparrow.

"God, Dad, will you ever fix this truck? Your muffler is, like, sonically loud."

"Nice to see you, too. How's your day?" He waited for her to buckle her seat belt before shifting into gear.

Rachel wedged her backpack between them. "Fine. So far. What's this shrink's name again?"

His daughter was thin, all arms and legs and elbows and knees. She looked more like her mother every time he saw her. It was hard to get used to. It made him miss Connie even more. He turned his eyes back to the road and began to drive.

"Dr. Brandt. She's a friend of your aunt Kristy's." At Rachel's elongated sigh, he added, "She sounded very nice on the phone."

Rachel's head fell back against the seat with a soft *thud*. "So do pedophiles."

He pressed his lips together. What was the correct parenting technique for chronic sarcasm?

Rachel continued to glower at the ceiling as if it had insulted her, and another sigh escaped.

Tom gripped the steering wheel. He wished it was his daughter's hand so he could squeeze it with reassurance, but he had none to offer. The inches between them yawned like a canyon. He drove on, letting silence fill the space.

"Do we really have to do this?" Rachel finally asked, her voice small, the question directed to the window.

"Yes, Rachel, we do. Didn't Kristy talk to you about this?"

"She did. But the whole deal is creepy. It's like I'm going to couples therapy with my dad."

It was, a little, and he chuckled. "It's not couples therapy. It's grief counseling. To help us, well . . . you know."

"Grieve?"

"Yes."

She slumped down farther on the seat. "I'm pretty good at missing Mom, you know. I don't think I need a professional coach to tell me how."

His chuckle evaporated. "It's not to help you miss her. It's to teach us how to live . . . harmoniously together without her."

Rachel turned her face toward him, her pale blue eyes flashing. "I live harmoniously at Grandma and Grandpa's house just fine. If you'd let me stay there, everything else would be fine, too."

His knuckles whitened on the steering wheel. His stomach felt full of rocks. Rachel had been living with her grandparents for more than a year, ever since the car accident, but he wanted his daughter back in his house. He missed her. He missed her constant singing, and the smell of her waffles toasting before school. He missed her soft kiss on his cheek, and the way she'd giggle when they'd watched television together.

"Sweetheart, I want you to come home and live with me. Is that so hard to understand?"

"But I want to stay where I am. Is *that* so hard to understand?" Her voice broke, and she twisted back toward the window, letting her hair once again shield her expression.

She didn't want to live with him. She'd made that fact abundantly clear, and so had her grandparents.

Rachel remained silent for the rest of the short drive, and he wondered if this counseling would be a waste of time. Even if it was, he had to try.

They stepped into a small, dimly lit waiting room full of plush, pale green furniture and an artificially floral smell. The adjoining door opened before they could sit, and Tom was relieved. The sooner they started, the sooner they'd be done.

Yes, he wanted this to work, but he wanted it to work fast.

A woman dressed in shades of pale cream crossed the room and extended her hand. "Hello. Are you Tom?"

He shook her hand. "Yes. And this is Rachel."

"Hello, Rachel. I'm Meredith Brandt. Why don't you both come into my office? It's right through here."

The next room had more overstuffed furniture and shelves full of books and plants. One wall was a floor-to-ceiling window letting in the golden afternoon sunshine. It was a beautiful day outside, the kind of September afternoon that clung to summer, but Tom felt a chill in this room. He wiped his hands on the front of his jeans, not sure what to do next.

"Sit wherever you'd like. Would either of you like a bottle of water? Or some coffee?"

Whiskey. Straight up. That's what he needed. "No, thank you," Tom answered, choosing a brown leather chair closest to the exit door.

Rachel dropped her gray backpack on the floor and flung herself into the seat by the window. She kicked off her little black shoes and pulled her feet up on the upholstery, wrapping her arms around dark-clad knees.

Tom frowned and gave a slight shake of his head, triggering the requisite eye roll from his daughter. She crossed her arms and frowned back. With exaggerated motions, she unfolded her legs and jammed her feet back into her shoes.

Dr. Brandt slid gracefully into her own chair. "We're very informal here. Rachel, if you're more comfortable with your feet up, feel free."

Rachel tossed a look of triumph his way and pulled her bare feet up once more. His own eyes might have rolled just then, before he sent his gaze toward the counselor.

Dr. Brandt was younger than he'd expected, maybe in her mid-thirties, like him. Everything about her was a generic sort of creamy beige, from her bobbed hair to her tiny tortoiseshell glasses. Even her voice was soothing, probably cultivated from years of talking to unstable adults and hair-trigger adolescents.

She smiled at him and then turned to Rachel. "I've spoken with your dad on the phone briefly, Rachel, about his goals for us. So why don't you share some thoughts on what you hope to gain from these appointments, too."

Rachel looked down at her black-polished fingernails. "Nothing."

"Rachel!" Tom's embarrassment flared, but Dr. Brandt raised her fingers from the arm of the leather chair, a tiny gesture that spoke volumes. "Tom, here in this office, there are no incorrect or inappropriate answers. We are each entitled to feel what we feel. You don't have to censor what Rachel shares."

Rachel relaxed more in the chair, flipping her thick hair over one shoulder.

"And Rachel, I hope that when your father shares his thoughts, you'll keep an open mind as well. Can you do that?"

A lifetime passed in a breath before Rachel finally said, "Sure." Her half-shrug, quasi-nod was not encouraging to Tom, but Dr. Brandt's smile brightened.

"Excellent. Now keep in mind, if you expect to gain nothing from these appointments, that's likely what you'll get. But since we're here, I'd hate to waste your time, so if you had to come up with something you'd like to work on, what might that be?"

Rachel's glance flicked over him, light as a mosquito and just as hard to capture. She wouldn't even make eye contact. She looked at the counselor instead.

"Fine. I guess we're here because even though I'm perfectly okay living with my grandparents, my dad thinks I should move in with him. I don't want to, so I think you're supposed to referee that argument." Her chin jutted forward, her posture tense once more.

Tom swallowed hard, realizing how sour an unspoken scolding tasted. Rachel was being deliberately abrasive, and as usual, he felt the blame directed toward him. There was a lot more to this situation than just getting Rachel to move back home.

Dr. Brandt nodded, though her hair remained motionless. "Referee? That's a good way to put it. Sometimes I feel like one. The difference is, in a game, there are specific rules to follow. There is a winner and a loser.

But in relationships, all those lines are blurred. The real challenge is to move from feeling like you're on opposite sides, competing with each other, to feeling like you are on the same team. Because when you're on the same team, you can both win."

Rachel shifted in her chair, the leather squeaking around her. "I don't see how that's possible when we want totally opposite things."

"Well, that's what we're here to talk about. Let's say your father didn't want you to move home. How would that make you feel?"

Rachel picked at the black polish. "That house isn't my home. We lived there for, like, six days before my mom died. It's just a beat-up old farmhouse out in the boonies. It probably doesn't even have Internet."

Her words were hornets inside his lungs. Rachel had been excited about the farmhouse when he'd bought it, thrilled at the prospect of getting her own horse and planting a garden with Connie. None of that had happened, of course. But some of it still could—if she'd just move there and give him a chance.

"Have you asked him?" Dr. Brandt said.

Rachel blinked. "Asked him what?"

"If the house has Internet."

Rachel squinted. Tom sensed this was a trick question, but as long as it wasn't his turn to answer, he'd just observe. He watched his daughter process her options carefully.

"No. I never asked him."

"Then why don't you ask him right now?" Dr. Brandt's voice was light and conversational. The light in the room cooled as a cloud passed in front of the sun. Rachel paused.

"Well . . . it's not just the Internet. It's all kinds of things."

"Yes, I understand that. But since you mentioned Internet, let's at least get that one question out of the way."

The walls in this office were painted a shade of terra-cotta red, and there was no artwork hanging anywhere. No pictures on the desk sitting over in the corner, either. Tom had time to notice all this while his daughter prolonged the silence.

Finally, she relented and turned her gaze his way. "Do you have Internet?" Her voice was as bland and impersonal as a traffic officer asking for license and registration.

"Yes, the house has Internet." Tom glanced at the doctor and wondered if he should add more. Like the fact that he'd fixed the broken step on the front porch, the one Rachel had stubbed her toe on just days before her mother died. Or that the barn was still empty, waiting for her to fill it with a horse. Or that he missed her.

"Is the kitchen finished?" Rachel blurted out, suddenly becoming animated. "Or the bathroom?" She turned to face Dr. Brandt, her cheeks flushing pink. "The last time I was there, he hadn't even unpacked yet. It's been more than a year. How am I supposed to live there with boxes all over the place?"

The doctor looked at Tom. "Have you unpacked?"

Her voice was mellow, the question innocent enough, but it felt like an accusation. He brought his ankle up over his other knee and tried to stop his foot from tapping. He'd meant to unpack. But the boxes were full of memories better left in storage. He and Connie and Rachel had moved into the old farmhouse barely a week before the accident. And once Connie was gone, and then Rachel was, too, he just never got to it.

"The house is completely functional, Rachel. I'm sorry it's not as nice as your grandparents' place, but we could fix it up and decorate it. I thought we might go through those boxes together."

"You want me to move home so I can do work and unpack for you?" More accusations.

"That's not what I meant, and you know it. See, Dr. Brandt? This is what happens. I say one thing, and she hears something completely different." He'd meant to stay calm, but frustration sharpened his tone.

The counselor's expression remained enigmatic as she gazed at him and then his daughter.

"Rachel, I think what your father means is that he'd like to have a shared experience with you of going through the boxes. Is it the labor of unpacking that bothers you, or the fact that the boxes are full of things that will remind you of your mother?"

Rachel sat up straighter. "I see reminders of her all over the place. I live with her parents, remember? They have pictures everywhere, and some of her old clothes and stuffed animals. I can even sleep in her bed if I want to. I don't need to go through boxes with him to help remember my mom."

Tom felt a hot flush of comprehension. That was something he hadn't thought of before. Of course Rachel would feel closer to Connie surrounded by her things. At the farmhouse, they hadn't built any memories together as a family. His wife's presence wasn't there. There hadn't been enough time.

Dr. Brandt seemed to reach the same conclusion. "It's important to keep those memories close to your heart, Rachel. You can cherish them, but you can't hide in them. Do you think your mother would want you sleeping in her old bed, or would she want you to go live with your dad?"

Rachel's jaw lifted again. "Well, it would be nice to ask her, wouldn't it? Except we can't—because she's dead."

The caustic words, flung so carelessly, were a gut punch to Tom. She wanted to wound him. She wanted to remind him that everything they were going through was entirely his fault. He'd been driving the car. If not for his mistake, Connie would still be alive.

It was the only thing he and his daughter agreed on.

CHAPTER *five*

"Of course I miss you. What kind of a question is that?" Seth's voice was mildly reassuring over the phone, but Libby couldn't shake the sense he was drifting away. Her job loss had hit hard, and maybe she hadn't been that easy to live with because of it, but she was making an effort to be a kinder, gentler version of herself.

She shut the door to her bedroom and sat down on the twin-sized mattress that had been hers since she'd grown out of her crib. Being back at home still felt like a visit, but she'd been there for almost six weeks. It didn't look like she'd be heading back to Chicago any time soon. Or that she'd be seeing Seth in the immediate future, either. Her stomach felt queasy, as if it were full of polliwogs, swishing around and bumping into one another.

"It's a logical question. I haven't talked to you in days." She meant to sound sad, but it came out cranky.

"Baby, I'm working my ass off in San Diego, and there's the time zone thing."

"It's a two-hour difference, Seth. It's not like you're in Australia." Now she *did* mean to sound cranky.

"I don't usually get back to my hotel room until midnight. You want me to call you at two a.m. your time?" A sharp spike of irritation stabbed into his tone, too.

She stared at the tape marks on her walls from spots where 'N Sync and Goo Goo Dolls posters had once hung, back when life was simple and easy. "I guess not. I'm just really frustrated. I miss you, and I miss my job."

"I know. I'm sorry. Any luck on the job front?"

Libby drew in a breath, about to tell him all the details of her last interview, hoping he might cheer her up and nudge away the boulder of doubt pressing down against her shoulders, but the soft clickety-click of keystrokes on a keyboard stopped her.

Seth was typing. He wasn't even listening to her. This was the first phone call they'd had in nearly a week, and he wasn't even paying attention. "Nope. Nothing to report," she said.

"Hmm. That's too bad. Listen, though. There's something we need to talk about."

The clicking in the background stopped, and Libby felt an urgent need to brace for impact. Those polliwogs in her belly morphed into full-sized frogs.

The last time someone had said, "There's something we need to talk about," she'd gotten fired.

"Okay," she said slowly, carefully, the way a bomb diffuser might say, "Now . . . cut the yellow wire."

Seth blew out a breath. "I'm pretty sure I'm being transferred to San Diego permanently."

She should have cut the red wire. "Permanently? As in *permanently* permanently?"

"Yeah. Permanently." He sounded more certain that time.

She fell back against the pillows on her bed, clutching the phone more tightly.

There were earthquakes in San Diego, weren't there?

Libby had never been in an earthquake. But she imagined there was a millisecond—just as the tectonic plates began to shift underground—when most people thought to themselves, *Holy shit. This is an earthquake!* She felt that way just now. Like everything around her was starting to wobble and there was no safe place to stand. "Wow. I was not expecting that."

"I know." He sighed. "I should have told you sooner, but I didn't want to say anything until I was more certain. It's pretty much a done deal now."

"What? How long have you known about this?"

"Awhile, but my boss told me right about the time you were getting ready to move back in with your parents. And you've been having so much trouble finding a new job I didn't want to make you feel worse by telling you I'm getting a huge promotion."

Plates shifting. Ground splitting. Libby falling in.

"You've known about this for two months and you're just telling me now? Seth, I've been trying like crazy to get a job in Chicago. Why didn't you tell me to look in San Diego?"

There was a long pause.

And that's when it hit her. Dinosaur, meet meteor.

"Oh." The word kind of wheezed from her lungs. "You don't want me to be in San Diego, do you."

It wasn't a question. A question needed an answer, and she already had hers.

"Now, Libby, it's not that. It's just that I'm working all the time. You wouldn't have anything to do out here. You wouldn't know anybody. And I really need to focus on my career right now. This promotion is a big leap forward, and I can't screw it up because I'm worried about my unemployed girlfriend. Wait. That came out badly."

It had come out badly. But it had also come out honestly. The land *had* shifted under her feet, and suddenly everything in Libby's line of vision looked different than it had sixty seconds earlier.

"Seth, are you dumping me?" How calmly she said that. Inside her head it sounded much louder and more screechy.

"No, no, I'm not. I just . . . I think maybe we should try seeing other people for a while."

Libby smacked her palm against her forehead and cursed Marti silently for seeing this before she'd seen it for herself.

"You mean see them naked?" Her voice roughened. She felt like a sea urchin had just burst inside her gut, with the pointy parts hitting every vital organ.

"Uh, God, Libby, that's not what I meant. I just . . . look, I should have talked to you about this sooner, and I should have done it in person. I get that. There was just no good time. The point is, I'm moving to San Diego. I don't want to break up with you, but I can't promise you more of a commitment right now, either. I don't think you should wait for me."

Breathing hurt. Not because she was shocked, but because she wasn't. She should have figured this out sooner, but she'd thought their emotional disconnect was because she was depressed about not having a job. But the truth was, even if she'd never been fired, Seth would've left for San Diego without her.

CHAPTER *six*

"Historic bricks are a lot softer, so you have to be careful about what mortar you choose."

Tom Murphy was presenting pre-twentieth-century brickmaking 101 to her father at the ice-cream parlor while Libby sat a few feet away on an overturned bucket and scraped at window grout with a screwdriver and a razor blade. Nothing about this project was glamorous. All those spunky remodeling shows on television apparently edited out all the tedious parts. But Libby didn't mind. This task was exactly what her brain could handle today.

It had been a week since her conversation with Seth. At first she'd been weepy, moping around, feeling tragic and raw, until even Nana started being nice to her.

Then a couple of nights ago Marti had taken Libby out and gotten her sloppy drunk. She'd made her talk about all of Seth's annoying habits. It turned out he had a multitude. He left his dirty clothes on the bathroom floor. His knife always screeched across the plate when he cut something. He never gave her cards on Valentine's Day. Or her birthday. He wasn't particularly intuitive in bed. Oh, and he moved to San Diego with zero warning. There was *that*, too. Turns out Seth was a lousy boyfriend. What Libby had thought was love might have just been a comfortable habit.

Libby had woken up the morning after Marti's intervention feeling like warmed-over hippo shit, but as her hangover faded, so did her heartache over Seth. She'd been making the break from him for weeks and weeks without realizing it. Now it was just official.

"What does the mortar have to do with it?" Libby's father asked.

She looked over at the two of them, her dad in khaki pants and polo shirt, as casual as he ever got, and Tom in well-worn jeans and a navy T-shirt with MONROE MAVERICKS printed on it. It was an old shirt, faded, with a tiny hole near the neck, and she wondered if he'd gone there for high school.

"The firing process used to be very unpredictable, so there is no continuity to the strength of the bricks, and if you use mortar that's too strong, you run the risk of the bricks crumbling around it. It's just something to be aware of. Are you sure you don't want me to go to the hardware store instead?"

"No, no. I can do this. I have the list you gave me. You stay here and make sure Libby doesn't break another windowpane." Her dad folded up a piece of paper and stuffed it into his pocket.

Tom glanced over and caught Libby's eye.

"Thanks for your confidence in me, Dad. By the way, who was it that broke the front railing? Oh, yeah. I think that was you."

Her dad nodded and shrugged. "Yep, that was me. Good thing you're here, Tom. If left to our own devices, Liberty and I might do more destruction than reconstruction of this fine building."

Tom just smiled and adjusted his red baseball hat.

After her dad left, it was just Libby and the enigmatic Mr. Murphy, working silently. He seemed to be a man with only two settings: Work and Off.

Asked about construction or restoration, he could answer with wikipedic knowledge, but when it came to the niceties of polite conversation, Tom was cagier. Personal questions left him flushed and monosyllabic, like maybe he had some secrets behind those black-coffee eyes.

There was one thing she had figured out about him, though. Marti was right. Tom Murphy smoldered. Maybe it was the leather tool belt strapped around those hips, or the work-rough hands that seemed capable of so many tasks. Or it could be the muscles flexing under a sweat-dampened T-shirt. Whatever it was, there was *something* . . . and she liked it.

She plucked at the front of her pink T-shirt, trying to move a little air against her skin. Her hair was twisted in a sloppy knot on the top of her head, and her back ached. Six days of painstaking labor at this ice-cream parlor was about six too many, but at least now she was wearing sturdy hiking boots. She'd nearly put a nail through her foot two days ago while wearing tennis shoes. Tom had been right about her needing thicker soles.

Libby moved off the bucket to sit on the ground and leaned back against the wall, stretching out her legs in front of her. She studied Tom discreetly. He was to the left of her, on his knees using a chisel and hammer to dislodge old baseboard trim from the wall.

She leaned over and pulled a cold bottle of water from a nearby cooler. It was hot for September, and this work made her thirsty. She held the bottle against her neck for a minute before unscrewing the top and gulping half the contents down.

Tom paused in his motions and watched her drink.

"Do you want some water?" She wiped her thumb across her lip, catching a leftover drip.

He blinked at her once, twice, and shook his head as if remembering where he was. "No, I'm good. Thanks." He looked back to the wall and hit the chisel with extra force. The *clang* echoed through the nearly empty room.

Libby pressed her lips together to capture her smile before it reached her lips. Tom Murphy had just checked her out. And she liked it. Take *that,* Seth.

"So, how long have you been a builder, Tom?" Judging from the size of his arms, he'd been at it for a while.

"A while," he answered, as if reading her mind.

She hoped he couldn't read the rest of it, because she was imagining those arms just then wrapped around her waist. She was being silly, of course. Tom was not remotely her type, all down-homey and baseball-hat-wearing. She liked her men metro and stylish. The kind of men she met in Chicago who wore expensive suits and used product in their hair. Right now she couldn't even see Tom's hair, except for the bits that stuck out from under his hat, which he was currently wearing backward. That was a look she had never appreciated—until now.

"Did you grow up in Monroe?" she asked.

He shook his head. "Nope."

"Where did you grow up?"

"Concord."

Concord was a small, one-traffic-light town just east of Monroe. Libby drove through it every time she made the hour-long trek between Chicago and her parents' house.

"Was it a nice place to live?" She took another sip of water.

"Nice enough." He readjusted the chisel and hit it again, not looking her way.

"Do you still have family there?"

"Nope."

This was starting to feel like a game. She could tell she was annoying him, but there was a certain thrill in watching his shoulders rise and fall, as if giving her an answer made him sigh with resignation.

"Do you have family anywhere?"

He stopped and stared at her now. "Don't you have something else you could be doing?"

She smiled. "Nope. I'm on a break."

A smile twitched at the corner of his mouth, and his voice held no heat. "Well, I'm *not* on a break, and all this chatter is a little distracting."

She smiled bigger, deciding to tease him just to see how that might go. "I'm sorry. I assumed you could talk and hammer at the same time."

His eyebrows rose a fraction. "Your father pays me by the hour, you know. Every time you slow me down it costs him money."

She thought of her sacrificed wedding fund. "Technically it's my money he's spending."

"What?"

"Never mind. Anyway, do you have family around here?"

Tom sat back on his heels and regarded her until she felt a flush creep up from the center of her body. "How about I ask you a question?" he said.

"Okay. Go ahead." This should be interesting. What could the steady, silent Mr. Murphy want to know about her?

"Why is your name Liberty Belle?"

Oh, that. She took a slow, deliberate sip of water before answering. "My father is a history fanatic, and at the time, my mother was a good sport. But don't ever call me Liberty Belle and expect to walk away unscathed."

He stared at her for a heartbeat, his eyes dark. "It's got a nice ring to it," he finally said with a smile, and then he turned back toward the wall and poised the chisel over the trim.

Libby crossed one ankle over the other and chuckled in response. "Oh, you're very clever. I've never heard that one before. I suppose your name is something very dull and typical, like Thomas James or Thomas Michael."

He flicked her with a glance. "Nope."

She took another sip of water. "Phillip?"

He jostled the chisel. "Not even close."

"Matthew? Mark? Luke? John? Paul?" She paused. "Ringo?"

"It's a secret," he said.

Libby pulled her legs in then, crossing them and leaning on her thighs with both elbows. "Oh, I love secrets." She also loved that they were very nearly having a conversation. Granted she was doing all the labor, but he hadn't left the room yet, and that was progress. It was the first time they'd exchanged information that didn't have to do with wiring or building codes.

But Tom shook his head. "Done talking. Working now."

"I'll make up something awful if you don't tell me what it is," she threatened.

He looked over his shoulder. His gaze roved over her in a less subtle way than it had before. "You couldn't make up anything worse than what it is."

Her heart thumped a little at the light in his eyes. "I'm very clever."

"I'm sure you are."

"Then you'd better tell me."

He sighed, a big, exasperated sound, and turned around. He leaned one shoulder against the wall and crossed his arms, holding the chisel in one hand and a hammer in the other. "Murlan."

A huff of laughter escaped before she could stop it, not that she would have tried. After all, the man had seen her bare-assed naked in the dirt. The scale of humiliation was still decidedly tipped in his favor. "Merlin? Like . . . the magician?"

He shook his head. "No, Murlan, as in M-U-R-L-A-N. It was my grandfather's name."

She nodded, and felt her smile widen. "You're right. That's pretty bad. But mine's still worse." She picked up the plastic bottle and tipped her head back, drinking the last of the water.

He watched her, and then abruptly turned back to the wall. He jammed the chisel in behind the wood and clanged the hammer so hard against it, the dry wood gave a loud crack and splintered into a dozen pieces. Tom jumped back and cursed, pulling his hand away and making a fist. He landed on his butt on the floor with a *thud.*

"Are you okay?" Libby leaned forward.

He opened his fist and looked at his hand. "Yeah, I'm fine. I just got a splinter."

"Let me see." She got up and moved closer.

He held his hand behind his back. "It's fine."

"Then let me see it. I used to work in a vet's office. I'm practically a nurse."

He smirked with humor, and after a moment's hesitation, presented her with his open hand. A thick splinter protruded from the side of his index finger.

"Oh, ouch. Do you want me to get the first-aid kit?"

He chuckled. "It's fine." He squeezed the pad of his finger, pulled out the splinter, and popped the injured fingertip into his mouth.

Libby watched with morbid fascination. "Wow. That is probably the most unsanitary thing I've ever seen. And I worked in a vet's office, remember?"

He pulled out his finger. "But efficient and fast. That's my motto. Get in, get done, get out."

His lips pressed together as soon as the words were out. The sexual innuendo could not be missed, nor could the instant infusion of color into his cheeks.

"Well," she said, very much enjoying his embarrassment. "Efficiency is what counts. As long as you get the *entire* job done."

He stared at her, blinking slowly, while she grinned back.

At last, with a tiny tilt to his head, he said, "I always get the *entire* job done, Miss Hamilton."

She felt her own cheeks flush at the thought. "I'm very glad to hear that, Mr. Murphy. Now I think I'll get you a bandage before you bleed all over my father's ice-cream shop." Libby turned away and felt an inexplicable sense of triumph.

I always get the entire *job done, Miss Hamilton?* What had possessed him to say that? It was practically a flirtation, and he had tried very hard over this past week to establish himself as disinterested in anything of that sort. He'd heard Libby and her sister talking about some commitment-phobic boyfriend out in San Diego, and Tom was not about to be her rebound experiment. It didn't matter how long those legs of hers were. Or that her smile left him weak in the knees. He wasn't interested. His only priority in this building was to do his job and turn this place into an ice-cream parlor for Peter Hamilton. Outside of that, his only priority was convincing Rachel to come and live with him.

But Libby Hamilton was a persistent flirt, batting lashes so long he swore they created a breeze. And then there were her tiny little T-shirts with the goofy pictures on the front, like a penguin wearing a red sombrero, or a honey badger. He'd been way off base thinking she was the serious sort. She might be practical, but she was definitely not serious. She was funny and bright and far too pretty. Everything about her knocked him off-kilter, from the purple socks peeking out of her boots to the way she couldn't seem to keep all of her hair inside her ponytail holder. Streamers of it were constantly swirling around her face, like she was in a shampoo commercial. That shouldn't annoy him, but it did.

And the fact that it annoyed him annoyed him even more.

When Tom sat down in Dr. Brandt's office a few hours later, that annoyance was still there. Right on the surface.

"You seem a little distracted today, Tom. Are you uncomfortable being here without Rachel?"

He rubbed his chin with one hand. "No. It just seems a little pointless for you and me to talk. These sessions are for her."

Dr. Brandt smiled her Mona Lisa smile. "These sessions are for both of you. No one grieves in a vacuum, and it's helpful for us to talk one-on-one occasionally. So let's start with whatever is on your mind today, shall we?"

He looked out the window. It was still warm, but some of the leaves had started to turn. Autumn was usually his favorite time of year. But the holidays would be here soon. He'd face his second Christmas without Connie, and probably without Rachel. Last year he'd hidden inside a bottle of Jack Daniel's and had paid for that with a hangover until January.

"There is this woman at work and she irritates me." He blurted out the words and wanted them back in an instant. But there were no take-backs in this office.

"Irritates you in what way?"

"I don't know, exactly. She's just . . . always *there*. Always wants to chat. And she wears these little T-shirts with cartoon characters on the front, so I constantly catch myself looking at her chest. It annoys me."

"Why does that annoy you?"

"Because I'm supposed to be working, not staring at her breasts all day. Her shirts are too tight. No offense, Dr. Brandt. I'm all for women's equality, but there's a reason why women shouldn't work construction."

Her smile seemed genuine for the first time ever. "All women, Tom, or just this woman?"

Tom pondered this a moment. He'd actually known plenty of women who could do his job, but those were sensible women who knew to wear steel-toed shoes. And long pants. He looked out the window at the park next to Dr. Brandt's office.

Smiling mothers sat on wooden benches and sipped coffee from paper cups, or pushed happy children on swings. The scene was idyllic, but it left him empty.

"Maybe just this woman."

"Are you attracted to her?"

His stare returned to Dr. Brandt. "Why would you ask me that? I just told you she annoys me."

She raised a brow a fraction of an inch, as if preparing to explain some significant revelation.

Before she could say anything, Tom shook his head. "You know what? Never mind about Libby. Could we get back to Rachel, please?"

The fake smile was back. Dr. Brandt would make a very good mannequin with that blank look. "In order to help Rachel, I need to know where you are in your grieving process, too. So, let's stick with this Libby a little longer. Have you dated anyone since Connie died?"

He blinked from the strike of her question and became acutely aware of how his chest could feel hollow and yet full of cement at the same time. It was a sensation he'd lived with since the day they'd put his wife in the ground. He took a slug of water from the glass sitting on the table next to him, but it did nothing to ease the dryness in his throat.

"I don't want to date this woman, Dr. Brandt. You're misunderstanding me. I'm annoyed because she dresses inappropriately for a job site and she's going to get hurt. And since I'm the only one on this project who knows a hammer from a hole in my ass, I'm responsible for keeping people safe. Let's move on."

Dr. Brandt folded her hands in her lap and regarded him as if he were an abstract painting at a gallery. "Let's talk about your goals again. What is it you want to change about your relationship with Rachel?"

The heaviness in his lungs lightened by an ounce. "I want to be a good father so she'll move back in with me."

Her head tilted to the left. "What does a good father look like? How does he behave?"

He wasn't sure where she was going with this, but it seemed like the answer was obvious. "A good father is dependable. Trustworthy. Patient. Protective. I'm not sure what you're asking."

"I'm asking you to describe what kind of relationship you want with your daughter."

"The normal kind, where she trusts me to take care of her."

"That's the second time you've used the word *trust*. Do you think Rachel doesn't trust you?"

The cement in his lungs expanded and cracked. "I know she doesn't. After the accident, when she needed me the most, I wasn't there."

"Where were you?"

It was always so goddamned stuffy in this office. He tugged at his collar, but it didn't cool him down any.

"Well, I was in the hospital for nearly four weeks. I missed Connie's funeral because of that. But even when I came home, I was still . . . pretty fucked up."

She adjusted her glasses. "Define 'pretty fucked up' in your terms."

He kept his voice level though it felt as if the room might be tipping. "I'm pretty sure it means the same thing in my terms as it does in yours, Dr. Brandt. I spent about three months washing down painkillers with whiskey and trying to pretend Connie hadn't died. By the time I got myself together, Rachel was settled in with her grandparents, and all three of them were convinced I was unfit as a parent. That's why they've convinced Rachel she's better off staying with them."

"Is she?"

That was an arrow dead center in his chest. It stole his breath even though it was a question he asked himself daily. "Do *you* think she is?" he finally asked.

Dr. Brandt's long pause filled his veins with ice.

"No, Tom, I think she'd be better off living with you. You are her father, and you're not unfit, but the fact that you're uncertain is something we need to work on. It's natural for Connie's parents to want to fill the void left by their daughter's death, but they shouldn't try to fill it with Rachel. And you shouldn't feel guilty for wanting your daughter back."

He looked out the window again at the happy mommies at the park, bouncing their fat, smiling babies on their laps. Rachel had been a fat baby. A fat, happy baby. "I should have insisted she come home. But she'd started school for the year, and if she came to live with me she'd have to transfer." His lungs felt full of ice water. "It felt selfish of me to make her go through another big change. Especially since this entire mess was my fault to begin with."

"Why would you say that?"

"Because it's true. Connie would be alive if it weren't for me."

"That's a pretty emotional answer. Is that what you believe intellectually? That Connie's death was somehow your fault?"

"It was entirely my fault. I was driving."

"Have you been in other accidents?"

"No."

"So, would you say you are typically a cautious driver?"

A sour taste sprang up in the back of his throat. He hated talking about the accident, hated reliving it. It was such a waste of time.

"Look, I get what you're trying to do here. And I appreciate it. I understand it was an accident, but if I'd had control of the car, Connie would still be here and Rachel would still have her mother."

Dr. Brandt leaned forward. "And you wouldn't be left all alone, and feeling guilty for staring at an attractive woman's breasts."

A vision of Libby sitting on the floor of the ice-cream parlor earlier that day popped into his head. She'd had cupcakes on her T-shirt. Little pink and purple sparkly cupcakes dancing right across her breasts. And all he could think of, every time he looked at her during the whole damn day, was licking off the frosting.

"Maybe."

Dr. Brandt leaned back again and crossed her arms. "Would it help if I said what you're feeling is normal and appropriate?"

"Not really."

"Well, it is. In a way, you take comfort in believing that you caused the accident, because then you have someone to blame. We all like to think we have some control over our destinies, so random events can be distressing. But now you need to decide. You can choose to stay stuck in this moment, live inside that fear and regret, and keep Rachel there with you, or you can be a mature adult, and a good father, by teaching her it's not the obstacles in our life that define us. It's the grace we display when overcoming them."

He didn't like Dr. Brandt very much in that moment. He couldn't tell if she was absolving him of guilt or calling him immature. Or both.

He looked once more into the park. The mommies were loading up their children into strollers. It was time to go home.

"I'm not sure how to do what you're asking," he finally said.

"I know," she said, smiling. "But I think you're ready to figure it out."

CHAPTER *seven*

"There is no way in hell I'm going to wear this, Marti. It's heavy and it stinks." Libby pulled at the garnet-colored velvet currently trussed around her midsection as she stood on a wobbly stool in the middle of A Royale Affaire Costume Shoppe and Medieval Armory wearing her little sister's farcical idea of a bridesmaid dress.

"And it's ridiculous," Ginny added from her spot on a tapestry-covered chair.

"I thought we were going to lunch," Nana said from her spot on the green velvet love seat. She was trying to button her cardigan sweater, which she wore in spite of the broiling temperature inside the cramped, tiny store.

Libby's mother reached over and fixed the button. "We are going out to lunch, Nana, but first we have to look at these dresses for Marti's . . . wedding." Libby could see her mother having to push out that last word. Her parents were still not in favor of this impending marriage, but there wasn't much they could do to stop it. Marti was a consenting adult, after all.

By legal standards, anyway.

A tall, reed-thin saleswoman with a tight black bun tugged brusquely on the laces in the back of Libby's dress, nearly knocking her off the stool. The threat was implied: *Stop complaining, or I'll hurt you.*

"Oh, relax, Libby. This is just a sample," Marti assured her. "The one you buy will be custom-made so it will only stink if you sweat it up."

"How can I not sweat it up? I'm hauling around two hundred yards of theater curtain. I'm wearing upholstery." She tried to lift the skirt as the salesclerk glowered.

Marti glowered, too. "Look, I already agreed to postpone my wedding until December so I can finish this semester *and* wait for Ginny to have her baby. I have been very accommodating. So stop bitching about the fact that I'm having a Renaissance-themed wedding, okay? If you don't want to be in it, then fine, don't be in it." Marti crossed her arms and all but stuck out her bottom lip.

"I don't want to be in it," Ginny said.

Marti's pout turned to crestfallen sadness as she turned from Libby to their older sister. "You can't mean that, Ginny. I was in *your* wedding."

"In my normal, traditional wedding where you got to wear a gorgeous chiffon dress."

"Gorgeous chiffon? Is that what you call it? I looked like a giant walking daffodil."

Libby nodded. "We looked like lemon meringue pies. But at least those dresses didn't weigh seven hundred pounds."

"I make excellent lemon meringue pies," said Nana. "But peach pie is my specialty. Your pies aren't very good, Beverly. In thirty years you never have made a decent crust."

Libby's mother leaned slightly away from Nana, trying to create space between them on the tiny sofa.

"My pies will never be as good as yours, Nana. Everyone knows that," Beverly answered mechanically, although that was obviously not the response going through her mind. When it came to Nana Hamilton, it was always best to agree.

Libby's sisters continued frowning at each other.

"My wedding was beautiful and elegant, and you looked lovely in that yellow dress," Ginny said, flipping her red-gold hair over her shoulder.

"Well, I think Libby looks lovely in this dress. And so will—" Marti paused and bit her lip. "Oh, I get it. I'm so sorry, Ginny. But don't worry. You'll lose that baby weight."

"What?" Ginny gasped.

Libby bit back a chuckle.

"You think that's why I'm objecting?" Ginny sputtered.

Marti leaned over from her seat on the other side of Nana and patted her sister's hand. "I know you're worried about getting your ass back up where it's supposed to be, but you will. And besides, no one's going to be looking at you anyway. They'll all be looking at me because I'm the bride."

Ginny snatched her hand away. "Then you don't need fat old me waddling down the aisle and distracting anyone."

"Girls, stop bickering." Libby's mother's tone was on autopilot. Either she was stewing about the pie comment, or she was still too emotionally numb that her youngest daughter was marrying a tattooed jousting instructor.

"Well, technically there won't be an aisle since we're getting married at the Renaissance banquet hall," Marti said.

"Where is she getting married?" Nana poked Libby's mother with an arthritic finger.

"We told you this already, Nana," Libby said calmly, hoping to keep her mother from breaking off Nana's skinny little hand. "Marti's wedding ceremony is going to be at the Renaissance banquet hall where she met her fiancé. Remember?"

"Oh, yes." Nana nodded. "I do remember that. Stupidest idea I ever heard."

"I'm right next to you, Nana. I can hear you." Marti pouted again.

"Ladies, perhaps we should focus on the bride today," said the salesclerk abruptly. A sheen of perspiration shone across her forehead. A room full of hostile Hamilton women was bound to have that effect on even the most experienced of bridal professionals. "Let's have her try on a few gowns, shall we?"

"Excellent idea," Libby said with relief. She wanted to get out of this circus tent and back into her own clothes. "Ginny, will you come help me in the dressing room?"

"Gladly." Ginny hoisted herself from the seat with a little effort and followed Libby down the narrow hall, muttering all the way. "Does she seriously think I don't want to be in her wedding because I'll be too fat?"

"Shh," Libby whispered back. "She doesn't mean it. You know how Marti is."

"Yes, I do. She's spoiled, and she wants everything all her own way."

Libby bit her tongue. There was no point in reminding Ginny she'd been exactly the same way over *her* wedding. "Just get me out of this thing, will you?"

Ginny shook her head as she worked at the laces. "Good Lord, this thing is a monstrosity. Oh, hey, I keep forgetting to ask. Can you help me at the high school for a couple of nights? The talent show is next weekend and I'm in charge, but I need some extra adults. It's like herding cats with these kids. Nobody is ever where they are supposed to be."

That was another downside of not having a job. Or a life. Everyone was always asking for favors. In the past week, Libby had taken Nana to the garden store for a new gnome, helped Marti try to wash her car without putting her hand through all the rust spots, and stapled two hundred exam packets for her mother.

Then, of course, there was the ice-cream parlor. She'd been there nearly every day, pulling old nails from pieces of wood that Tom and her dad wanted to reuse, scraping toxic lead-based paint from the exterior that was sure to give her a raging case of lung cancer, scrubbing twenty years of grime from the windows, and even crawling under the front step, through an enormous spiderweb, to reach a valve because she was the only one small enough to get under there.

She didn't have to be at the ice-cream parlor, of course. There were plenty of ways she could help from a distance. But being around brawny Tom Murphy was fun. He still wasn't much of a talker, of course, but he wasn't as evasive as he'd been at first, either. Every day she peppered him with questions just to see his reaction. Teasing him until he either got annoyed or started to laugh was Libby's favorite new hobby.

"Well, that's one rehearsal behind us. Five more to go." Libby brushed her hands together as she and Ginny stood near the back of the Monroe High School auditorium. "And that wasn't nearly as painful as I expected it to be. These kids are more talented than we were in high school."

"Speak for yourself. I was incredibly talented in high school." Ginny stretched, pressing both hands against her lower back. "Thank you so much for helping me out. I'm usually the one running between the dressing room and the stage, but I just can't keep up right now. And I can't let these students see my weakness. They can smell fear."

Libby laughed. "They seem like a pretty decent group."

"Most of them are very sweet," Ginny agreed and lowered her voice. "But I need to keep them a little bit afraid of me."

"I hope that's not your parenting philosophy, too." Libby picked up her bag and started walking toward the exit with her sister.

"What's that supposed to mean?" Ginny stopped and stared at her.

"Uh, nothing. It was a joke."

Ginny knotted the handle of her purse. "It wasn't funny. You do think I'll be an okay mother, don't you?"

"Of course I do. I was kidding." Libby put an arm around her shoulders and nudged her hormonally hypersensitive sister toward the doors again. "You'll be a wonderful mother."

"Really? Do you think so? Because I always thought Mom and Dad were pretty good parents, but then I look at Marti, and I realize it's all a crapshoot."

Libby burst out laughing. "There's nothing wrong with Marti. She's just a dreamer, like Dad."

"But what if this baby is a dreamer? I can't handle that. I'm too shallow. What if I'm horrible to her because she wants to get a nose ring someday? Or grows up to be a rodeo clown? What if she hates golf? Ben and I love to golf."

Libby's laughter paused at the serious tone in Ginny's voice, and then erupted again. "Ginny, that's ridiculous. You'll love her no matter what. And you'll be a fabulous mother, just like you're a fabulous teacher and a fabulous wife."

Ginny stared at her. "Wow. I must be really pathetic. You have never been this nice to me."

Libby nudged her toward the door again. "You are completely pathetic and I am loving it. This is the first time in my life I've been skinnier than you are. Now let's get you home so you can put up those puffy cankles."

"Are they puffy? I can't see them."

They walked out the back door of the auditorium into the evening light, and Libby spotted a lone girl sitting on a nearby bench, her blond hair blowing in the breeze.

Ginny walked over to her. "Hi there. Isn't your ride picking you up in the front? That's where everyone else is."

"I told him to come to the back. He should be here soon."

Libby saw the indecision slide across Ginny's face. She couldn't leave with a student waiting.

"You go on, Ginny," Libby said. "I'll wait here until everybody's picked up."

"Thanks. I'd appreciate that. My feet are killing me. I'll see you both tomorrow then." Ginny waved and duck-walked toward the teachers' parking lot.

Libby sat down on the bench next to the girl and smiled at her. The sun was just dipping below the horizon, scattering shadows in every direction.

"You play the piano, right?" she asked the girl, trying to recall her name.

The blond nodded. "Yeah."

"I loved your song. You have a beautiful voice."

The girl blushed and twisted a lock of her hair. Something about her seemed vaguely familiar, but then again, half the girls in the talent show had blond hair and blue eyes. It was hard to tell them all apart.

"Thanks. Are you Mrs. Garner's sister?" she asked Libby.

"I am. And Mrs. Hamilton's daughter."

The girl nodded again, her hair swishing in front of her face. "I had Mrs. Hamilton for social studies. She's nice. Are you a teacher, too?"

Libby chuckled. "No, I'm the black sheep of my family. Even my dad is a teacher, but I didn't get the gene."

The blond smiled. "Oh, that's right. Your dad is Hot Air Hamilton, right? The balloon guy who crashed in the football field?" Then another furious blush stole over her cheeks. "Oh, my God. I'm sorry. That was rude."

Libby's laughter bubbled over. "I haven't heard him called that in a while. He'll be so glad to know that story hasn't died down."

"Everybody knows that story. I wasn't there when that happened, but I heard all about it." The girl tapped her feet against the ground, suddenly seeming shy. "Was that sort of, like, embarrassing for you guys?"

"I was living in Chicago at the time, but it was a little hard on my mom and sisters. I think they got teased more than my dad did. And quite frankly, he does that kind of stuff all the time. It's just not usually so public."

The girl nodded and looked down at her fingernails. "God, dads can be so humiliating."

"It's part of their job, I think. Being weird and trying to embarrass us." Libby nodded.

"My dad is completely weird. And he drives so slow it makes me crazy. That's why he's always late."

Libby smiled. "Mine goes around the house adjusting everybody's lighting, and then he leaves the room. It's like 'If I wanted that lamp on, I'd have turned it on.' It's maddening. Does your dad do that?"

The girl shrugged. "I don't know. I live with my grandparents, so I'm not sure what he does. I just know he sucks at driving."

A muffler sounded in the distance, and the girl sighed. "Oh, that's him. Thanks for waiting with me."

She hopped up and hurried off, and Libby watched in quiet surprise as a familiar old blue truck came to a stop in front of the steps, and Tom Murphy stared at Libby from behind the steering wheel.

CHAPTER *eight*

Mornings were usually the toughest part of Tom's day. That moment when he first woke up and in the haze of sleep, forgot, and reached for Connie. For a while he'd tried sleeping on her side of the bed, but that just made his heart ache, and so he'd moved back to his own side where it felt like he had no heart at all.

But this morning was different. Today he woke to a pounding thunder in his chest and the remnants of a dream, a most unimaginably explicit dream about cupcakes, and frosting, . . .

. . . and Libby.

He pushed the covers off and let the air cool his skin.

Last night she'd been sitting next to Rachel outside the high school. He wasn't sure why, and his daughter said only that she was there helping one of the teachers. Now, for the first time in weeks, Tom didn't want to go to work. Libby's interrogations about his life and interests were persistent enough. Now that she'd seen him with Rachel, she'd have a whole new line of questioning ready to aim and fire.

She was tangling up his emotions like an old rope. He didn't need this new knot. He found himself thinking of her during the times he'd normally thought of Connie, and it felt like betrayal.

He kicked off the remaining covers and got out of bed. A cold shower and some hot coffee would set him to rights. He and Peter were scheduled to work on the flooring today. Tom would just focus on that and keep his interactions with Libby to a minimum. That was the plan.

But his plan got shot to hell an hour later when he walked into the ice-cream parlor and the first thing he saw was Libby's perky little ass, way up high on a six-foot ladder.

His heart plummeted to his gut. She was on the top. The very top, and leaning forward against the window frame.

"Goddamn it, Libby!" His work bag thumped against the floor as he crossed the room fast. He grabbed the ladder to steady it with one hand and reached up with the other to clasp her calf. He wasn't too agitated to notice the shape and feel of her leg in his hand. But he *was* too agitated to appreciate it. "What the hell are you doing?"

She looked down at him. "It's a little early in the morning to start swearing at me, isn't it?"

"Don't you know better than to stand on the very top of a ladder?" His lungs felt overexpanded, pressing against the wall of his chest.

"I couldn't reach from any lower." She leaned forward even farther, a fraction of an inch from falling. His lungs collapsed then, and that felt even worse. The ladder creaked and swayed as she hooked a metal end to the window frame and let a tape measure fall to the ground, the yellow strip sliding along the side.

It hit the floor with a resounding *clunk*. She stared at it for a second, and then laughed. "I guess it's good you showed up, though, because I can't read the measuring tape from up here. Bend down and tell me what that says."

His grip tightened on her leg, and he worked to keep his voice level. "Libby, climb down from there, and I'll show you how to measure something without risking a broken neck."

She pushed back from the window frame, and the tape measure retracted with a metallic hiss. The ladder moved with her, even as Tom held tight.

He let go of her leg but kept his hand raised, ready to catch her as she climbed down. Her perky little ass tilted from side to side as she went from rung to rung, and it was all he could do to stop his head from tilting in unison. Christ. He looked away and dropped his hands.

Libby hopped off from the last rung and turned to face him. Her smile was sunshine bright.

He wanted to kiss her.

And then he wanted to shake her for being foolish enough to stand on the top of an old, creaky ladder.

But he couldn't do either, so instead he picked up the tape measure from the floor and flicked the yellow strip upward, alongside the window frame. He extended it up above their heads. When the tip reached the top of the window frame, he bent down to stretch the tape measure to the window's lower edge. He pointed at it with his other hand. "This is how you measure something. From the bottom up, not the top down. Got it?"

She leaned against the ladder. "You're grouchy today."

He stood up and handed her the tape measure. "I'm always grouchy when someone is careless at work. If you fall off that ladder, you know who gets blamed? Me."

"Uh . . . I think I can decide for myself if I want to climb a ladder." Her smile held, and her tone was more mocking than conciliatory.

He crossed his arms. "How'd those tennis shoes work out for you?"

She mimicked him, crossing her own arms. "Not that bad."

"Uh-huh. Well, see this label here?" He uncrossed his again and tapped hard at the ladder right next to her face. "The one that says, 'Danger. Do not stand on top step'?" He moved his hand and slapped the top. "Yeah, this is the step they're talking about."

She looked at him, not cowed in the least. Not that he wanted to scare her; he only wanted to make his point. But she just kept smiling. It was infuriating.

It made him want to kiss her even more.

There was a raccoon on her shirt today. Wearing sunglasses. Yesterday she'd worn one with a fire-breathing unicorn on it. Where the hell did she find these shirts?

"So that was your daughter last night, huh?" she said at last.

And there it was.

That's why she was so smiley. She knew he didn't want to talk about Rachel. All those hours of working together he'd managed to avoid any mention of his daughter, or of ever having been married, or anything more personal than the size of his shoe and the fact that he liked pistachio ice cream. But now she had him cornered and she knew it.

He ran a hand across his jaw and stared out the window. He looked back at Libby.

"Yep."

"I didn't know you had a daughter."

He stepped away and folded the ladder to lean it against the wall. "Well, now you do."

"I think it's kind of interesting you never mentioned her."

"I think it's kind of interesting you think it's any of your business." His tone was harsher than he intended, and he could see by her change in expression that his words had stung. His cheeks went hot with remorse. He certainly hadn't intended to hurt Libby's feelings, but he also absolutely didn't want to tell her about his fractured relationship with Rachel, or the reasons behind it.

"I'm sorry," he said, after a pause. "It's complicated."

It was late in the afternoon when Marti showed up carrying two grocery bags. "Daddy! Tom! Oh, my gosh! Look how much progress you've made! It looks amazing."

"Hey, I've been working, too," Libby reminded her, although she wasn't sure why she'd stayed. After Tom snapped at her, it had been a very dull and quiet day.

Dante ambled in behind her sister, holding up his hands as if framing a shot. A video camera swung from a strap around his neck. "The light is perfect right now," he said. "Hey, Dad Hamilton, can we do some interviews for the documentary? We brought beer."

Libby's dad sat back on his heels from his spot on the floor and stretched his back. The scowl on his face at the sound of Dante's voice faded when he heard the word *beer*. Every man has his price, and Peter Hamilton's was roughly the cost of a six-pack. He glanced at his watch and then at Tom, who had been working next to him. "It's almost four o'clock. You ready to call it a day?"

"I'll finish this section. You go ahead." Tom nodded at him.

Marti set down the bags and pulled out a few bottles, expertly popping off the tops. Libby took two, grabbing the bottles by the neck.

All day, the weight of her curiosity—and Tom's reaction to it—had pushed her down. Maybe his daughter *wasn't* any of her business, but she thought they'd become friendly over the last couple of weeks and that the whole gruff demeanor was kind of an act. Maybe it wasn't. Maybe she really had been annoying him as much as he'd pretended.

Or maybe, like he'd said, it was complicated. Either way, she felt like they'd had a fight, and it didn't feel good.

She crossed the room to where he sat on the floor and held out a beer.

He looked at it like it was a mousetrap waiting to snap on his fingers, but after a pause he reached up and took it. He gave her a single nod. "Thanks."

"You're welcome."

"Libby," he said quietly, after she'd turned away.

She looked back over her shoulder.

"I'm sorry about this morning. I just don't like to talk about it."

She smiled and felt a little better. "I'm sorry I ask so many questions."

Tom gave her a tight smile back. "You do ask a lot of questions."

"I know. But I'm a good listener, too. In case, you know, you ever do want to talk about it."

He took a sip from the beer. "I'll keep that in mind."

She wanted to say more, but then again, she always wanted to say more. She sipped her beer instead and walked back over to her sister. "Holy shit, Marti, what's that on your leg?"

Marti had plastic wrap around her ankle and halfway up her shin. But underneath it was something scaly and green.

"Oh, check it out. It's my new tattoo. I just got it today."

Libby's father choked on his beer. "Your what?"

Marti grinned. "My tattoo. An early wedding present from Dante." She tugged at the plastic and plucked it away, revealing a slightly smaller version of the same dragon adorning her fiancé's arm. Its tail curled around her ankle as its mouth breathed bright-orange fire halfway up the back of her calf.

Libby felt the urge to laugh and gasp at the same time, but she watched her father's face turn purple and decided to quietly drink her beer instead. He'd be breathing fire of his own in a second. She turned around and tiptoed back toward Tom.

"Martha, what have you done?" her father sputtered. "Tattoos are permanent!" He stood up with a lurch and moved quickly over to his freshly decorated daughter.

Marti lifted her leg and put her foot up on a box, turning so he could get a better look at her new ink.

"I know they're permanent," she said. "That's why they're so totally worth how expensive they are."

Libby heard Tom chuckle, but when she turned to him, his face was sober as a Baptist minister. He looked straight ahead, avoiding her eyes, and sipped his beer.

"Tattoos are dangerous, Martha! You'll get an infection. You could get hepatitis. This was very irresponsible."

Irresponsible like a man who buys an ice-cream parlor without telling his wife? Or like a boyfriend who moves to San Diego with virtually no warning? It suddenly occurred to Libby that she knew a lot of madly impetuous people.

"I'm being super-responsible, Daddy. That's what the plastic wrap is for. Ivan said it was the best way to keep this clean for the next few hours. Anyway, it's too late to be mad. It's already done, and I love it. So let's talk about these interviews for the documentary." She gently set her foot back on the floor. "Do you want to go first, or should we talk to Tom?"

"Who is Ivan?" her father demanded, as if that made any difference.

"My cousin," Dante said from his spot near the door. "He's a true artist, Dad Hamilton. He's done all my tattoos. You know I wouldn't take Marti to somebody disreputable."

"No, I don't know that." Libby's father shook his finger at Dante, his voice full of bluster. "Anyone named Ivan sounds plenty disreputable to me."

Marti put her hands on her hips. "That is completely prejudiced, Daddy. Ivan is family now. And he's a preacher, which is, like, the most reputable thing ever. He's performing the marriage ceremony for Dante and me."

"Wait. Your cousin is a tattoo artist and a preacher?" Libby asked. Tom gave another quiet chuckle.

"I know. Isn't it awesome?" Marti grinned. "He got his preacher's license online just so he could marry us. Dante's family is the coolest ever." Marti sighed with joy as her father deflated like a leaky Thanksgiving Day parade float.

"So, are we doing these interviews or what?" Dante asked. "This good light won't last all day."

"I'll go first," Tom offered, moving toward Dante. "I think Mr. Hamilton could use a minute."

"Great," Dante responded. "Libby, can you help us, too? I could use somebody to hold the microphone."

They chose a spot on the front porch. Dante pulled out some folding chairs and a few pieces of camera equipment from his car and positioned everyone. Libby quickly found herself holding a long tube with a tiny microphone on the end. She dangled it over Tom's head as instructed by their intrepid director.

"Try not to conk me with that thing, okay?" Tom asked, raising his hand up over his head. "You're a little clumsy."

"I'm not clumsy at all. You just keep assuming I'm clumsy because I'm a girl."

Marti sat in the chair next to Tom with some blue index cards in her lap. "Whenever you're ready, baby." She laughed at Tom as his brows lifted. "Oh, not you. Him." She pointed at Dante.

Tom nodded and repositioned himself in the chair, crossing and then uncrossing his legs.

"Okay, babe," said Dante. "We're rolling. Let me check the audio first, though. You guys just talk for a minute."

Marti smiled at Tom. "Don't worry about any of this. Dante says the magic happens in editing, so say whatever you want, or ask questions or whatever. Okay?"

Tom nodded and ran a finger around the collar of his navy T-shirt.

"What is your name?" Marti asked.

"Tom."

She smiled. "Okay, now say your full name and address so Dante can check your audio."

"Oh." Tom flushed and cleared his throat. His gaze moved to Libby and caught there. She felt an unexpected ripple of anticipation, as if she were holding a raffle ticket and waiting for her name to be called.

A smile hooked the corner of his mouth. "My name is Thomas Murlan Murphy."

Libby caught herself smiling back.

"Murlan?" asked Marti. "That's pretty funky. But not as bad as mine."

Tom's gaze moved from Libby to her sister, and Libby found she was a little sad about that.

"What's yours?"

"Martha Washington Hamilton."

Tom winced.

"I know. It's awful." Marti nodded.

"Okay, we're good for sound, babe. Ask him the real questions now."

Tom's glance flitted back to Libby again, as if for reassurance, which she found interesting. And appealing. The unease from that morning's conversation had disappeared, leaving behind it a new understanding. Or if not that, exactly, at least a new tolerance.

"Okay, you ready?" Marti asked. "When was this building constructed?"

She went on and asked him a dozen or so questions about the characteristics of the schoolhouse and the challenges unique to restoring old buildings. He answered thoughtfully, using lots of words without any extra prompting.

"Okay, one last question," Marti said after they'd been filming for almost half an hour. "What is it about restoration projects that appeals to you the most?"

Tom looked at his hands for a minute as he paused. Libby could see he was thinking this through, not giving some flip response. "When you build something, you can see it. It's solid and you can grab on to it. I like that about building in general. Tangible results. But especially with these old places, you can see the attention and care that went into constructing them. They were built to be permanent, crafted with materials meant to weather just about anything that blew their way. A run-down old place like this has seen hard times. I guess I just like giving it a second chance and a new purpose."

CHAPTER *nine*

"Was that Seth you were talking to on the phone this morning?"

Libby and her dad were sorting through countertop samples while sitting on two overturned crates in the ice-cream parlor. Tom was off on some mysterious errand.

Her dad's question pinched at her mood. She tossed a sample down onto the pile with a little flick. "Yes. He's got some stuff of mine packed up back in Chicago, and he wants me to come pick it up so he doesn't have to ship it."

"Hmm. Are you going to go?" Peter took off his glasses and started cleaning them on his shirt.

"I don't know. I kind of want to make him ship it." She dropped another sample, and it skidded to the edge of the pile. "It would be a huge inconvenience for him to get to the post office. Seems like he deserves that." *Petty, table of one, your table is ready.*

"Yes, it does. But knowing how cheap Seth is, he'd probably send you the shipping bill." He put his glasses back on, and Libby chuckled.

"I'm sure he would."

Recovering from Seth was a process, like sore muscles the day after a strenuous workout. There were sharp twinges, a surprised intake of breath, the realization that something hurt, but also the knowledge that it would fade, that the next day she'd feel even better. And want to exercise again. This breakup could have soured her on relationships, but it hadn't. It just made her want to go out and find a better one.

Tom Murphy strode in the door right then, as if on cue.

Libby tried to douse the flame abruptly flickering in her belly. He was not her type. She dated men who wielded smart phones, not power tools. They had nothing in common. Plus as soon as she got a job, she'd be heading back to Chicago. But it was getting harder and harder to remember that.

Tom wore dark jeans today and a collared shirt. His mystery appointment must have been something important. He wasn't even wearing a hat.

The two of them had come to an unspoken agreement since the awkward exchange over Rachel three days ago. She tried to stop pestering him with personal questions, and he tried not to get all huffy if she slipped up and asked him something he thought was out of bounds.

Her dad stood up. "Afternoon, Tom."

"Peter. Libby." He nodded at them both, but his eyes caught on hers. She sat up straighter. His eyes dropped to her shirt and lingered. She had on her favorite cupcake shirt—the one she'd stolen from Marti, so it was actually a little small. Tom seemed to like it, too.

He twitched his head a little and turned toward her father. "Did you get that new packet of pictures from the historical society yet?"

"Oh, drat. I forgot. What time did you say they closed?" Her father patted his pockets as if searching for his keys.

"Today I think they're open until four. You can still make it if you leave now." Tom reached over and picked up a set of car keys from another crate. "Here you go."

"Excellent. Thank you. I'm on my way. Libby, I'll see you at home."

Her father left with a wave.

They watched his exit, and then Tom turned back to her.

"Hi," he said.

Libby chuckled at his sudden awkwardness. "Hi. How are you?"

"Good. You?"

"Fine."

"Good." He hesitated, and she smiled up at him. His eyes were chocolate brown. She'd been noticing that a lot lately, but it was especially nice to see them without the ever-present shadow of a baseball cap.

He ran both hands through his hair, clutching it for a second. Then he spoke in a rush. "Do you know how to make a collage?"

"A collage?" That was a most random question.

"Yeah." He nodded.

"Do you mean like a . . . picture collage with . . . pictures?" Libby slid the samples together into a pile as he sat down on a crate next to her with a thump.

"I guess. I'm not entirely sure." He sighed, a big heavy sound, and splayed his hands out on his knees.

Libby's curiosity clicked up a notch, but she bit her tongue. The other thing she'd figured out over the last few days was that, if left to his own devices, Tom would eventually *start* a conversation.

He looked around, but since her dad had left, it was just the two of them. He tapped his foot for a second before speaking.

"So, my daughter and I don't have the greatest relationship. I'm sure you figured that out. But we're working on it." He paused again, and Libby's heart gave a little *whump* as she silently urged him on. "And this family counselor we go to wants us each to make a collage."

He shook his head. "I guess it's supposed to express our feelings or something, using pictures. Because apparently I'm not very, um . . . what's the word?"

"Articulate?"

He chuckled. "Yeah. And neither is Rachel, quite frankly."

Libby couldn't argue with him on that. She'd seen his daughter at rehearsal the last couple of nights. She was sweet, and everyone seemed to like her, but she didn't bubble over with silliness like the average teen. Of course, now that Ginny had filled Libby in on the car accident, that made sense. It shed some light on Tom's personality, too, but it still didn't explain why Rachel lived with her grandparents. Someday she'd like to ask him about that.

"She's very expressive when she sings, though," Libby said. "She has an amazing voice."

Tom's shoulders went back, and he looked at her with curiosity. "When did you hear her sing?"

"At rehearsals. I'm helping my sister with the talent show."

"What talent show?" His forehead creased as he frowned.

"Um, the high school talent show? Didn't Rachel tell you?"

He was silent just long enough for Libby's heart to go *whump* one more time.

"No. She didn't tell me."

"But you picked her up from school."

He nodded slowly. "Yeah. She told me she was working on a history project in the library. I'm not that surprised."

Well, Libby was. Her parents had never missed a school event, or a soccer game, or a volleyball tournament. Or lemonade stand, for that matter. Granted, her parents were insatiably overinvolved, but still . . .

"I know it's none of my business," she couldn't resist saying, "but why would she not tell you?"

He regarded her for a minute, as if translating the question in his mind. "Because she'd rather I didn't go."

"Why?" That question popped out in a burst.

He shrugged and shook his head. "Because she lives with her grandparents and she doesn't like me. I told you, it's complicated."

This time his tone had none of the heat from the other day, none of the snap. It almost seemed like he *wanted* to talk about it. He tapped his palms on his knees a couple of times, staring out the window, and then he turned back to her.

"I don't have a clue how to make a collage. Will you help me?"

Will you help me? That was the last thing in the cosmos she'd expected to hear from a man like Tom Murphy.

He hadn't intended for it to come out that way. What he meant was for her to *tell* him how to make a collage, not for her to actually help him make it. But she'd nodded her consent so somberly, staring at him with those big, dark blue eyes, and said, "Yes, of course. I can help you make it tonight."

And so a few hours later he found himself with clammy palms and a dry mouth, standing in a convenience store with Libby, searching for magazines with pictures he could use. Pictures to demonstrate to Rachel who he was, and what he felt, and what he longed for.

None of which he wanted to share with Libby. Not because he didn't trust her, but because trusting her would be so easy. And he didn't want to.

She pulled something from the rack and smiled. "*Knitter's World.* Do you knit?"

"No."

"Figured that was a long shot." She tucked the magazine back into the rack as she laughed.

The sound had a melody to it, one that had grown on him. During those first few days of working at the schoolhouse, her humor had tested his patience, distracting him. Now he rather liked the cadence of it. He liked the way she tipped her chin up as the sound burst out. She really was beautiful.

But still a hazard. Still a complication he didn't need. Libby had seeped under his skin and into his thoughts, where she didn't belong.

He fidgeted with the sunglasses display next to the magazine rack.

"How about *Kitt 'n Kaboodle*?" Libby asked.

"What's that one about?"

"Kittens and puppies." She laughed again.

She needed to stop doing that. It was too enticing. Lately, it seemed as if all the sexual energy he'd locked away after Connie died had surged forward, a tsunami of base desires. Dr. Brandt was supposed to throw him a life preserver and pull him free from that, but all she'd done with her absolution and her permission was toss him into the deep, way over his head. She thought pursuing Libby might be therapeutic.

Dr. Brandt was a terrible influence.

He crossed his arms. "Do I seem like a kitten and puppy kind of guy?"

Libby turned and looked him up and down, her gaze finally meeting his. "No, you seem like more of a . . . rattlesnake kind of guy."

His laughter surprised him. "A rattlesnake?"

She nodded and held up a hand with two fingers curled out, like snake fangs, wiggling her arm a little. "Yes, you know. Coiled up tight, making all sorts of warning-type noises."

"Really." He tried to frown—and failed. "You know, rattlesnakes only make noise when something aggravates them."

"You are easily aggravated."

"You are a professional irritant."

She smiled at that. "Well, there's one job I've never applied for."

She turned back to the magazine rack, and Tom shook his head at his own foolish thoughts.

Somehow they managed to find a handful of magazines he hoped would be useful. There were a few about remodeling, one about fishing even though he rarely fished anymore, and one about organic gardening. That one he almost left behind. The garden had been Connie's dream, but he'd plant one with Rachel if ever she asked, and he wanted her to know that.

He and Libby kept the conversation light as they paid the convenience store cashier and left. Once outside, he tipped his head toward the sandwich shop next door.

"Come on. I'll buy you dinner for helping me out," he said.

"Ooh, someplace fancy, huh?" The color heightened in her cheeks, and for the first time, her laughter sounded more nervous than sincere.

He opened the door, and she stepped inside the shop, sliding her hands into her pockets. The place was small and smelled of toasted bread and burnt cheese. A few rust-colored booths ran along one wall, and other than the two yellow-smocked sandwich makers behind the red laminate counter, the place was empty.

"This might not be the best choice," Tom murmured.

"The food is actually pretty good," Libby whispered back. "It's just empty because it's Friday night."

It was Friday night? He didn't even realize that. He worked nearly every day, and so the weekends didn't mean much to him. But Libby should be out doing something social. Like being on a date. Not that it was any of his business. Maybe she was still pining over that jackass who'd up and moved to San Diego.

He frowned at the back of her head. What kind of woman fell for a guy like that anyway?

She turned and smiled at him, her thick gold hair sliding over her shoulder. "They have a chili dog here that is scrumptiously divine."

Oh. That kind of woman. The kind with sapphire blue eyes and a luscious mouth who used expressions like *scrumptiously divine*—but wasn't too girly to chow down a chili dog.

Well, it didn't matter to him what kind of mouth Libby Hamilton had, or how soft her lips might be, or what sort of words she used. As soon as they'd eaten and she'd explained to him how the hell to make a collage, he'd thank her and say good night. He could manage from there well enough. He was not going to sit next to her for hours, sifting through magazines while her hair fell all over his arm.

They ordered their food and sat down near the front window to wait for it. The evening light was fading slow, casting shadow fragments over the table. Country music played from the overhead speakers, some guy singing something about a truck.

"So, explain to me again the purpose of this collage," Libby said, taking a sip from her straw.

He stalled, drinking from his own cup, trying to decide how much he was prepared to share. "Well, you've met my daughter, right?"

Libby nodded.

"Do you know anything about . . . our situation?"

Libby glanced down at the table but then quickly back at him. There wasn't any judgment there, or pity either. Only calm regard. "My sister told me Rachel's mother died in a car accident about a year and a half ago."

Tom set down his drink. "Did she tell you I was driving?"

"Yes, she told me that, too. And that Rachel lives with her grandparents. Why is that?"

He looked out the window and watched cars drive by, people going on their way, never thinking how that turn in the road might be their last. "She moved in with them while I was recuperating. It was supposed to be temporary. Now it's going on a year and a half, and I can't seem to get my daughter back." He looked back at Libby.

She straightened in her seat. "That doesn't make sense. They can't just keep her there. I mean, she's your daughter. They don't have custody, do they?"

Tom felt a brief moment of gratitude that it hadn't come to that. "No, there is nothing legally binding her to stay there. I just . . . I want her to come home because she wants to. Forcing her would just make her dislike me even more."

"I'm sure she doesn't dislike you."

"I'm pretty sure she does. I was kind of . . . useless for a while after her mother died."

"Useless?"

He didn't want to tell her the details. She didn't need to know about the pills and the booze. Not because she'd judge him, but because she might not. And if she looked at him with any kind of tenderness in those pretty blue eyes, he'd be lost.

"Rumor has it I was a little unpleasant to be around," he murmured.

"And that's why you're going to a counselor together?"

The yellow-smocked waitress set red plastic baskets full of chili dogs and French fries in front of them. "Here you go."

Tom waited until she was gone before answering Libby.

"Yes, that's the reason for the counselor. And why I'm doing this art project with paste and scissors. Dr. Brandt says I need to meet Rachel at her level, and try to communicate in a method she can relate to, which leaves me at a distinct disadvantage."

"How so?" She took a bite of her chili dog.

"Because I don't understand high school girls any better now than when I was in high school. Maybe it's just my opinion, but she seems a little touchy."

Libby smiled, covering her mouth with the back of her hand. "I don't recall being particularly rational during high school."

"So it's not just her, then?" He took a bite from his own chili dog.

"No, it's pretty much a universal phenomenon, crazy-girl syndrome. She can't really help it—raging hormones, peer pressure, schoolwork, stupid boys."

"Are you referring to me?" He took another bite. This was a damn good hot dog.

"No." She chuckled, wiping mustard off her finger. "I'm referring to the boys at Monroe High School."

He dropped the remaining half of his chili dog into the basket. "Please don't remind me that my daughter is surrounded by high school boys." This topic he was completely too familiar with and yet entirely ill-equipped to handle.

Libby shook her head and wiped her mouth with a napkin. "I don't think you have to worry too much about that. She doesn't seem like the very flirty type."

"Does she make eye contact?"

"I assume so."

"Then she's flirty enough."

Libby laughed, but he didn't. Something deep inside pulled at him to tell her the truth. All of it. "I met Rachel's mother when she was just seventeen." He paused for a breath. "And she was pregnant pretty soon after that."

Libby felt her smile freeze. "You did? She was?" Ginny must not have known about that.

Tom's nod was slow as he pushed the basket to the side. "I worked at the grocery store where her family shopped. Connie would always come in and get a Coke and then go sit in the parking lot. Somehow I always managed to find myself out there at the same time so we could talk."

He picked up a French fry, looked at it for a minute, and then tossed it back into the basket. "I was eighteen. I had a car, so she used to sneak out the basement window at night. We fell hard, you know? We were reckless. Needless to say, her parents didn't like me much then. And they don't like me now. The way they see it, I've stolen their daughter from them twice. And now I'm trying to take their granddaughter."

Libby felt a French fry lodge in her esophagus. She had wanted to hear this, to know about Rachel and why they lived apart. But she hadn't given much thought to what went on before that accident, during the time he'd spent with a wife he loved and a family he adored. Thinking of it now was like tripping over something unexpected, a shove from some unanticipated force knocking her to the ground.

She'd known he'd been married, of course. It hadn't bothered her that much when Ginny mentioned it. But it bothered her now, when he talked about it. *We fell hard, you know?* The idea made her feel a little jealous.

A crease formed between Tom's eyebrows while he paused. "I've made a lot of mistakes, Libby. Falling for Connie wasn't one of them, but getting her pregnant in high school was. Crashing that car was another. And being a shitty father, well, that's the one thing I hope I can still fix."

His life *was* complicated. Nothing in hers came anywhere close. She'd lost her job because of a stupid mistake, but that didn't compare. Even losing Seth couldn't help her comprehend what he'd been through. "What does Rachel say about all this?"

His smile was meager as he slouched down in his seat. "Nothing, except that she wants to stay with her grandparents. That's why we need the collages, I guess. I can't tell where her opinion ends and her grandparents' takes over. Rachel's aunt Kristy has been running interference for me for months. It was her idea that we see this counselor."

"Do you think it's helping?"

He looked around the sandwich shop for a minute, and Libby's heart thumped a little erratically, hoping he'd say yes. He tipped his head, a small nod.

"I suppose so. It gives us a reason to be together. Otherwise she finds excuses to avoid me. Like not telling me about the talent show."

"I think you should go anyway."

Tom chuckled in unamused amusement. "I'm sure her grandparents would love having me show up unannounced."

A sense of injustice welled up inside her. "But they're not being fair to you. You have every right to see your daughter, even if she didn't invite you."

Her cheeks felt hot with indignation on his behalf, but he was calm over on his side of the table. "You think so, huh?"

Libby nodded. "I'll be there. I'll be backstage helping my sister, but you can sit with my parents."

Now Tom chuckled. "Oh, that would be easy to explain."

"What's to explain? You work with my dad every single day. My mom's a teacher at the school. And besides, isn't Rachel performing enough of a reason? I'm no counselor, but I'd bet you ten thousand dollars she secretly wants you there."

He looked at her now, his eyes dark but his tone light. "You don't have ten thousand dollars."

"Okay, fine. I bet you six dollars she secretly wants you there."

Tom laughed, and Libby felt her heart lighten by an ounce, or maybe two. He was sexy when he laughed. He should do it more often. He was a good man. A little surly, sure, but he had some good reasons. She wanted to help him. It was the neighborly thing to do, after all. It didn't have anything to do with his oxlike shoulders or the way her ankle sizzled every time his foot bumped against hers under the table.

"Six dollars, huh?" he said, picking up his chili dog again.

"Worth every penny you'll be losing."

He took a bite. "When is it?"

"Tomorrow night at seven. I'll tell my parents to save you a seat."

"I'm not sure I'm going."

"You have to go. For Rachel." And for him, too.

"I might sit in the back."

"No, you should sit up front. They'll save you a seat. And you might bring Rachel some flowers. Girls love that."

"You don't think it would embarrass her?"

"Maybe. But it proves you were thinking of her and went to the trouble of buying them."

Tom's smile broadened. "You seem pretty sure about all this."

"I'm an event planner. I am *all* about the details. Besides, all women love to get flowers. Even fifteen-year-olds, and even from their dad."

Tom moved his foot under the table, bumping hers, because his legs were long. They were probably strong, too. Just like his arms. Libby felt the tingle from her ankle zip all the way north.

She couldn't stop her thoughts. And she didn't try. Sex with Tom Murphy would be delicious. All that work he did with his hands? That could only be to a girl's advantage, right? *I always get the entire job done, Miss Hamilton.*

Yes, it would be good. Very good. But he was not a rational choice. Not for a fling and certainly not for a boyfriend. Tom Murphy was an emotional flight risk with more baggage than an airport lost-and-found, and a teenaged daughter to boot. She didn't need such a complicated man. She needed a simple white-collar businessman.

Still, sex with Tom would probably be heaven.

CHAPTER *ten*

The Monroe High School auditorium was full when Tom arrived. Probably because he'd sat in his truck in the parking lot for the better part of twenty minutes before deciding if he would actually go inside. But he was in there now, looking for a seat in the back in the darkest corner.

"Tom," Peter Hamilton called out, waving at him from the center aisle.

Tom gripped the carnations in his hand and heard the cellophane wrapper crinkle. What the hell was he doing here? He should leave. Rachel didn't want him there, or she'd have invited him. He scanned the crowd, looking for her grandparents, but didn't spot them in the crowd. They would not be glad to see him either.

But Peter Hamilton certainly was. Libby must have told him the whole story. And her mother, too, whom he'd never even met. This was exactly why he liked to keep his business just that. *His* business.

Tom raised his arm just long enough so Peter might know he'd been spotted, then worked his way in that direction. Peter held out his hand, and Tom shook it.

"Good to see you, Tom. Libby told us you'd be coming. Please allow me to introduce you to my lovely bride, Beverly."

Beverly Hamilton's smile was warm, nearly as sunny as Libby's, and Tom relaxed some.

"Hello, Tom," she said, standing up in her seat. "Peter has told me so much about you. I'm sorry I haven't been down to the . . . ice-cream parlor to meet you myself."

Tom smiled back. He'd heard all about this from Libby, about how her mother refused to set foot in the place because Peter hadn't told her he was buying it until the deal was done. He could see her point.

"It's a pleasure to meet you, Mrs. Hamilton."

"Oh, call me Bev. Are those flowers for your daughter? Aren't you sweet. If you give them to that usher over there, she'll take them to Rachel before the show."

Before the show? If he did that, Rachel would know he was there. He wasn't so sure that was a good idea. But then again, wasn't that the whole point? To prove to her his dedication? Still, maybe she'd enjoy herself more not knowing until the end that he'd come at all.

"Go on," Beverly urged. "The show is about to start."

Beverly nudged him toward the usher. He handed off the flowers and quickly made his way back to his seat next to Peter and Beverly. The lights dimmed. He felt a thrill and a tremor and a sense that he was right where he should be and yet somehow in the wrong place. He didn't know where he fit in when it came to Rachel. Parenting was supposed to be hard, sure. But it wasn't supposed to be this hard.

The first performer came and went, a painfully dull magic act where the only highlight was a pesky rabbit that did not follow instructions. After that came several mediocre dance routines, and a kid who played bagpipes. Tom's mind drifted. He thought about the ice-cream parlor and how much wood he should order for the counter. He thought about when he might have time to change the oil in his truck. And he thought about Libby, and how she'd looked last night when he'd said he could make the collage on his own. She'd looked disappointed, but for the life of him, he could not imagine why.

Three girls with hula hoops came onto the stage next and did an awkward routine. Tom wished he could leave. This wasn't entertainment. This was purgatory.

But then he saw Rachel. It was her turn. She walked out onto the stage wearing an elegant black dress and her hair twisted up in a fancy style, and Tom knew again that he was right where he should be.

Connie had taught her to play the piano, and the singing came naturally. But he hadn't heard her perform in over a year. As she started to play and her voice filled the auditorium, the emotion of missing her was suddenly as raw as it had been the day she'd climbed into her grandparents' car to leave him.

Listening to her now was a terrible, wonderful thing. His chest burned. Breathing took effort.

He watched Rachel's expression change as the music tore down her usual reserve. She lit up as she sang. It was a syrupy ballad but full of sweet emotion. She seemed happy and relaxed up on that stage, in front of all those eyes. He could see it in her smile and her posture and the fluid way her hands moved over the keys. A sense of paternal pride washed over him, and even though he could claim little ownership of it, he gave himself this moment to enjoy. And he knew then that he'd do anything to keep her looking that happy all the time.

After all the performances were over, and the parents milled around waiting for their little prodigies to emerge, Tom spotted Connie's sister, Kristy. Surprise lit her features when she met his eyes, but she smiled and moved his way.

She leaned close and hugged him. "Tom, it's good to see you. Rachel didn't mention you were coming."

"She didn't know. She didn't invite me." He sounded more terse than he'd meant to.

But Kristy nodded, her lips pressed together in a tight smile. "I told her she should tell you, for what that's worth."

"Thank you. Kristy, this is Beverly and Peter Hamilton. I'm working on a project for Mr. Hamilton right now. An ice-cream parlor."

They exchanged greetings and chatted, but all the while, Tom watched the crowd for two familiar faces. Rachel, whom he'd come to see. And Libby, whom, if he was being completely honest, he'd also come to see.

Moments stretched, but finally, there they were, Libby and Rachel walking down the stage steps together. Libby said something and his daughter laughed, and suddenly his legs felt like overcooked noodles. How long had it been since he'd seen Rachel laugh?

He'd known Libby was helping with the talent show, of course, but it hadn't occurred to him until just that moment she'd been getting to know his daughter. The idea pleased him and shook him at the same time, and he felt quite certain this was something that might come up with him and Dr. Brandt.

Libby raised her head and caught his eye, her smile brightening. She pointed and said something else to Rachel. His daughter's expression dimmed, but she sought him out and offered a hesitant wave when she spotted him. In her hand was the tiny cluster of flowers, making his heart take an extra thump. She wasn't annoyed. She might not be thrilled he was there, but at least she wasn't pissed. That was progress.

"There's my rock star!" Kristy exclaimed as soon as Rachel was within reach. She pulled her in for a tight hug.

"God, Aunt Kristy, I can't breathe." Rachel giggled. Her cheeks were bright pink, and a curl from her fancy hairdo was starting to unwind. She looked flushed and happy as she turned to Tom. She held out the flowers awkwardly. "Hey. Thanks for coming. And thanks for these. That was nice."

He wanted to hug her then, too, with all of the enthusiasm Kristy had shown, but he held back, not wanting to embarrass her. "Hey yourself. You did a great job."

"Thanks." Her cheeks went a deeper pink. She looked around at the cluster of them. "Um, hi, Mrs. Hamilton."

"Hello, Rachel. That really was a lovely song you played. I enjoyed it so much."

Peter leaned forward. "A fabulous job, young lady. You should be very proud of yourself."

"Thanks," she said again, and twisted the flower stems in her hands.

Libby leaned closer to Rachel. "That's my dad," she murmured. They exchanged a smirk that Tom had every intention of asking Libby about later.

Rachel turned back to Kristy. "Where are Grandma and Grandpa?"

Some of Tom's elation dimmed, but he tried not to take her question personally. Of course she'd be expecting them.

"They're over there," Kristy answered. "We'll catch them in a minute. Your dad was just telling me he's working on an ice-cream parlor."

Rachel's glance darted his way but just as quickly moved beyond him. "Oh, there's Jamie and Sarah. I need to catch them. Some of us are going out for pizza. Thanks for coming, everybody."

And just like that, she was gone.

"Rachel," Kristy called after her, but Rachel's slender form was folded into the crowd. "Well, I guess she's done with us."

Tom hadn't expected a marching band or confetti or anything just because he'd shown up to watch her in a talent show that she'd never invited him to, but this felt a little anticlimactic. He'd hoped they would have a chance to talk for a few minutes. He put his hands in his pockets and looked down at his shoes.

Still, he smiled toward his feet when Libby moved closer and murmured in his ear, "You owe me six bucks."

"I am incredibly happy that's over," said Ginny as she took a sip of her ice water. "Remind me the next time I'm eight and a half months pregnant to just say no to the talent show."

Ben rubbed her back as they sat across the table from Libby and Tom at the darkly paneled Monroe Street Pub. The place was crowded with Saturday night regulars, and the booth they had squeezed into was tiny.

Libby didn't mind. It gave her a good excuse to press close against Tom Murphy. He was wearing a hint of cologne tonight. It smelled good, kind of spicy sweet, but she almost missed the eau de sawdust-and-varnish that usually surrounded him. And his pinstriped shirt was a surprise. She'd pictured him as a purely plaid and mostly flannel kind of guy. But she liked the stripes. She liked him, too, and was very glad when he'd agreed to come have a drink with them after the talent show.

"So, Tom, what's it like working with the professor?" Ben asked, spinning his cocktail napkin with his index finger.

"It's all right. A little more chatter than I'm used to." He offered Libby a sideways glance.

"He means me," she said. "Apparently I talk too much."

Ben smiled. "This is the first time someone has told you that? Ah, good. Drinks." He reached out and took his from the waitress before she could set it down.

"Relax, Ben. She's not going to take it back," Ginny chided. But he gulped half of it down anyway, before the waitress had even left the table.

"Why so thirsty, Ben?" Libby asked. He wasn't typically much of a drinker.

He shook his head. "Absolutely craptastic day at the office. My boss is an idiot. But you know all about that, don't you, Libby? Maybe I should send an email and get fired."

Embarrassment slapped at Libby, even though she knew he was just teasing. Ginny shushed him, but the damage was done.

"How do you get fired from an email?" Tom asked Ben.

Libby took a big breath and raised her hand. "That was me. I got fired because of an email. I meant to send it to one friend at work, but I accidentally sent it to about thirty-five hundred employees. I think it might have gone out to all of our clients, too."

Tom took a sip of his drink. "That seems like an honest mistake. Why did they fire you for that?"

Ben started to chuckle, and Ginny shushed him again, but her own smile was evident.

Libby took another breath, like the one right before a bandage gets ripped off. "Probably because in the email I said the only thing more inflated than my boss's ego was her breast implants. I think I may have also mentioned she had a nose like a narwhal."

Tom burst out laughing, and so did Ginny and Ben. Libby smiled, and for the first time since getting fired, she realized the absurdity of the situation. She shouldn't have written that email, and she sure shouldn't have sent it, but all things considered, it *was* actually kind of funny.

"A narwhal?" Tom finally asked. "You mean like the dolphin?"

"It's a whale, actually. Ask my dad. He can tell you all about how early European explorers used to find their tusks and assume they were unicorn horns."

Tom laughed again. "Oh, well, in that case, it sounds much less insulting."

Libby nodded and took a drink. "Go ahead and laugh. You should see this woman's nose. Anyway, Ben, I do not recommend it. I am having a terrible time finding a new job. But at least I have the ice-cream parlor."

Ben pointed his finger at Tom while still holding his drink close to his lips. "Well, that doesn't sound half-bad to me. Can I come and work for you, Tom? I have virtually no carpentry skills, but I can pound a hammer."

"That kind of help I already have." He tilted his head toward Libby.

"Hey." She might have been offended had he not chosen just that moment to lean into her and smile, and she noticed that he had the tiniest cluster of freckles high up on his cheek, like a little constellation. She'd never noticed them before. She'd also never been this close to him. She liked it there.

"Actually, Libby has been a lot of help," Tom told them. "And I especially enjoy the updates about Marti's dungeon-themed wedding."

Libby laughed into her glass and bumped him with her elbow. "It's not dungeon themed. It's medieval."

"Just like marriage," Ben teased. He kissed Ginny's temple and then motioned to the waitress to bring another round.

"Speaking of medieval, have you seen that tattoo?" Ginny asked, crossing her arms over her expanded belly. "She's hiding it from Mom, you know."

"Good call. Maybe Marti hasn't gone completely crazy."

"In spite of her ring tone," Tom said, sipping from his beer.

Ginny looked over at her. "What ring tone is that?"

Wow. Everyone was dumping out secrets tonight. This one might require some finesse, but Libby was fast on her feet.

"Oh," she answered. "I was showing Dad how to assign unique ring tones to specific numbers, so he assigned that old Patsy Cline song for Marti. You know, 'Crazy'?"

Ginny's eyes narrowed, making the next logical leap. "What's the ring tone when *I* call your phone?" Her tone was as suspicious as her expression.

Libby smiled, prepared with an answer. "'Sisters,' from *White Christmas*. You know, 'Sisters, sisters. There were never such devoted sisters.'" She sang the line to sound convincing, but it was a big, fat lie. Her ring tone for Ginny was "Baby Got Back," but no way in hell was she telling her that.

Tom coughed a little into the neck of his beer and took a hearty swallow.

She thumped her knee against his under the table, a warning.

His knee tapped hers back. A promise to keep her secret.

She very nearly reached her hand down to give his leg a squeeze, but something held her back. Common sense, maybe?

"So how did you escape without getting a historical name, Ginny?" Tom asked, deftly changing the subject. Libby tapped her knee against him one more time for thanks.

"Oh, I have one. I'm Virginia Dare, named after the first European baby born in North America. Lucky for me, no one knows that." Ginny repositioned again and pressed her hand against her back. "And speaking of babies, this one has been kicking me all day. My back is killing me."

The evening rolled on, and as they talked and laughed, shared stories and ordered more drinks, a glow warmed Libby from the inside out. A glow that had nothing to do with her rum-and-Coke and everything to do with Tom Murphy. This was starting to feel like a double date.

It wasn't, of course, and that was a good thing. Probably. But . . . it felt nice. It was fun and comfortable and good. The kind of good you don't realize you're missing until suddenly it's there. A shiny gift from a secret admirer left on your doorstep.

There were so many more layers to Tom Murphy than she'd thought at first. More than any other man she knew. His job might be straightforward and obvious, but he was complex. And the more she learned, the more she liked. She knew she liked looking at him. A lot. That part was easy. But she also liked the way he extolled the virtues of run-down old buildings, and that sad but determined glow that lit his eyes whenever he talked about Rachel. She liked the flush that came over his face whenever he laughed at something she'd said. And at this moment, she very much liked the way he was looking at her, as if he might be seeing something more to her as well. Maybe he wasn't such a bad decision after all.

Butterflies fluttered to the tips of her fingers and toes, tickling everything in between.

"What?" he asked.

The butterfly in her throat made it hard to talk. "My car is parked back at the high school. When we leave, can you give me a ride over there?"

He nodded and set down his drink. "Um, sure."

"Well, I will be driving us home," Ginny said, tipping her head toward Ben. "I think Captain Craptastic has had a couple too many."

Ben offered up a lopsided grin and hugged her to his side. "You drive us home, but I promise I will absolutely h-h-h-hook you up when we get there." His slightly slurred words ended in a hiccup, prompting laughter all around.

Ginny shook her head. "Oh, that would be super, honey. I can hardly wait. You're so romantic."

"Romantic enough to knock you up." He tipped back the last of his drink.

"Okay. We're done here." Ginny shook her head again and pried herself from the booth. "Tom, I'm sorry you had to witness this. I shouldn't have let him order scotch. My husband really can't handle the hard stuff."

"I'll give you hard stuff, baby." Ben giggled like a frat boy.

Libby gasped with more laughter. She'd never seen her brother-in-law drunk before. Tipsy maybe, but never drunk.

"Oh, my God, Ben. You are humiliating yourself." Ginny laughed as she tugged on his arm to get him up out of the booth. "Come on. Let's go home."

"Let's give her a hand," Tom murmured, and Libby slid instantly from her seat.

They left the pub and, with some maneuvering and a lot of laughter, got Ben settled into the passenger side of Ginny's sedan. It was dark and after midnight. Thunder rumbled in the distance.

"Are you sure you're all right from here?" Libby asked her sister.

"Oh, I'll be fine. Ben may end up sleeping in the car, but I'm going to bed."

Ginny hugged her as best she could and reached a hand out to Tom. "Hey, we didn't get a chance to talk about this tonight, but Rachel is a really sweet girl. I know it's not perfect with you guys right now, but she'll come around."

"Thanks." That usual warning note was nowhere in his voice. He almost sounded relieved.

They watched Ginny drive away and then walked over to his old blue truck. The door creaked as Tom opened it for her. A gentleman. She climbed in and dropped her purse on the floor as he walked around and got in on the other side.

He looked at her expectantly, and she smiled back. "What?"

"Put on your seat belt," he said.

"Oh!" She thought for one second about sliding over to the spot right next to him, but that seemed a little bold. She wanted to, though. She could sidle right up beside him and blame it on the rum. But she stayed put instead, way over on her own side, and sighed.

Tom turned the key, and the truck came to life with a jerky vibration, the rattle and hum filling the silence in the cab. Conversation, which had been so easy all night, stopped, and suddenly Libby felt as twitchy as this truck. She was wide awake, and she didn't want to go home.

"Are you tired?" she heard herself asking.

Tom paused. "Not especially."

"Hmm. Me neither."

She waited for him to make a suggestion.

He didn't.

She stared at his hands on the steering wheel, those broad, work-rough hands. Maybe he'd be inept with them under the blankets, but even as she thought it, she knew that wasn't likely. How many times had she watched him glide his palm across a board, just to appreciate the grain? Tom Murphy paid meticulous attention to detail. Another tiny sigh rose up and halted in her throat.

"Thanks for the ride," she said as they arrived back at Monroe High School ten minutes later.

"No problem," he answered quietly. He pulled his truck into the spot right next to her car and stared out into the dark. "Thanks for making me come to the talent show tonight. I'm glad I did."

That little sigh of hers escaped, a breathy whisper. "I'm glad you did, too. And so was Rachel."

"Okay, okay. You'll get your six bucks." He finally met her gaze, and his joke fell flat.

Libby turned toward him. "You can keep your money. I just . . . you know . . . want you guys to be happy. I want you to be happy."

He stared at her, his face half in shadow, half in moonlight, until her heart somersaulted against her ribs. A clumsy, flailing sort of somersault. The kind that left one breathless. The kind that left bruises.

"You want me to be happy?" His voice was nearly lost in the space between them.

The atmosphere inside the cab shifted. A flash of lightning blinded Libby with its brilliance and then left them both in the dark.

"Yes."

He turned the key and cut the engine.

CHAPTER *eleven*

Tom heard thunder in the distance. Or maybe it was in his chest. He shouldn't have asked her that. Because they both knew what he really meant.

Do you want me to be happy for an hour? Maybe two? Will you wrap those legs around and squeeze me tight, and then let me be on my way?

Because he couldn't really offer her more than that.

And she shouldn't offer him half that much.

The snick of her seat belt unlatching sounded as loud as china shattering against a concrete floor.

The seat shifted as she moved closer, but he stayed still. Then Libby reached over and undid his seat belt, too. She may as well have been unzipping his pants for the message *that* sent.

He should stop her. He should warn her about his mistakes and all the damage he had caused. But the truth was, she already knew. He'd told her everything. In bits and pieces, he'd revealed all there was to him. And she wanted him anyway. And he wanted her. The notion struck, reverberating through him like a metal bat against a chain link fence.

Her face was always alluring, but he was unprepared for this. She gazed at him with open desire, and such certainty. She looked at him with . . . trust.

No one had looked at him like that in a good long while. He'd freeze that moment if he could, but Libby's hand reached up and touched his cheek, running her fingertips along his jaw and down his neck. His head tilted against the seat. His breath hitched, and every red blood cell in his body rushed straight to his groin. If the sheer force of an instantaneous erection could tear through denim, his was about to do it.

She leaned in close, not taking her eyes from his, but he reached out to pull her closer still, aching to feel more of her. All of her. He ran his hands through her hair, that dark gold hair he'd wanted to get tangled up in for weeks now. She rose up, letting it cascade down around both of their faces, and in that safe shelter, she kissed him. Sweet but firm. A simple kiss that was anything but. A begging-for-more kind of kiss. Her hands were on his face again, and she sighed, her breath soft against his mouth. Her motions were innocent enough, but flames shot through his veins like wildfire.

He kissed her back, deeper and more insistent, unwilling to resist. Ignoring all the warning bells pealing in his mind. The pull between them was undefeatable. It was magnetic, mindless, and elemental.

He ran one hand down her side, lingering over her breast, filling his palm and squeezing until she offered up a tender little moan and arched toward him. His other hand caught her chin. He leaned back, capturing her gaze, reading her expression. She did want this. She wanted him. Right here, right now.

He slid away from the steering wheel, toward her, and caught her leg with his hand, pulling her so that she straddled his lap. The move was sudden, but she followed his lead, and pressed down against him with another breathless gasp.

"Goddamn." He couldn't stop the words from slipping out any more than he could stop the motions of his hands or the violence of his heartbeat.

He'd been eighteen years old the first time he kissed Connie, and she'd been the only one since. Until now. He hadn't forgotten how, but somehow he'd forgotten the pure bliss of it. The discovery and the revelation of pure, unhindered want. Libby's body rubbed against the fire in his pants, and he knew there was no turning back. He wanted to taste every part of her, to memorize the curves and swells and valleys of her body. Even knowing that once he had, his life would never be the same.

He kissed her harder, breath mingling with breath. They melded together like honey and butter, slick and sweet, the perfect complement. Libby's soft little sighs and urgent gasps nearly undid him. Her hands traced his face and tugged at his hair, and when she slid her fingers inside the open collar of his shirt, he thought his heart might rip right through the wall of his chest.

She tugged at the buttons with an impatient gasp, loosening one and then another until his skin was free for her to explore. She pushed the edges of the fabric far apart and chuckled, an earthy, seductive sound. Her sultry gaze lifted to meet his eyes. She leaned forward, and he felt her smile against his lips.

"I'm going to hook you up, Tom Murphy." Her voice was a breathy tease, a challenge and a promise, and he exhaled in a burst. She dropped her mouth to his shoulder and scraped the muscle with her teeth. He groaned and grabbed her hips to guide her movements, wishing with all his might that he could melt away pants with the heat of his body.

He tugged at her shirt then, thrilling at the touch of her velvety skin underneath. She lifted her arms so he could pull it off over her head. He dropped it to the floor and soaked in the vision of Libby in the dim light in her lacy little bra. It was something he'd imagined, but his imagination had not done her justice. She was perfect. Just enough muscle, just enough curve.

He pulled her close and pressed his mouth against the lace even as he reached around and fumbled with the hook.

Libby gasped, and reached behind her back to make short work of the clasp. He slid the straps down her arms and chuckled to himself as he hung it from his rearview mirror.

"Nice." Libby smiled and pulled his face back to hers. He kissed her, hard and fast, but there were breasts to be discovered, and he wanted to know everything about them. His mind cleared of thought and flooded with nothing but desire.

This was Libby, here in his lap, kissing him back and grazing her teeth along the tight muscle of his shoulder. He opened his eyes and leaned back to see her, to watch her face. He ran a finger along inside the waistband of her jeans. She sighed, and smiled. Her thighs squeezed his hips, and she reached between them, tugging open the button of his jeans.

"I like big butts, and I cannot lie . . ."

Libby's eyes went round and met his. "That's Ginny calling," she gasped. "But it's so late. Something must be wrong."

She arched, trying to reach the floor of the cab to grab her phone from her purse. Tom winced as she scrambled and accidentally bumped her knee against his very optimistic hard-on.

"Sorry," she said, and then answered the phone. "Hello?"

"Hey, I'm sorry if I woke you up," Ginny said, her voice strained. Libby turned so she was sitting on the seat next to Tom while he pressed one hand against his forehead. He looked at her from one squinted eye.

"No, you didn't wake me. But it's almost two in the morning. Are you okay?"

"Sort of. I think my water just broke, and my husband is passed out in the car." There was a slightly hysterical quality to her giggle.

"Oh, geez. Are you kidding me?" Libby looked at Tom, who was now looking back at her with obvious concern. "Her water broke, and Ben's passed out in the car," she told him.

"Who are you talking to?" Ginny asked.

"Um, Tom."

"Really? Well, that's, oh—" She paused and took a deep breath. "Hang on. Contraction time."

"Contraction time? God, Ginny. How long ago did those start?"

"Well, I guess a while ago. I mean, I was having the fake kind all day, and tonight during the talent show, on and off. But I guess maybe they weren't fake."

"The fake kind? What the hell is a fake contraction?" Libby reached down on the floor and grabbed her shirt, holding it in front of her. She really couldn't have this conversation with her sister while sitting topless in Tom Murphy's truck.

"They're called Braxton Hicks, and I've had them for months. They were really bothering me today, but I thought I was just stressed out about the talent show. But now I don't know. They're getting kind of intense."

Libby's throat went dry. "Did you call your doctor?"

"Yes, and she said I should come to the hospital. But she told me not to drive myself, and Ben is useless to me right now." The hysterical giggle evaporated, and Ginny burst into tears. "How am I supposed to tell my doctor I can't come to the hospital because my husband is too drunk to drive? They'll take my baby away if I tell them that."

Libby held the phone away from her ear because Ginny's personal volume was rapidly increasing in decibels. She turned to Tom. "She says—"

"I heard her," Tom said. "We'll go and get her. Tell her we're on our way."

"We're on our way, Gin. Get your stuff together." She tossed the phone back in her purse and pulled her bra from the mirror.

"You don't need to take me. I can just drive over there myself." She said it, but she didn't mean it.

"You take care of your sister. I'll deal with Ben."

A swell of adoration wrapped around Libby. She looked at him, sitting there with his shirt pushed wide open looking very much like a sexy man, and all she wanted to do was climb back on his lap. "I'm sorry about this," she said.

Tom gave a little shake of his head. "Babies don't wait."

He would know about that, wouldn't he? He'd had one. It was easy to forget he was somebody's dad when she saw him here in the moonlight with the button of his jeans undone. But he was. And she realized she didn't really mind that at all.

CHAPTER *twelve*

The maternity waiting room at Monroe General Hospital was decorated with bunnies and kittens, just as Libby might have imagined, had she ever given any thought to that sort of thing. Tom was perched on the edge of a baby-blue vinyl chair when she walked in. He looked as tired as she felt.

"Well, Ginny is all settled in her room, and Ben is with her," she said, sinking into the chair next to him. "Thank you so much. This would have been twice the adventure without your help."

It had been a mad scramble getting her sister and brother-in-law to the hospital, but Ben sobered up pretty quickly once he realized this was no drill. And Tom's cool thinking kept everyone's panic at a manageable level.

Libby leaned back in her seat and looked at his broad shoulders. They were like mountains. He was hunched over a little, elbows resting on his knees.

"I'm glad to help, but you would've managed fine once Ben was upright."

Her chuckle ended with a sigh. "Not quite how you and I expected this night to end, though, huh?"

He shook his head and looked down into the paper coffee cup he held in his hands. He tipped it back and drank the rest. "Not quite. Listen, I'm going to head out now. Okay? You called your parents, right? They should be here soon."

She put a hand on his back, and his muscles tensed beneath her touch. Something unwelcome knocked against Libby's good mood.

He turned and gave her a faint smile that faded fast, and suddenly all of his walls were back up. Reinforced.

There were a lot of reasons that might be, and Libby wasn't sure what to say. She only knew she didn't like his frowning. They'd had a good time tonight. A great time, in fact. A time that would've gotten even better if Ginny hadn't called. But suddenly Libby felt very far away from those moments in his truck.

Tom stood, and her hand dropped to the chair.

"Hey," she said softly.

He looked down at her, his expression guarded.

Unease rippled through her core. "Are you okay?"

He crumpled the empty coffee cup in his hand and stared at it like he wasn't sure why he was holding it. "As good as I ever am in a hospital at four o'clock in the morning."

She sat forward, a little stung by his mood. She hadn't asked him to come. He'd insisted, but regret was splashed all over his face. She gestured to the empty waiting room. "I'm sorry about all this."

He shook his head and tossed the cup into a nearby wastebasket. "Don't be sorry. It's probably a good thing we got interrupted when we did."

It didn't feel good at all. It felt awkward and scratchy. A fluorescent light buzzed overhead. "A good thing?"

"Don't you think?" His tone formed an edge.

"Um . . ." Libby stood up and faced him. "Not really. I was pretty happy with where things were heading tonight. Weren't you?"

He rubbed his hand across his jaw, now rough with whiskers. "Tonight was . . . reckless."

"Awesome?" she said at the same time.

"Reckless," he said again. "Libby. I'm just . . ." Tension creased lines across his forehead.

The old Tom was back, the one who didn't say much with words but spoke volumes with his silence.

"Let me guess. It's complicated, right?"

He paused. "Yeah."

His resistance was a force field, but she'd broken through it once. She'd do it again. "I'm pretty good at puzzles. I think I can figure you out."

He shook his head again. “I have professionals working on that. I’d rather you didn’t get caught in the muck.”

That’s what he was doing? Trying to protect her? “Well, I appreciate that, but maybe I’ll just put on some waders and try it anyway.”

He met her gaze. “It would be easier for me if you didn’t.”

His voice was tender, but the words were rough as sandpaper scraping at her skin. And they didn’t sound all that different than Seth saying, “Don’t wait for me.”

Embarrassment burned her cheeks. “Oh. Oh, okay, I get it.”

“No, you don’t. Libby—”

“Tom! I didn’t expect to see you here.” Libby’s father came around the corner into the waiting room, his hair a little flat from sleeping.

Her mother was right behind him. “Goodness, it’s early. Why are babies always born so early? All three of you girls—oh, hello, Tom.”

Tom took a step back from Libby, and she felt the distance multiply with every breath.

“Hello, Peter. Bev. I was just on my way out. Looks like you’re about to become grandparents.”

“A blessed event,” her father said, yawning and nodding.

“Which room is Ginny’s?” Libby’s mother asked.

It took a second for Libby’s mouth to work. Her heart felt like clay, cracking as it dried.

Tom looked at the kitten wallpaper, and at his shoes, and avoided her.

Libby swallowed down her sigh and finally answered. “She’s down the hall. Come on, Mom. I’ll show you.”

“So how exactly did you get drafted into transportation service?” she heard her father ask as she and her mother moved down the hall, but Tom’s answer was too quiet to overhear.

Theodore Roosevelt Garner was born at 6:04 a.m., weighing in at a robust seven pounds, nine ounces—an impressive amount considering he was born almost three weeks ahead of schedule.

“Thank God you had him early,” Marti said from her pleather chair in the corner of Ginny’s hospital room. She stroked the baby’s cheek. “Imagine what a porker he’d have been if you cooked him any longer.”

"Stop touching his face, Marti. Did you wash your hands?" Ginny said from her bed.

"Germs," said Nana from the other chair. "You mothers today are all too worried about germs. We used to play all day in the dirt and drink from a garden hose. And look at me. Eighty-six years old and still healthy as a mule."

"And as stubborn as one," Libby's mother muttered to no one in particular.

It had been two days since Ginny delivered her baby, and the Hamilton women were gathered in her hospital room to coo and sigh.

And bitch.

"How fares the prince?" her father asked, poking his head in through the doorway.

Ginny smiled. "He's perfect, Daddy. They're letting us go home today."

Libby's dad lifted his brows and stepped into the room. "In that case, I'd better get back over to your place and finish putting together that baby swing. I have to stop by the ice-cream parlor first, though."

He took a look at Marti with a baby nestled in her arms and blanched. He turned to Libby instead. "Want to come with me?"

To the ice-cream parlor?

Where Tom was working?

She hadn't talked to him since he'd left the hospital just before the baby was born. She'd thought he might try to call. They'd left some very pleasant business unpleasantly unfinished, and now that she'd had a couple of days to stew about things, she couldn't help but think his change in attitude had been triggered by all this baby stuff. It must have been a little overwhelming for him when his own baby was just out of reach. Not to mention how a late-night visit to a hospital may have stirred up distressing memories.

He hadn't told her any details about his car accident, and it didn't feel right to ask. She didn't want to push him where he wasn't ready to go, or force herself on him if he wasn't interested. But he'd seemed interested enough when her bra was dangling from his rearview mirror.

Plus she just plain missed him. She missed Tom Murphy in a way she had never missed Seth. That concept gnawed at her. Maybe there wasn't much point in it if Tom didn't miss her back, and yet she couldn't seem to help herself. The memory of his urgent kisses and the heat of his skin under her hands was impossible to block from her mind. Not that she'd tried.

"Sure, I'll come with you."

Tom's truck was there when Libby and her father arrived. A foolish but irrepressible bubble of hope rose within her. Tom had been tired and overwhelmed at the hospital. Surely by now he'd had time to get his bearings.

Her father grabbed a long coil of rope from the backseat of the car before they headed inside.

"What's the rope for?" she asked, her curiosity percolating.

"I'm going to tie it to the bell so I can ring it."

She felt a blip of relief. Her family had all been studiously mute about the fact that she'd been with Tom Murphy at two o'clock in the morning, yet for a second there she'd thought maybe her dad was about to string him up for making improper advances. Although technically, she'd done most of the advancing.

"Uh, I'm not sure the neighbors around here want to hear that bell. Isn't there a noise ordinance or something?"

"First of all, there are no neighbors close to here. Second, that ordinance question would be an excellent thing for you to look into."

He chuckled at her sigh as they climbed the steps.

Tom was inside, his back to the door as he measured a board across a couple of old sawhorses. Her heart hiccupped at the sight of him in his faded jeans and the blue shirt he often wore, the one with the tiny hole in the shoulder seam that she found herself wanting to sew for him, which was hilarious since she could hardly thread a needle.

This attraction to him was as impossible to ignore as it was illogical to pursue.

"Greetings, Tom. The proud grandfather has arrived." Her father adjusted the rope he'd slung over his shoulder.

Tom's smile did not quite reach his eyes.

She'd hoped for an enthusiastic welcome, some hint he'd reconsidered those words from the hospital and was glad to see her, but her wishful thinking clunked inside her, like driving with a flat tire.

"Congratulations. How's Ginny?" Tom adjusted a pencil behind his ear and glanced her way.

Her father beamed. "Mother and child are both doing well, thank you. And Ben has been forgiven. Thanks for helping out that night. You are quite the hero."

Tom looked her way again, his glance wary as if he was worried she'd told everyone about their *reckless* behavior. Her ire rose a bit. They hadn't done anything wrong. A few kisses in the dark that he seemed determined to forget about.

"Just in the right place at the right time," Tom answered.

She found his words utterly ironic.

"Well, nonetheless, our family is beholden to you," her father said. "Now I'm going to take this old rope and tie it to the bell so I might herald my grandson's birth."

Tom frowned and reached out to take it. "That bell is pretty high up there, Peter. Why don't you let me do that?"

"Nonsense. I may be a grandfather, but I can still stand on a chair and tie a good solid knot. I'll holler if I need you."

Tom looked like he wanted to argue, but Libby knew the bell wasn't that high up. Her dad could handle it. It was pretty obvious Tom knew that, too.

Her dad's footsteps faded away as he climbed the tiny back staircase leading to the bell tower.

Tom looked at her and adjusted the pencil behind his ear again. His skin flushed, and his stare grazed over her body.

"Hi," she said, when he said nothing.

"Hi. How's Ginny?"

"My dad just told you. She's fine. How are you?"

Tom shook his head and looked down. He took off his hat and then immediately put it back on. "I meant to call you."

Libby crossed her arms and tapped her foot. "Really? Because I would have answered if you had."

A small chuckle passed through his lips at the snap in her tone, and his dark gaze lifted, a sheepish expression on his face. "I'm sorry I upset you."

"Good. You should be. Because now I'm embarrassed."

"Embarrassed? Why?" Genuine surprise brought his head up, and he faced her squarely.

"Because *you're* acting embarrassed. You're acting like we did something terribly wrong, but we didn't. It wasn't that big a deal, Tom."

He huffed at that and frowned, and took his hat off again to run a hand through his hair. Finally his arms crossed.

"I'm not embarrassed, Libby, but where I come from, kissing a woman is a pretty big deal." His voice was quiet but firm.

Her heart plummeted. "That's not what I meant."

"Well, I'm sorry. I don't know what else to say. You caught me off guard the other night. And you're catching me off guard right now. Hell, everything about you catches me off guard."

His gaze dropped to her mouth and lingered like a touch, until he huffed again and turned his face away.

Though it made no sense, his frustration pleased her. He *did* want her. She could see it in the tension on his face, the way his hands squeezed into fists. She could practically see him remembering, reconsidering.

And so she waited, knowing this was one of those times she needed to let him talk first.

After a pause, he turned back, and reached out a hand. "Libby, I know I—"

A combination of sounds ricocheted around the room just then, the *clang* of an old schoolhouse bell, wood splintering, and Libby's father shouting out. And then an ominous silence.

Their gazes crashed together in shock, a moment frozen, before Tom turned and sprinted to the bell tower steps. Libby paused, stunned for the space of a heartbeat, but followed seconds later.

Her father lay in a twist in the middle of the stairs, arms flung out and his head lower than his feet. Or his foot, rather, because one leg was straight out, while the other was somewhere underneath him. He was motionless, and Libby's stomach jumped into her throat.

"Fuck, fuck, fuck." Tom's voice was eerily calm. "Libby, call nine-one-one."

Her father's eyes were closed. Why were his eyes closed? "Dad?" she called up the remaining stairs.

Tom turned and clasped her shoulders, giving her a gentle shake. "Libby, listen to me. Do you have your phone?"

"It's in the car."

"Mine is downstairs in my jacket pocket. Grab it, or get yours, and call nine-one-one."

She couldn't move her feet. "The car keys are in his pocket."

"Fuck." Tom pulled her back down the stairs. She should stay with her dad, but she let Tom lead her away. Was that blood on the steps?

Tom jerked his phone from the pocket of his jacket and punched the numbers. He handed it back to her. "Tell them to send an ambulance. Do you know the address here?"

"What? Oh, yes. Of course."

"Good." He spun back around and disappeared back up the steps.

"Nine-one-one dispatch. What is your emergency?"

Time slowed to a crawl as Tom staggered up the stairwell back to Peter's side. This couldn't be happening again. Not another person broken right before his eyes. He couldn't bear that. Peter Hamilton wasn't moving so much as an eyelash.

"Peter," Tom called, pressing two fingers against his neck. He had a pulse. Barely. But Connie's pulse had been there, too. Until it wasn't. "Peter, can you hear me? You fell on the stairs."

There was no sound except the hammering of his own heart. He took a breath and swallowed the knot pressing against his throat. He patted Peter's cheek gently. "Come on, old man. Wake up. No sleeping on the job."

He looked up, trying to figure out what had happened. The iron school bell was at the top of the steps, flipped on its side, its support beam dangling from above and split in two. Fuck. He should have checked that and reinforced it. He shouldn't have let Peter go up there alone.

He looked down again. Peter's leg was broken—that much was for sure, the way it was jacked up behind him. There was blood underneath him, too, coming from the back of Peter's head. He couldn't tell how bad any of this was. But it looked bad enough. And he didn't want Libby to see it. Because these kinds of visions stuck for a lifetime.

Libby came clamoring back and stood at the base of the steps, breathless. "Is he awake?"

Tom shook his head. "No. Stay down there, okay?"

She came up anyway, just as he knew she would. Her blue eyes clouded with worry. Her lips trembled. "Shouldn't we lift his head up?"

"We should wait for the ambulance. Moving him could make things worse."

Libby moved closer and sank down on the step opposite Tom with Peter in between. She touched her father's face then snatched her hand away as he twitched and let out a sharp gasp.

"Dad?"

He squinted and blinked and then tried to sit up. Tom caught him by the shoulders and held him still. "Whoa, whoa, Peter, hold on. You've had a nasty fall. Take it easy."

"Dad, are you okay?"

Peter looked at her, forehead wrinkled in confusion. "What happened?" He tried to sit up again.

"Libby, grab my coat to put under his head," Tom said.

She paused, looking as dazed as her father, but then hurried back down the stairs.

"You fell down the steps in the bell tower, Peter. Do you remember?" Tom asked.

Peter was inverted on the steps, blood seeping from his head, and every instinct Tom had told him to help Peter move, but he knew better. It was safer to let him stay put until the ambulance arrived.

Libby came back with the jacket, and Tom rolled it up and wedged it gently beneath Peter's head.

"What hurts, Peter?" he asked.

More confusion passed over Peter's face. "My head. My foot." His eyes drifted closed again.

Maybe that was good. If things hurt, then he wasn't in shock. Yet.

Libby's breath was loud, her face pinched with anxiety. Tom wanted to reach over and clasp her hand and tell her everything would be fine. But he'd broken so many promises in the past, he was done with making ones he couldn't keep. All he could do was remind his lungs to do their job, and help all of them stay calm.

She looked at him in the dim light of the tiny stairwell. "Can't we do something?"

The question tore at him because he had no answer, and he should. He should have learned something from the last accident, but all he'd learned was how fragile a body could be.

"We just wait," he said.

"But there's blood," she whispered.

"He's tough, Libby," he said. It was as much comfort as he dared to offer.

The sirens wailed minutes later, though it felt like decades.

"Go flag them down. I'll wait here."

She hesitated.

"Go," he said again.

He heard the paramedics, and Libby's strident answers, and seconds later they were in the stairwell, their shirts crisp and white, their actions efficient.

"We're going to need some room, sir," one of them said. "Could you wait downstairs, please?" Tom patted Peter's shoulder and moved from the stairs into the ice-cream parlor to stand next to Libby. She was silent, her fist pressed against her mouth. He knew her heart was in overdrive with worry. There was nothing he could do about it, but when her father yelled in pain as they repositioned his leg, Tom wrapped his useless arms around her shoulders and held her tight.

At last they had Peter moved to a backboard, and then the metal gurney. Libby rushed to the stretcher once they'd maneuvered it into the main room, and Tom followed.

"Dad?" She leaned over. Peter's eyes were glassy when he turned to her.

"I didn't get to ring the bell," he said, and then his eyes drifted to a close once more.

"Can I ride with him?" she asked as a dark-haired paramedic carrying a red medical bag stepped around them.

"No, ma'am. I'm sorry. But we'll take good care of him. He's headed to Monroe General."

"I'll take you," Tom said, watching them slam shut the ambulance door.

She looked at him, still no tears in those dark blue eyes. Just a depth of concern he understood completely.

"You don't have to. I can drive my dad's car."

"I don't think so. Get in the truck."

Outside, she grabbed her purse and a jacket from her dad's car. Then she went back to get Peter's jacket, too, not really grasping that he wouldn't need it at the hospital. Like locking the door when a tornado is coming.

She climbed into the truck and buckled in. A wavering breath escaped. He wanted to say something, anything that might help. But he didn't know anything.

"I should call my mom. Shouldn't I?" She looked at him with uncharacteristic uncertainty, as if there were a protocol for this type of situation.

"You dial. I'll talk to her, okay?"

She didn't argue, just pulled her phone from her purse with trembling hands. She pressed a few buttons and handed it to him. "It's ringing."

"Hello?" Beverly Hamilton's voice was chipper, thinking it was her daughter calling. He was about to ruin that.

"Beverly, it's Tom Murphy. I've got Libby's phone."

"Oh, hello, Tom." She sounded curious, but still not worried.

"Listen, Peter took a little tumble at the ice-cream parlor. I'm afraid he may have broken something."

"Not something of yours, I hope." She laughed, and he wondered if his tactic of downplaying the seriousness would backfire.

"No, but maybe his leg."

"His leg? Are you certain?" Worry seeped into her voice.

He thought of how Peter's foot had been in completely the wrong place. "Yes, ma'am. Pretty sure. He's on his way to Monroe General in an ambulance, and I've got Libby with me. We're heading there now."

"An ambulance? Monroe General? Oh. Oh, my goodness, we just left there with Ginny. Let me get her home, but then Nana and I will come right back."

"Beverly," he said, trying to sound calm but insistent, "you should hurry a little bit, okay?"

"Of course. I'll be there as soon as I can."

Tom disconnected the call and handed the phone back to Libby. She was staring at him, forehead furrowed in a frown.

"A little tumble? My dad fell halfway down the steps of a bell tower." Her voice broke, his composure nearly breaking with it.

"You want your mother knowing that when she's trying to drive? She'll find out more at the hospital."

She turned back to the front, staring. "I guess." Her breathing came in short puffs. After another minute she whispered, "Tom. Can you pull over? I think I need to throw up."

CHAPTER *thirteen*

For the second time that week, Libby found herself surrounded by members of her family in a waiting room at the local hospital, but this time was very different. Her mother had arrived with Nana nearly half an hour after she and Tom had gotten there. Marti and Dante joined them shortly after that.

"You again?" Libby overheard Dante ask Tom as he settled into a beige plastic chair next to him.

Tom nodded slowly. "This family is like quicksand, kid. Get out while you still can."

Dante drank from a can of Red Bull. "Nah, I'm already in. Marti's worth it."

His simple declaration threatened to nudge out the tears loitering in Libby's eyes. Maybe it was just the stress of the day that made her irrationally sentimental, but Libby suddenly had an overwhelming sense that Dante was indeed the one for Marti.

But while Dante was there of his own choosing, Tom Murphy seemed to be struggling to get away. She didn't want him to feel that way. She wasn't a burden. She wasn't a trap. If that's how he felt, then maybe he really should go.

But she didn't tell him that, because she wanted him to stay. And he didn't leave. That had to mean something.

It was Tom who had told the others all the details of the fall, downplaying the more gruesome aspects while being honest about how badly her dad was injured. It was Tom who helped her climb back into the truck after she'd puked up her breakfast on the side of the road. And it was Tom who'd asked a burly nurse for a toothbrush when they got to the hospital so Libby could freshen up.

On second thought, no wonder he wanted to get away.

"What's your name again?" Nana asked Tom after they'd all been sitting there for what felt like ten hours but had really been less than two.

"That's Tom, Nana," Libby's mother said.

"Oh, yes. My son, Peter, has been telling me all about you. He says you're very smart. Are you very smart?"

Tom sat up straighter in his chair. "Not really, ma'am."

"Yes, you are," Libby said. She'd give voice to his skills, even if he wouldn't. "Tom is very smart, Nana. He knows everything there is to know about restoring old buildings. You should see what he's done at the ice-cream parlor. It was a disaster before he got there, but now it looks fantastic."

"Your father told me it wasn't in that bad of shape," her mother said.

"Um . . ." Libby realized her mistake too late. "Honestly, Mom, it was a train wreck. We figured it was best to keep that to ourselves until we had a chance to get some work done. Thank goodness for Tom, though."

His skin flushed. "I've restored lots of old buildings. This one looked worse on the surface than it turned out to be. Structurally it was still in good shape." He paused before adding quietly, "Except for the bell tower."

The conversation halted at that, and Tom stood abruptly and walked to the window in the waiting room, his back to them. His muscles bunched as he crossed his arms tightly across his chest. "I should have checked that."

His misplaced guilt was a neon sign, frustrating Libby. He'd done nothing but rescue members of her family this week. Why couldn't he see that?

He pulled a phone out of his pocket and walked into the hallway outside the waiting room to make a call.

Marti moved over to sit next to her. "How are you?" she whispered.

"Shitty. But better than Dad," Libby whispered back. "You should have seen him on that staircase, Marti. It was awful."

Marti's green eyes glistened with unshed tears, and she clasped Libby's hand. "I'm so grateful Tom was there."

Pinpricks pierced all over her heart. "Me, too."

"What's up with you guys, anyway? Ginny told me you were with him the night she had the baby."

Libby glanced up. She could see Tom pacing in the hallway, talking into his phone.

"It's complicated," Libby heard herself saying. She pulled her hand free of her sister's.

"Because of his daughter?"

Libby nodded. "Because of lots of stuff." His daughter. That car accident. Connie. Libby was competing with all kinds of ghosts.

Marti shook her head, making her hair sway. She had two long, skinny, white feathers woven in just behind her ear. "Please tell me it's not because you're still hung up on Seth."

Libby scoffed at the question. "No, I'm not. Not even a little bit."

For the first time, she knew she meant it. She hadn't talked to Seth in ages, or even exchanged a text. She'd told him to ship those boxes of her stuff just so she wouldn't have to deal with seeing him. The days had gone by, and she'd filled them with work and family and the talent show. And Tom.

Maybe he wasn't ready for her, but she was most certainly ready for him.

He came back in the waiting room a few minutes later, tucking his phone into his pocket and looking just as exhausted as he had the other morning when they'd brought Ginny here, and Libby felt some guilt of her own. Her family *was* like quicksand. And poor Tom Murphy was masochistically helpful.

He sat down next to her, and Marti moved back over by Dante, leaving Tom and Libby a hint of privacy.

Tom had a stain on the front of his shirt, round and dark, and she realized it was blood. The vision of her father, bent and in distress, exploded in her mind. She didn't know any details of Tom's car accident, but it must have been even worse than this. And today would certainly dredge that up.

She leaned closer to him, wishing she could wind her arm through his, to hold his hand. But she didn't. "I'm sorry," she whispered instead.

He looked back at her, his eyes as dark as espresso and just as intense. "For what?"

She gave a little shrug. "For the stuff that makes you sad."

A molasses-slow smile turned up the corners of his mouth, and Libby saw some of those walls start to come back down.

Another half hour passed before a pretty, dark-haired young woman in scrubs and a lab coat came through the double doors of the emergency department.

"Are you the Hamilton family?"

Libby's pulse jumped to attention as everyone stood up and clustered around the doctor.

"I'm Beverly Hamilton," Libby's mother said, stepping in front of them all.

"I'm Dr. Hoover, Mrs. Hamilton. It's good to meet you. First, let me say your husband is currently resting comfortably, and I believe he should make a full recovery. He appears to have struck his head quite hard. He had a one-inch laceration that we've stapled with no complications."

"Stapled?" Dante said.

Marti wiped away a fresh tear.

The doctor smiled. "Stapling is standard procedure. It's not as bad as it sounds."

Libby shuddered at that image anyway. Maybe it wasn't as bad as it sounded, but it still sounded pretty awful.

The doctor continued. "As I understand from what the paramedic told me, Mr. Hamilton fell from a chair and then down some stairs, and then was unconscious briefly, is that correct?"

Libby nodded. "Yes. We were with him." She reached over and tugged the sleeve of Tom's jacket, bringing him closer.

"Well, he's been seen by our trauma team, and they plan to admit him for observation to evaluate his mental status. That's standard whenever someone loses consciousness. Mr. Hamilton has demonstrated some amnesia for the event, which is also quite typical. He may never fully remember, which is common with a concussion." The doctor's phone chimed, and she pulled it from her pocket to glance at it.

Dante wrapped one arm around Marti and the other around Libby's mother.

Looking back to Libby's mother, the doctor continued. "We've completed a CT scan of his brain, and there doesn't appear to be any serious injury that we can detect at this time. However, people respond to concussions in different ways, and it's difficult to predict if he'll have ongoing problems such as headaches or memory problems. This is something you'll want to watch for. But there's a very good chance he'll suffer no lingering side effects."

Libby slipped her hand into Tom's. He squeezed it back. A tiny thing, but monumental just then.

"Now, regarding his right leg," the doctor said. "He has a tibia and fibula fracture just above the ankle. The breaks are fairly clean, and I suspect he'll regain full use of his leg, but he will need surgery. He's been seen by our orthopedic team, his leg has been splinted, and they're taking him to surgery. Despite his injuries, Mr. Hamilton seems to be in good spirits, although he's slightly combative about the fact that he'll be non-weight-bearing on that foot for six to eight weeks. He tells me he's opening an ice-cream parlor, is that right?"

"Yes." Libby spoke again, clearing the frog of emotion from her throat.

The doctor smiled. "And I got the impression from our conversation that he's taking a very active role in the construction, yes?"

Libby nodded, but the doctor shook her head. "Not for a while on that. The surgeon will give you more specifics, but I can guarantee strenuous manual labor will be out of the question for the next several weeks."

Libby nodded, not sure if she felt relief or despair. Thank goodness her father was all right—but this changed everything.

"Mrs. Hamilton, could you come back with me, please? We have some forms for you to fill out, and then you can see your husband before surgery. I'm afraid the rest of you will have to wait until he's out of recovery. You may just want to come back tomorrow."

Libby's mother looked slightly dazed and uncertain.

"Go on with the doctor, Mom. We'll wait for you out here," Marti said.

"Can I see him? I'm his mother," Nana said.

The doctor's smile was practiced. "I'm sorry, ma'am. They're holding the operating room for him, and we have a very full house tonight. There will only be time for one visitor. But we'll take very good care of him."

Libby's mother turned to look at them. "Someone should take Nana home."

"We've got it, Mom. Don't worry. We'll be here when you're done with Daddy," Marti said.

The doctor led their mother away while the rest of them exchanged glances of varying levels of concern and relief. Tom pulled his hand from Libby's and slid it into his pocket.

"Why don't you take Nana home, Libby?" Marti said. "Dante and I can stay and wait for Mom."

"I don't have my car."

She heard Tom's soft sigh from over her shoulder. "I can drive you."

She turned around to face him. "Are you sure? Seems like you've done enough."

His smile was tired but sweet. "It's nothing. I'll take you and your grandmother home."

Getting Nana into Tom's truck was no easier than it had been getting a drunken Ben into Ginny's car, but at last they hoisted her up and in, and she now sat between Tom and Libby as they headed down the road.

"I haven't been in a truck since I was a girl," Nana said. "But it's just as bouncy as I remember. And it smells the same. Now, young man, my son tells me you're a widower. Is that so?"

Libby pressed her fingers against her temples. Her grandmother couldn't remember anybody's name or how to button a sweater, but *this* detail she had crystal clear. Libby tried to steal a glance at Tom without being too obvious, but Nana's fluffy white head was in the way.

"Yes," he answered, his hand seeming to grip the steering wheel more tightly.

"That's unfortunate. What happened to your wife?"

"Nana, please. That's not what anyone wants to talk about right now."

She should've just used her mother's car and brought Nana home in that. But the truth was, she and Tom had some things to talk about, and she'd hoped to do that as soon as they were alone.

"She died in a car accident, Mrs. Hamilton. I was driving too fast, hit a slick spot in the road, and crashed into a tree." His voice was neutral, as if he'd explained this a dozen different times and the words held no more emotion, but his knuckles whitened on the steering wheel and Libby saw a muscle twitch in his jaw.

"Oh, my. That's very sad." Nana reached down and double-checked her seat belt.

The muscle twitched again. "I don't drive too fast now, Mrs. Hamilton."

"I'm glad to hear that. I'd expect you to be extra-careful now that you're seeing my granddaughter."

"Nana, we're not . . ." Libby took a breath. "We're not seeing each other." She waited for him to disagree, but she knew he wouldn't. After all, they weren't seeing each other. She didn't know what they were doing. Maybe nothing.

"You're not? Well, maybe you should let your mother know that, because she thinks you are."

Libby turned toward the window, picturing Tom struggling in Hamilton family quicksand, his strong arms useless and waving madly.

"You're not getting any younger, you know, Liberty," Nana went on. "I had four children by the time I was your age. Whatever happened to that boy from Chicago? Sam? Simon?"

Libby considered rolling down the window and jumping out. Or maybe she could chuck her Nana out instead. That might be easier.

"The boy from Chicago is now in San Diego, and I didn't want to move there." She also hadn't been invited, but that hardly mattered. Seth was old news.

Nana nodded. "Well, I can't blame you for that. California is full of nuts. Still, I thought you'd be married by now."

This day could not get worse. "Well, at least you have Marti's wedding to look forward to."

"Oh, don't get me started on that. That young man of hers needs a haircut. And another thing . . ."

Nana went on, but Libby stopped listening. And, she hoped, so had Tom.

The hot Indian summer had finally given way to a wet, messy autumn evening, and it started to rain in earnest just as Tom pulled into the driveway and took his keys from the ignition.

"Give me your keys, Libby. I'll unlock the door so Nana doesn't get all wet."

"I don't have my keys, but you can go in through the garage. There's a keypad."

Tom nodded. "What's the code?"

"Seventeen-seventy-six."

He started to get out of the truck, then looked back at her, a smile curving up his mouth. "Seventeen-seventy-six. Seriously?"

She shrugged. "You know my dad."

He laughed then, and the sound of it warmed her through. He'd been so quiet and guarded at the hospital and on this drive. Just a few nights ago they'd been halfway to naked in his truck, but then Ginny went into labor. Then her father broke his leg, and something between her and Tom had broken, too. She didn't know if it had to do with Rachel or Connie or both. But she'd seen a glimpse of how he *could* be, and she wanted that back.

The garage door rolled open. Libby hopped from the truck. She reached up to help Nana, but Tom was right there, doing it for her.

They made their way through the garage and into the Hamilton kitchen. Tom paused to wipe his feet on the rug and brush rain from his jacket.

"Thank you for the escort, young man," Nana said. "My son is very lucky to have you around. I guess we all are. Libby, make that boy a sandwich. I'm going to my room. Where I'm sure I won't hear anything, no matter what you two decide to do."

"Nana," Libby gasped, but her grandmother just flicked her hand in Libby's direction and walked out of the kitchen.

Libby turned to Tom, feeling suddenly awkward and uncertain. "Do you want some coffee or a sandwich or something? We never had dinner."

Tom's posture seemed stiff, and he stood on the rug as if it edged up to a cliff, like he wanted to turn around and bolt right back to his truck now that the cushion of Nana between them was gone.

Her heart paused as if it was about to be launched from a slingshot. She wanted him to sit down. She wanted him to stay and talk to her. She wanted him to kiss her, too.

He shook his head and gave her half a smile. "I had about fourteen gallons of coffee at the hospital."

"A sandwich then? I'm sure we've got something here to eat. Maybe some pasta or leftovers?"

He brushed a droplet of rain from his face, and he sighed. "I probably should go. It's been a very long day. For both of us."

The slingshot went slack, and her heart tumbled down to the ground. "It's been a long couple of days for both of us. I'm sorry you've gotten sucked into all this family drama. I never meant to be your quicksand."

His head dropped, and he rubbed the back of his neck before he looked her way.

"I didn't mean for you to hear that. And I didn't mean it the way it sounded."

He finally left the rug and walked over to stand close, so close she could see the flecks of bronze in his brown eyes. She saw the uncertainty in them, too. He stared, as if willing her to understand something that made no sense to him. Her heart jumped back into the slingshot as he cupped her face with both hands and kissed her, firm and fast.

Relief chased surprise along her nerves. His lips felt every bit as good as she'd remembered.

She slid her arms around him and leaned in. He wrapped her in a loose embrace and pressed another kiss along the curve of her neck. He was solid and safe and strong, a haven of warmth. They stood like that a moment, fending off doubt and worry, if only for the moment.

"I'm trying, Libby," he whispered against her skin. "These last few days have been a lot to take in. And I just don't know quite what to do with you."

"It seemed like you knew what to do with me the other night."

He shook his head without lifting it. "You know it's not that simple."

"It could be."

But it couldn't be, really. Not for Tom. There were aspects of his life she couldn't begin to comprehend. She knew that intellectually, but she still wanted him. Selfishly and completely.

She also wanted him to feel the same way.

He moved his hands to her shoulders and took a step back, his emotions pulling away just as physically as he did. "I'm tapped out right now. Can we talk about this later, please? I can't think straight when I'm this close to you, and I have to figure some things out before this gets any more complicated, okay?"

She saw it in his eyes then, a flickering sense of possibility.

She just needed to wait.

CHAPTER *fourteen*

"Thanks for seeing me on such short notice, Dr. Brandt." Tom settled into the leather chair of the counselor's office and sipped his coffee. He'd made it double-strong this morning. It tasted like hot mud, but he needed that extra jolt of caffeine.

Dreaming about Libby had become a bad enough habit, but the last few nights all he'd had to do was lie down in bed and visions of her started dancing through his mind. Libby in the moonlight, laughing at the pub, pressed against him in her parents' kitchen. He hadn't slept in days.

"I don't mind, Tom," said Dr. Brandt, putting on her glasses. "It sounds like you've had a rough couple of days. How is your friend?"

"I don't know much more now than I did when I called you from the waiting room at the hospital, but he should be okay, eventually. Broken ankle. Concussion."

"Fortunately, bones heal. It's often those other injuries that can be harder to treat."

He took a gulp of coffee sludge. "Oh, are we talking about me, now?"

Dr. Brandt smiled. They'd developed a nice rapport over the last few weeks. He'd be sarcastic. She'd patiently lead him around with questions until he figured out what he was supposed to understand.

"We can talk about whatever you'd like to talk about, Tom."

"Let's talk about Libby."

He blurted that out rather unceremoniously, but he paid this counselor by the hour. Today he was going to get his money's worth.

Her brows lifted, and she took her glasses back off. "Libby would be the woman with the cupcakes on her shirt, yes?"

"Yep. That friend who fell down the stairs? That was her dad."

"Oh, goodness." Glasses back on. "So, tell me more."

"I kissed her." There. He'd said it. That made it true.

Her face remained impassive as ever, as if he'd said *I'm wearing brown loafers today*. She didn't even blink. "Did you? And how did Libby respond to that?"

Yes, that was the Dr. Brandt he'd grown to appreciate. Always clinical.

Still, heat stole over his face as if he were a sixteen-year-old at confession, because just as a sixteen-year-old might have, he'd kissed Libby in the cab of his truck. They'd been no more cautious or wise than a couple of hormonal kids steaming up the windows in a parent's car and throwing caution to the roadside. Just as he and Connie had. He hadn't learned one damn thing in all these years.

Once he and Libby had gotten to Ginny's house and he saw her in labor, the similarities had slapped him. Hard. They'd even been sitting in the same high school parking lot where he'd first kissed Connie. The sense of betrayal to his wife was like a cleaver to the chest. But it was the look on Libby's face in that pink and blue waiting room at the hospital that haunted him now, even more than Connie's memory. He'd hurt her feelings with his dismissal, but it had to be done. He'd been letting himself think this flirtation with her was harmless. Victimless. But it wasn't.

"How did she respond?" he replied to Dr. Brandt. "Um, enthusiastically."

"And how did that make you feel?"

It made him feel like his blood had turned to gasoline and he was holding a lit match. "I'm not sure I understand the question."

"If Libby is receptive to starting a relationship with you, I'm wondering how that makes you feel."

"I'm not receptive to starting a relationship. I shouldn't have made her think I was. And I don't know how I'm supposed to feel. That's why I'm here."

She rested her chin in her hand. He recognized the gesture. It meant *pay attention to the point I'm about to make.*

"First of all, there is no *supposed to*. And second, I suspect you do know how you feel, but you're here looking for validation. And absolution."

Is that what he was doing?

All he really knew for sure was that from the first moment he'd set eyes on Liberty Belle Hamilton peeking over the top of that Dumpster, it had been one thing after another pulling him into her life, and the harder he fought, the more impossible it became to get free. But maybe it wasn't Libby he was struggling against at all. Maybe it was memories. Or maybe it was just him.

Kissing Libby had been a wake-up call, a blinding reminder of what life *could* feel like. The rush and the fever and the full speed ahead.

And it scared the shit out of him.

He would have explained that to Libby at the ice-cream parlor if Peter hadn't taken a swan dive down the staircase.

"I'm not ready for a relationship. Rachel is my only priority." Even to his own ears it sounded like he was reading from a cue card.

Dr. Brandt folded her hands in her lap. "Of course Rachel should be a high priority, but I advise against pursuing that at the expense of any other relationship. You have to live your own life, too, Tom. At what point do you feel it would be appropriate for you to start dating? Two years? Five? Ten?"

"I don't know."

"That's because there is no clear-cut answer. If you are as attracted to someone as you seem to be to Libby, maybe you are ready for a relationship."

He thought of Libby in the kitchen last night, the smell of her skin at the curve of her neck when he'd pulled her close. The feel of her body and her mouth. He shifted in his chair.

"All right, then let me put that another way," Tom said. "Let's say, hypothetically, I do know how I feel, and maybe I am ready for a relationship. How am I supposed to explain that to Rachel? She and I have made some progress lately, and I don't want to rock that boat."

Dr. Brandt nodded at this. "I understand that concern. It's difficult for most parents to balance their own personal needs with those of their children, and even more so with single parents. But this could be a real opportunity for you to demonstrate to Rachel that life does move on, that you're looking toward the future. Have you two talked any more about her moving back in with you?"

"Not really. It just starts a fight, so I don't bring it up. She had a talent show, and she didn't even tell me about it."

"So you missed it?"

"No, I went anyway, and actually Rachel seemed okay with it. Although I haven't had a chance to talk to her since then." He'd been a little busy running members of the Hamilton family around town.

"When is the last time you spoke with her grandparents?"

When was the last time? It was during the summer. He remembered that. Maybe he should have tried harder, but Anne and George had made it pretty clear they had nothing to say to him. "About three months, give or take."

"So Rachel is the only link of communication between the three of you?"

Tom sensed a gentle scolding coming on. "Do you think that's a problem?"

"I think it puts a burden on Rachel. Similar to a divorce situation, the child sometimes gets stuck being an intermediary when the adults aren't communicating. This will often encourage them, subconsciously, to choose a side so they have at least one safe place to be."

A roll of unease swelled inside Tom. He hadn't been a safe place for Rachel in a very long time.

"See, that's just the thing. I want to be that for her. But if my attention gets divided between her and Libby, Rachel's going to feel like I've abandoned her again. It's just too soon for me to get involved with someone, no matter how I feel."

"You have a right to privacy, too, Tom. Don't forget that."

His coffee was cold now, but he drank some anyway. "Privacy?"

"Yes. You should always be honest with Rachel, but that doesn't mean you have to tell her all the details of your adult life. If you chose to date someone, it's really none of her business. Use your best judgment about when to tell her and what to share. I'm sure you and Connie had a romantic life that you kept separate from Rachel. This is no different."

He hadn't thought about it in that way. Of course he and Connie had kept parts of their life separate from Rachel. It hadn't been deceitful. It was a case of protecting her from grown-up concepts she wasn't ready for. If that were true, then nothing that happened with Libby had to impact

Rachel at all. These two areas of his life simply didn't intersect. At least, not for now.

He set his coffee cup on the table. "So, you're not just going to tell me what to do?" He was being facetious, and she'd know that.

Dr. Brandt smiled. "I'm a counselor, Tom. I counsel. I don't make decisions for you."

"Okay, but if you were me, what would you do?"

She laughed at that. "You know it doesn't work that way. But I will say this. You can't be the father you want to be for Rachel as long as you are still wounded yourself. Guilt is a destructive force, and it's not productive. Take what you know now and move forward. I know your main goal is to do what's best for Rachel, and that's commendable. But it starts with your own peace of mind. So in an ironic way, you owe it to Rachel to take care of yourself first."

Tom took the long way home, the way that took him past the curve in the road where Connie had died. He'd driven by that awful spot at least a hundred times since the night of the accident. The scars on the tree had weathered, so much so they couldn't really be seen unless one knew where to look. Lots of scars were like that, it seemed.

He pulled into his driveway a few minutes later and went inside. He turned on all the lights and looked around his little farmhouse like he'd never seen it before. It was full of tiny, impractical rooms he'd once had big plans for, but now he couldn't really remember what any of those plans were. He stood in his kitchen and let his thoughts rove over the past, through old hopes and faded dreams. There were some good ones in the mix, memories of their old house and Connie and Rachel putting on makeup together, or the three of them having pancakes on a Saturday morning and watching cartoons. Those moments he'd cherish, always, but just as Dr. Brandt had told Rachel, he could keep them, but he couldn't hide in them. Not anymore.

Thunder rumbled in the distance, and another memory flooded his senses. A recent and delicious vision of Libby on his lap. The sound of her breath and her laughter. That was where he wanted to live now—but there were things he needed to do first.

He picked up his phone and dialed Connie's sister.

"Hello?"

"Kristy, it's Tom. I was hoping to ask for a favor." He could hear the television and her kids playing in the background.

"Of course. What do you need?"

"I was wondering if you could come over tomorrow and help me sort through all of Connie's stuff. Rachel doesn't want to, and, well, I can't really blame her. But I could sure use the help."

The long pause on the other end left his palms sweaty.

"I will absolutely help you do that. You could've asked me sooner, you know."

A pressure that had taken root and wound around all the muscles in his shoulders a lifetime ago began to unwind. This was the right thing. "I know. I wasn't ready. I am now."

"Can I ask you something?" Kristy said.

"Um, sure."

"Does this have anything to do with the pretty blond from the talent show?" Her voice was light and teasing.

"If I said no, would you believe me? Because it really doesn't. It's just time. It's past time."

Kristy chuckled into the phone. "It is past time. I'll be over first thing in the morning."

"Thank you. This means a lot to me, Kristy." He exhaled, not realizing he'd been holding his breath.

"I know. And Tom?"

"What?"

"Connie would be glad to see you finally clear all that stuff out of your house. Donate it to charity or something so someone can benefit from it."

"You think?" He looked at a stack of cardboard boxes that had been lined up behind the sofa for more than a year.

"Of course. And for what it's worth, I think she'd like the blond, too, even though this has nothing to do with her."

Tom caught himself chuckling back. "You met her for two minutes, and you think you can make that assessment?"

He could hear the smile in her voice. "Rachel likes her. She told me so. That's all I need to know. See you around nine."

Tom hung up the phone. *Rachel likes her.* He hoped that was true.

CHAPTER *fifteen*

"Daddy, are you going to eat your pudding?" Marti asked as she leaned over her father's hospital bed. She bumped against some random button, setting off a high-pitched beep.

Their father was not a model patient, and Libby and Marti had been tasked with entertaining him while their mother visited with Ginny and sweet baby Teddy.

"You may have my pudding if you go find me a pot roast and some real mashed potatoes," her father answered. "I've had three days of nothing but cardboard meat and gritty mashed potatoes. No wonder the Pilgrims thought potatoes were poisonous. They must have been using this same recipe. Honestly, how do they expect me to recover?"

"You're coming home tomorrow, and Nana is going to make you the biggest and best meal you've ever had," Libby told him. "If Mom doesn't stuff her into the oven first. Now stop being so grumpy, because I have some pictures to show you."

"What sort of pictures?" he asked. "And what is that infernal beeping? My God, everything in this room is rigged with an alarm."

A plump nurse bustled in and flipped a switch. "Please stop touching all the buttons, Mr. Hamilton."

"I'm looking for the one that ejects me out of here, Nurse Ratched." He smiled at her as he said it.

She smiled back, weary but obviously not insulted. "I sure will miss your special sense of humor when you leave us. But in the meantime, please stop touching all the buttons. And I can take that tray for you, if you're all finished with lunch."

"That wasn't lunch. That was leftover POW rations from World War Two. Say, speaking of World War Two, it's rumored that Hitler only had one testicle. Do you know the medical name for that?"

Marti scooped up the pudding cup and a spoon as the nurse lifted the yellow plastic tray from the bedside table.

The nurse chuckled. "No, Mr. Hamilton, I don't, but I'm sure you can tell me."

He nodded as he readjusted his covers. "Monorchidism." She took a Styrofoam cup from the table and added it to the tray. "Fascinating. Please stop touching the buttons." She turned and left, shaking her head.

"Really, Dad," Marti said as she scooped pudding from the container. "Why would she want to know that? Why would anyone want to know that?"

"Anyway," Libby interrupted, desperate to never learn how her father knew so much about missing testicles, "I wanted to cheer you up, so I printed out some pictures of possible décor for inside the ice-cream parlor. Window treatments and little bistro tables and stuff like that."

He frowned. "How am I supposed to get that place finished with this bum leg? The doctor says I can't put any weight on it for two months. I can't believe I fell off a chair."

"Well, you did. And we are all very grateful you didn't break your neck. Because trust me, I saw you, and you looked like you had a broken neck."

Sympathy would only make her father feel worse and act grumpier. The best way to perk him up was with no-nonsense gumption. He was usually a very big fan of gumption.

"Do you suppose if a giraffe broke its neck, its head would drag on the ground?" Marti asked.

Their father's eyes perked up, and he pointed at Marti. "Actually, what's especially fascinating about giraffes is that they have the exact same number of vertebrae in their necks as humans. Just seven. Can you imagine? Of course each vertebra is huge, ten inches, and weighs nearly eighty-five pounds."

"Eighty-five pounds? That's crazytown. So two of them would weigh more than my entire body. Right?"

Libby was losing them. Fast. "Do you want to see these pictures, Dad?"

"What? Oh, pictures. Yes. Say, have you talked to Tom? He's still working, isn't he?"

Libby nearly dropped the pictures on the tiled floor. Her lungs wobbled together like bowling pins teetering from a strike.

"I talked to him for a few minutes the day after you got here. He said he needed to do some work at his own house for a couple of days, but he'll start back at the ice-cream parlor next week."

Her conversation with Tom had been short and cryptic, in that monosyllabic way he had. He wasn't one to emote in person, and he definitely didn't do it over the phone, so she'd tried to read the sound waves in his voice to get some sense of what he might be thinking. At the end he'd sounded moderately upbeat and said, "I'll see you soon, okay?"

It wasn't much to pin her hopes on, but it was all she had.

"Oh, before I forget," said Marti, tossing the empty pudding cup and spoon into the trash basket. "We're supposed to go have a bridal fitting tomorrow afternoon, Libby. Can you do that? My wedding is coming up soon, you know."

Peter tried to adjust in the bed, tugging at his hospital gown impatiently. "You know, I can't walk you down the aisle for at least two months, Martha. How would you feel about postponing this wedding thing until springtime?"

She leaned over and kissed his cheek. "Nice try, Daddy. Dante says if you're not mobile by the wedding we can just launch you from a catapult into your seat. But he called it something else. A treble clef or something."

"A trebuchet?"

"Yes. How did you know that?" Her voice squeaked in amazement.

Their father pointed at his chest. "History teacher, remember?"

Marti nodded as she pulled her vibrating phone from her pocket and looked at the screen. "Oh, yeah. Okay, well, anyway, looks like I have to go help Ginny now. She just texted me to say Nana is driving her crazy and she's about to lock her in the bathroom." She turned to Libby. "So, are we on for tomorrow?"

So many awesome options. Hang out at the hospital with her grumpy dad, go to Ginny's and listen to her argue with Nana about baby-rearing, or get trussed up in the most absurd version of a bridesmaid dress ever.

"Yep, I'll go with you," she told Marti.

"Perfect. I'll pick you up at two."

Marti left, and Libby took a seat next to her father. "Ready to look at these pictures?"

He looked at his leg and sighed. "This wasn't supposed to happen this way, Liberty. I wanted to fix up that old schoolhouse with my own two hands. I wanted to be the one to transform it into an ice-cream parlor."

"I know, Dad. And I'm sorry. I guess you could tell Tom to postpone the work until you can join him again." Even as she said it, she prayed he'd reject that notion.

"I can't. I've sunk too much money into that place, and I need to start turning a profit as soon as possible. I'm up to my shoulders in debt already, and your mother didn't speak to me for two weeks after I bought it. I have to prove it was a good idea. But falling off that chair just proves she was right."

Libby leaned over and hugged him. "She'll get over it, Dad. As soon as she sees it full of happy little kids all excited about their ice cream, she'll jump on board." She sat back down in the chair.

Her father shook his head. "If I can get her to go. She still hasn't set foot in there, you know. And now that I've broken this leg she thinks the place is cursed. Maybe it is."

"It's not cursed. It was just an accident with a wobbly chair and some old, weather-weakened wood. But we do need to get her inside to see how cute it's all turning out. I was just thinking that if I invite her and Nana to go out to lunch, I can offer to show it to them. You know Nana will say yes, and then Mom will have to go, too."

He pursed his lips for a moment before speaking. "That's quite devious."

"Do you mind?"

"Not if it helps my cause." He smiled, but it didn't last. "What about another job for you, Liberty? My ice-cream parlor is taking up all your time, and I haven't heard you mention any interviews in quite a while."

Libby looked down and fidgeted with the pictures in her hands. "I have been thinking about that. My unemployment lasts a couple more weeks, and until your ice-cream parlor is finished I kind of feel like that is my job. I do have a few résumés out there, but everybody is cutting back, and companies just aren't hosting big events like they used to. Plus, I'm not so sure about Chicago anymore."

Libby hadn't really admitted that to herself, but there she was, saying it out loud.

"Really? Well, that's quite a shift in thinking. What brought that about? Or should I say, who?"

She looked into her father's dark blue eyes, the same shade as her own. He looked small in that industrial hospital bed, frail, with plastic tubes jabbed into his veins. His leg would heal and he'd be fine, but the fact remained that her father was getting older. Someday he would go the way of that anglerfish and just fade away. For those long moments when he'd been unconscious on those steps, she'd thought it might have already happened.

"You really, really scared me when you fell, Dad."

He looked away and fussed with his covers.

"It was just a clumsy accident. You can't plan your future worrying about something like that."

"I know, but it got me thinking about what's really important. Chicago was great, and I had fun there, but part of that was because I loved my job, and now that's gone. And the other part was because of Seth, and he's not there anymore either. I'm not sure what I'd be going back to, because the things I care about now, and the people I love, are here in Monroe."

Her father smiled, and moisture sparkled in his eyes as he reached over to squeeze her hand. "There's no place like home, is there, Dorothy?"

"Nope, I guess not. Plus I love that there is parking, like, everywhere. I sure never found that in Chicago."

She squeezed his hand back. "Now I just have to find a real job. No offense, but being your handygirl doesn't pay very well."

"Ah, but there are other perks. Like maybe a man you've got your eye on?" He arched a brow and twirled an imaginary mustache.

This was not a road she wanted to travel with her father, especially given his propensity for sharing tidbits about bizarre mating rituals. The last thing she needed was her dad asking Tom if he was familiar with bonobo monkeys.

"Yes, there is a man, Dad. I'm completely in love with him. His name is Teddy Roosevelt Garner."

"Ah, yes. Teddy sure is a cute little bugger, isn't he? There's nothing quite as wonderful as holding a baby. Especially your own. I was a master diaper changer, you know." He beamed with accomplishment. "Even your mother said she could never change a diaper so fast or so efficiently as I could."

Libby smiled. "You haven't figured that out yet, huh?" She leaned back in the pleather chair.

"Figured out what?"

"That Mom only said you were the best and fastest so that you'd do it and then she wouldn't have to."

His face fell. "No, she didn't."

Libby patted his hand back. "Yes, she did, Daddy. Where do you think my devious streak came from?"

"And that is how you make my famous peach pie," said Nana as she pulled her golden-crusted masterpiece from the oven.

It smelled divine and might taste delicious enough to justify spending two hours shut up in the Hamilton family kitchen with Nana and Marti. With their help, Libby had finally mastered a pie.

"Now," said Nana. "I want you to take this pie to that nice Mr. Murphy and tell him I said thank you for taking care of Peter when he fell. And for giving me a ride home. I did enjoy bouncing in his truck."

"Seems like there's a lot of that going around lately." Marti snorted with laughter, and Libby flicked her. She never should have told her sister what happened with Tom, but they were at that stupid bridal shop for hours yesterday afternoon, and somehow Marti had gotten it out of her.

"Ouch! Geez, don't take it out on me just because you can't close the deal," Marti said.

Libby flicked her again. "Shut up, Marti."

"Girls, stop roughhousing. Libby has a pie to deliver," Nana scolded. "And I'm not quite sure what you two are talking about, but I have a pretty good idea. I'm not that old." She handed the pie to Libby. "Trust me. This will work. How do you think I got your grandfather's attention?"

Libby pretended she didn't want to take that pie over to Tom's house. She pretended they were being ridiculous. But the truth was, Nana's idea was brilliant. Maybe it wouldn't close any deals, but at least it gave Libby an excuse to drop by Tom's place and see him. Not in a crazy-girl stalker way, but more as a friendly social call. With pie.

She sent him a text before she left her house. *RU HOME? I HAVE SOMETHING TO DROP OFF FROM NANA.*

There. That sounded innocent enough.

So did his one-word response. *YEP.*

She stewed about that for a minute, and very nearly asked Marti's opinion, but if he didn't want to see her, he would've ignored the text or said he wasn't home.

She drove to his place, breathing in the aroma of peach pie and trying to admire the beautiful fall colors, deep red and gold in the setting sunlight, but her palms were damp and everything inside felt slightly wobbly.

She pulled in and parked behind his old blue truck and smiled. She liked that truck. It was kind of faded and dinged up, but it had a lot of character. Very much like Tom Murphy. Same for the outside of the white farmhouse, with its unadorned porch and empty landscape beds. Lots of potential but none of it realized.

When he opened the door, though, Tom didn't look faded or dinged up at all. He just looked good, wearing a shirt she'd seen a dozen times, the gray one that said COLLEGE in block letters across his chest.

"Hi," he said.

"Hi." She held up the foil-wrapped pie. "This is from Nana. She said thanks for the ride home. And thanks for helping with my dad. Well, she said, 'Thanks for helping with my son,' but you know what I mean. And my mom said to tell you thanks again, too."

She suddenly felt a little foolish. Maybe she'd just drop off this pie and leave. He was going to let her ramble. She could see it in his posture as he leaned against the doorframe making himself comfortable. She lifted the pie higher. "Here. Take it."

He smiled, his eyes warm. He pushed the door open wider. "Come on in."

The inside of Tom's house was quaint, but plain, as if he hadn't quite moved in. Nothing hung on the walls; nothing was modern. She was expecting artsy craftsmanship, like the stuff he'd done at the ice-cream parlor, but there was little here that seemed like him. She stepped inside into a small, clean kitchen that overlooked a tiny family room. A hallway next to the refrigerator led off to the rest of the house.

She set the pie on a beige laminate counter.

He leaned over and pulled up the foil, the muscles flexing in his arm. "This is still warm."

"Fresh from Nana's oven. Well, not Nana's oven. My mom's oven, actually." Rambling again. He seemed happy enough to see her, but her heart gave a little hop, skip, and a jump when he pulled two forks from a drawer.

"How's your dad?" he asked.

"Pretty good. Anxious to be home. Driving the nurses crazy with random trivia."

Two forks?

Tom chuckled. "I'll bet he is. I'll give him a call in a couple of days to talk about our next steps for the ice-cream parlor."

The air pressure around her seemed to double. "He wants you to finish it. I already asked him. You'll do it, won't you?" He *had* to stick with it. If Tom gave up on this project, and on her, Libby might seriously consider joining a convent. Which was going to be a real challenge because she wasn't Catholic.

"Of course I'll finish it. I always get the job done, remember?" His voice was quiet as he leaned against the counter. "Are you going to help me?"

He looked at her expectantly, his expression almost flirty. Tom Murphy really should come with some directions, or at least a compass so she could tell which direction his emotions were heading.

"Do you *want* me to help you?" It seemed like maybe they were talking about more than the ice-cream parlor.

"Yes." He didn't hesitate with his answer, and her stomach gave a little flippity-flop toward optimism.

"Okay, then. I will," she said.

He walked toward her, holding up the forks. "Good. Are you going to stick around and help me eat some of this pie?"

Now it seemed like they were talking about more than pie. Nana was very wise. "Do you *want* me to eat some pie?"

Setting down the forks, he stepped around behind her and tugged the jacket from her shoulders. He slid it down her arms and hooked it over a chair. His breath was warm on her ear. "Yes. Pie's no fun to eat alone."

She turned to face him, trying to gauge his expression. "No, I guess it isn't. But eating it alone is . . . less complicated."

He leaned closer. He looked at her mouth, his gaze so heavy it was nearly a kiss. Then his deep brown eyes came back to hers. "Liberty Belle

Hamilton, my life got more complicated the very first time you smiled at me."

Her lungs joined her stomach in a jig of optimism. It felt good, but it was hard to breathe.

His hands came up and cupped her face, his thumbs lingering at the corner of her lips. "I find myself wanting to make promises to you, but I can't. I can't guarantee what comes tomorrow."

She reached out then, clutching the material of his shirt. "No one can. And anyway, I don't need a guarantee. I just need you to kiss me."

There it was, that look of possibility in his eyes, a certainty of purpose, and Libby flooded with desire.

Tom leaned closer still and nuzzled his lips near her mouth. "Okay, but if we start this, I'm not stopping. No matter who goes into labor or who falls down the stairs."

All of her breath escaped in a single burst. "Good. Me neither."

He kissed her then, hard, with no preamble, his lips firm and insistent. His tongue delved into her mouth, and she welcomed it. She'd been waiting for this kiss for days and days. Maybe even all her life, because never in her past had she been kissed like this before.

Tom pulled her tight, and pressed her back against the edge of the counter, pinning her with the width of his body and the force of his desire. He was hunger and pleasure and turmoil sealed in one kiss. His mouth was delicious, full of texture and heat. She ran her hands up his back, aching to peel that shirt away and touch every part of him.

He caught her lip in his teeth, and her knees buckled. He wasn't being gentle, and she didn't want him to be. This was the Tom she'd imagined, all primal and uncontrolled, ruled by reckless passion.

She pushed up the hem of his shirt. "Too . . . many . . . clothes," she uttered between breathless kisses.

He pulled it off in a single motion, tossing it behind him to the floor. In the moonlight, he'd looked mysterious and sexy. In the bright light of the kitchen . . . he was still mysterious and sexy.

"God, look at you." She ran her hands up his chest and over his shoulders. His skin was smooth and warm and quivered beneath her touch.

"Let's look at you," he whispered back.

He pulled at the first button of her shirt, and it popped through the opening as if it had been waiting for his touch. He nudged the fabric with one finger and leaned down to kiss her skin at the gap. She sighed with the certainty of delicious things unfolding and ran a hand over his hair.

Then another button, and another kiss. Lower and lower until, at last, her shirt dangled open, the cool air a delicious contrast to his warm lips and her sizzling skin. He bent low and kissed her belly button, circling his tongue around it. She stepped back from the tickle of it, but he wrapped his arms around her, under her bottom, and picked her up.

She was floating, with Tom her only anchor to the ground. She bit his earlobe as he walked down the hall to the bedroom, and he let out a low rumble deep in his throat.

The room was small and uncluttered, just a big bed, nightstands, and a dresser. The evening light came through the windows, casting shadow fragments across a faded quilt.

He loosened his hold, and her body slid down his, her skin taut with anticipation. He was so solid, everywhere. She wanted to surround herself with him, and surround him in return.

Tom looked down at her, lips parted, breath erratic. "Are you absolutely positive? Because I'm just about at the tipping point here."

"Absolutely positive."

She had been ready for this since the first time she'd heard him laugh. She just hadn't known it. She slipped her hand into her pocket and pulled out a foil packet. "Marti made me bring this. Just in case."

A smile spread across his face like water flowing. "You brought a condom?"

"I brought two. Presumptuous, I know, but Marti insisted." She pulled out the second one and tossed them on the bed.

Laughter bubbled up between them.

"Remind me later to tell her thanks."

"How about you thank me right now?"

Desire chased away the laughter on his face as he pushed Libby's open shirt down her arms. It landed on the hardwood, buttons clicking. His fingers tangled into her hair, tugging, tipping her head back. A happy moan escaped as he lavished her throat with kisses.

Libby tugged at the waistband of his jeans. "Still too many clothes."

Tom picked her up again and slid with a bent knee over the bed, tipping until they fell together across the foot. He landed on top, pressing the air from her lungs in a pop, and pulled her wrists above her head. She couldn't breathe, and she didn't care.

Tom smiled with the patience of a Sunday afternoon driver. "Libby, I haven't done this in a while. I'm not going to hurry."

His words sent her heart tumbling over itself with sublime expectation. She was dazzled.

"Sorry. Carry on," she whispered breathlessly.

"I intend to." He kissed her again, a tiny shallow kiss, teasing her with nips and nuzzles across her jaw, until at last his own breath deepened and he kissed her deeply, with slow sweeps of his tongue. He pressed his body down, and she wrapped her legs around his waist, denim meeting denim, friction increasing.

Tom let go of her wrists and rolled to the side. His fingers traced a path along her collarbone and skimmed over a breast. The sensation was electric, and she arched in reflex, her sigh ardent, even to her own ears. Tom watched her face, his eyes on hers as tantalizing as his touch.

The frenzied passion of the kitchen had transcended into a maddeningly seductive meander over her body as he kissed her neck and pressed soft lips against the hollow behind her ear. Her hunger doubled as he bit her earlobe, and when his fingers splayed against her stomach, she wished with all her might that he'd keep going. But he slid that hand up and underneath her instead, to unhook her bra. She sat up so he could slide it off her arms, and soon it joined her shirt in a twist on the floor.

She turned his way then, pushing him, unresisting, to his back and straddled him. He wasn't playing fair and so neither would she. She leaned over, letting her hair trail over his chest. He was all man beneath her, smooth skin over sleek muscle. "I haven't done this in a while either, you know."

She pressed her lips against his belly and moved upward. She felt the thumping of his heart beneath her hands and knew its pace matched her own. Frenetic and wild.

"God, Libby." His breath came in waves. He threaded his fingers through her hair and pulled her face back to his, time and again, for another searing kiss. But when she trailed her fingertips down his belly and pressed her hand against the obvious swell in his jeans, he groaned and flipped her back over before she could resist, pinning her with one leg.

"Still in such a hurry?" he whispered.

"Stop teasing me."

His smile was full of mischief as he ran his hands down her sides until they reached her waistband.

"Seriously, stop teasing me." She'd never been so desperate to be naked in her life.

He popped open the button of her jeans, and she bit her lip. His eyes stayed on hers as he tugged down the zipper. She lifted her hips, and his teasing stopped as he eased the fabric down. He caught the waistband of her panties with his fingers and pulled them, too, over her thighs and knees and ankles, until at last she was as bare as she longed to be. What little modesty she had left fled. His gaze slammed into her like a heat wave. He slid his hands up her legs and body, pausing to kiss her stomach before lying down, half-covering her with his body.

She pulled at his waistband. "These, too."

"Soon." He reached between them then, and her arguments faded against his lips as his palm pressed against her. Her knee rose up, granting him access, and she thought she might explode right then and there as his fingers sought then delved inside her. She rose up against his touch, her body melting with a quivering ache. Longing seized her under the pressure of his touch. She got lost in it, the sound of his breath rasping against her neck faint behind the roar growing in her ears. Sensations swelled and retreated, and swelled again.

"You're so beautiful." His words floated past her on a reverent sigh.

She kissed his mouth, hungry. She reached down, the need to touch the length of him all-consuming. He didn't stop her as she yanked against the zipper and slid her hand inside his pants. His skin scorched her fingers as they wrapped around and stroked him. His erection thrummed against her hand.

Tom groaned into her mouth and pulled away to strip off his jeans. He grabbed a foil packet and tore the wrapper with his teeth. Libby held her arms out to him, impatient as he rolled the condom into place, and finally he rejoined her. At last there was nothing between them but sweat and desire.

He pressed between their tangled legs, and rose up on his elbows. He looked into her eyes, and she could sense the breadth of his craving. She felt it, too, and arched her hips upward against him.

"Please." A breathy plea whispered from the depths of her longing.

He pushed into her then, sinking deep and settling in, with a labored breath and a long, slow blink.

"God, Libby," he said again.

He moved against her, and nothing before had ever felt so good, or so right. The certainty of this moment was spontaneous and powerful and impossible to ignore.

"I know," she whispered, and pulled him tight with her arms and her legs, wanting to lock him in that place and bring him closer than physically possible. They moved, and swayed, and found a rhythm, pleasure building and cascading.

He reached between them again, finding that spot, and she moved, pressing against his exploring fingertips until he understood just what she needed. His hand was gentle but sure, just as she'd known it would be.

He stroked and circled until tendrils of release eased out, slow at first, building in her toes and coiling inward until, at last, she burst forth with her climax and tumbled into ecstasy. Hot, sweet perfection, so ridiculously good. Libby started to laugh. She couldn't help it. Her joy bubbled forth, and Tom paused his movements, gazing down at her.

She covered her face with her hands and squeezed her legs around him. "I'm sorry," she said as she floated downward and laughed harder. "I'm sorry. I'm just really, really happy."

He pressed his hips against her and plunged a little deeper. "Me, too, almost."

He moved again, a little more abrupt, deeper still, again, and again until she caught up with his need. The muscles of his back were taut and tight under her palms as she pulled him close, his breath a primal rhythm in her ear. She arched her hips to meet his strokes, encouraging his pace. She pulled the soft hair at the nape of his neck, and his teeth grazed her shoulder as he came, exhaling in a fevered rush of incoherent pleasure.

Tom thought maybe he'd imagined it—the glory of making love. After the accident, he'd thought it was just grief that made his memories of it so compelling. But no, it was every bit as magnificent as he remembered. Libby was marvelous and wicked. Hot and sweet. Demanding and responsive. Her laughter at the ending had caught him completely by surprise, saving him from what might have otherwise been too vulnerable of a moment.

She was, after all, only the second woman he'd ever made love to.

"Why are we at the foot of the bed?" Giggles still trembled through her limbs as they lay sprawled out on top of the covers.

"I was in a hurry." He chuckled, happy.

"God." Libby rolled against him. "If that was you hurrying, we'd better start right now for the next time."

The next time. His body quickened at the thought. There could be a next time, and a time after that. He could spend the next one hundred days in bed with Libby Hamilton and not miss the world going by.

Except for Rachel.

The complications he'd neatly tucked away in the back of his mind inched forward again like ants across a picnic blanket, but he flicked them aside.

"Get under the covers. I'll be right back."

He made a quick trip to the bathroom, then trotted into the kitchen with his bare ass and his good idea, and grabbed the pie and the forks, returning to the bedroom just as Libby slid under the sheets and blanket.

"Hungry?"

Her eyebrows lifted. "You want to eat that in bed?"

"I think in the spectrum of reckless behavior, this is lower on the scale than what we just did." He set the pie on the bed and slipped in next to her. He handed her a fork after she adjusted the pillows behind her head.

She frowned. "'Reckless behavior'? Why would you say that?"

"What?"

"That what we did was reckless. We were careful." There was an edge to her voice, and he tried to rewind the last fifteen seconds to see where he'd made the wrong play.

"I didn't . . . I mean, we're not . . ." He stared at her. "It just was reckless. I'm not saying I regret it."

She glared back with love-tousled hair and her arms firmly crossed. "Oh, good. I'm so relieved you don't regret it."

Shit. Shit. Shit. "God, Libby. You remember the collage. Don't get frustrated with me now for not knowing how to explain something."

Her face relaxed a little. "I'm sorry. I just don't want to feel guilty about this. I was really, really happy, and now you're acting like I made you do something bad." She pulled the sheets up tighter over her breasts.

He shook his head. "That's not how I feel at all. Of course it wasn't something bad. And you didn't make me. You compelled me, though.

And I mean that in the most flattering way possible. You're a force of nature, Libby. Don't you know that?"

"No."

"Well, you are. And I'm glad. You've woken me up." He leaned over and kissed her, because her lips were lush and pink and he just couldn't resist. Then he leaned back against his own pillows. "It's just . . . a little terrifying, you know? Sometimes you look at me and I worry that you think I'm a much better man than I am. I'm just trying to keep the bar set really low, I guess, so I don't disappoint you."

Libby pushed the hair away from her cheek and tucked it behind her ear. "Can I ask you something personal?"

He pulled the pie closer. "We're a little past that point, don't you think?"

"No, I'm being serious here. You talk about disappointing people, but I'm just not sure who you're referring to. I mean, I see how hard you're trying to make things right with Rachel, and it seems like if her grandparents weren't telling her otherwise, she'd see that, too. So who else have you disappointed? Honestly, Tom, I get the distinct impression you confuse accidents with failures. You're a little hard on yourself."

He took a bite of the pie, not because he wanted it now but because it was easier than giving her an answer. "You sound like Dr. Brandt," he finally said.

Libby twirled the fork in her hand, then scooped up a bite. "Well, I'm very smart, and obviously so is she. And if my dad were here, he'd say you were like a blind man trying to describe an elephant."

Tom laughed around his next bite. It was tangy-sweet, like Libby. "And what the hell would your dad mean by that?"

"He'd mean that you can only feel the part that's right in front of you and not the whole elephant. Everybody else can see it's an elephant, but all you know is the trunk, or maybe a foot." She took another bite.

"Help me out here, Lib. I still have no idea what you're saying."

She stared at him, direct and guileless. "I'm saying that the rest of the world can see the whole you. The helpful guy, the smart guy, the hard-working guy. The loving-dad guy. We can see all of that, all at once. But all you see is the guy who crashed the car."

The pie was suddenly too sticky and too sweet. He set the fork down.

Libby's eyes were big, luminous in the fading light. She reached out and touched his arm. "You're all those good things, Tom, so stop focusing on just that one part."

He looked away and wished he knew what to say to that, but he didn't trust his voice just then. Her words had touched him, the same way her hands and her kiss had, gentle but insistent. And she was right. He only saw those dark bits of himself, the scars that had faded to everyone else but were bright and rough and raw in his eyes.

He set the pie on the nightstand and turned back, gathering her close. She wrapped her arms around him, and pressed her lips against his in a honeyed kiss, a kiss that asked for more.

He rolled her back against the pillows and showed her without words just how he felt.

CHAPTER *sixteen*

Tom woke up the next morning smelling like peaches but feeling like a man. He smiled at the empty pie tin next to the bed. His memory of the evening sizzled, and his body responded before he could even blink. He'd made love to Libby twice before they'd finished that pie, naked and laughing in the bed. She'd stayed a few more hours and went home looking thoroughly satisfied, and Tom enjoyed the best night's sleep he'd had in over a year.

He stretched and wondered why he, of all men, should get a chance in life to feel this good. It made him want to accomplish things today. He jumped out of bed, brushed some pie crumbs off his arm, and got in the shower.

Twenty minutes later his sipped his coffee and dialed a number on his phone that he called far too infrequently.

"Hello?" Her voice was raspy.

"Rach, it's Dad."

"Yeah, I know. I have caller ID. Do you know it's, like, eight thirty on a Sunday morning?"

"Sorry. I thought you'd be up. I was hoping we could have breakfast. Or lunch. Can you? There's some stuff I want to talk to you about."

"Today?"

"It doesn't have to be today, but I'd like to see you. I'll take you to that place with the chocolate-chip pancakes."

He heard her snuffled giggle on the other end, and his hope lifted. "Dad, I don't eat chocolate-chip pancakes anymore."

"All right, well, we can go wherever you want. Is that a yes?"

She sighed. "Yeah, okay. Brunch. Pick me up at eleven. I'm not done sleeping."

He hung up the phone and felt like he was standing on the tip of a knife. One wrong move could leave him in shreds. But at least he could feel it.

His daughter was waiting outside her grandparents' house when he guided his truck up the driveway. He hadn't been inside there since before Connie died. Since his recent talk with Dr. Brandt, he knew that was something he needed to fix. But not today. Today was just for him and Rachel.

She climbed into the truck wearing a red beret and a sparkly scarf. She'd loved to play dress-up when she was little. Always a flair for the dramatic.

"Hey. Nice hat. You hungry?"

She shrugged. "I guess. That was the whole idea, wasn't it? To go eat?"

"And to spend some time together."

She looked at him, but she wasn't scowling. Practically a declaration of peace.

"Where do you want to go?"

"Someplace with good soup."

He didn't know of any place with particularly good soup, since soup was what he ate while he waited for his meal.

"How about Flanagan's?"

"No, their soup sucks. How about Licari's?"

"If that's where you want to go, that's where we'll go."

She looked at him, eyes narrowed with what looked very much like suspicion. "You're agreeable this morning."

"I'm just glad to see you."

He was. It wasn't just his night with Libby that had him smiling. It was also the fact that Rachel had said yes and not found some excuse to avoid him.

They arrived at the restaurant and ordered their meals without much extra chatter.

"Have you finished your collage?" he asked as they sat down with trays of food.

"Mostly. It's kind of cheesy, though. Are you done with yours?" She took a slurp of soup.

"Almost. It's pretty awful, I have to warn you. But I tried hard. I even asked Libby to help me. She said my cutting and pasting skills were substandard."

Libby hadn't really said that. He hadn't let her help with that part. He was just trying to make Rachel giggle because he loved the sound of it more than anything else in the world.

She didn't giggle. "Libby?"

"Libby Hamilton. You know, from the talent show? I'm helping her and her dad with that ice-cream parlor."

"Oh, you mean Mrs. Garner's sister. Hey, did you hear Mrs. Garner had her baby on the night of the talent show?"

He choked a little on his soup. "I think I did hear something about that."

"Is it true Hot Air Hamilton fell out of the bell tower and nearly broke his neck?"

Tom coughed outright at that. "Not exactly. He fell down some stairs and broke his ankle. Where did you hear that?"

Rachel shrugged. "Twitter. So what did you want to talk to me about?"

Tom set down his spoon and put his clammy hands in his lap. He shouldn't be nervous talking to his own daughter, but he was. "I went through the boxes with Aunt Kristy." He said it fast, like ripping off a bandage.

Rachel looked down at her soup, hovering her spoon over the bowl for a fraction of a second before dipping in. "And?"

"And I wanted you to know they're all unpacked. I was planning to donate a lot of the stuff, but I wondered if you wanted to go through any of it first." It all came out in a rush, as if he had to say it all before he lost his nerve.

But his daughter sat quiet, continuing with her soup. She seemed to take the news in stride. She was calm. Not sullen calm, or like the calm before the storm, but serene. "Donate it where?" she asked.

"Kristy has a place in mind, a homeless shelter, I think. She said that's what your mom would have wanted me to do with it." His heart went *thud*, and he waited.

Rachel's lips trembled for a second before she took another bite. She swallowed the soup and met his eyes. "I think that's what she'd want you to do with it, too. I already have a bunch of her stuff that I took when I moved to Grandma's house, so I guess I don't need to look through the rest. You should just get rid of it."

And *thud* again. "Are you sure? Because I don't want to get rid of anything you're not okay with."

She nodded. "I know that, Dad. Go ahead and donate it. Did you unpack all the boxes?"

"All of them."

She set down her own spoon and straightened her shoulders. "Why now?"

"Why now *what*?"

"Why did you finally unpack them? I've been asking you for, like, ten months."

"I don't know." He wished he had a better answer, but the truth was he wasn't sure. Maybe it was Libby. But it had to be more than that. Maybe it was just time. He'd never be over Connie's death, but he'd started to realize he could at least move past it.

Rachel twisted her scarf. "Well, thanks for doing that. Did it suck?"

"Yep. Pretty much. But now it's done, so neither one of us has to worry about it. I did save this, though, and I thought you might want to have it."

He pulled a charm bracelet from his pocket. Kristy had actually come across it in Connie's jewelry box. It was made of silver beads and little blocks with letters on it. He handed it to his daughter.

She took it and looked it over. "It says 'Rachel.'"

"I know. Your mom had it made when you were a baby. She used to wear it all the time. I'm not sure when she stopped."

Rachel turned it over in her hands and pressed her lips together in a tight line. She sniffled, and his own eyes went moist.

"You don't have to keep it if you don't want it."

"No, I want it." She tried to hook it around her wrist but fumbled.

"Here, let me." Tom reached over and hooked the clasp. Then he just couldn't help it. He held her hand. He kept his voice low. "I love you very much, Rachel. You know that, don't you? Even if you're mad at me, and even if you hate me, I'm still always going to love you."

She gently tugged her hand free and put it in her lap, staring down. "I don't hate you. And I'm not sure who I'm mad at. I just know I'm mad."

"Do you think Dr. Brandt is helping?"

Rachel nodded and dabbed at her nose with her napkin. "Yeah. And I like her." She looked back at Tom. "I talked to Grandma about you after you showed up at the talent show."

His stomach twisted in a knot. He'd rather Rachel not see how much he didn't want to hear about that. "How'd that go?"

Rachel shrugged, and picked her spoon back up. "Not that bad. I don't think she hates you either, but she won't stand up to Grandpa."

Not many people could. "Well, Grandpa's got some strong opinions. Your mother didn't agree with him very often."

"She didn't?" Rachel's eyebrows arched.

Dr. Brandt's comments about Rachel choosing a side and needing a safe place bounced around inside his mind just then. He shouldn't push her into a corner anymore by criticizing George. "No, but now that I'm a father I can see his point of view a little better."

Rachel took another bite of soup. "How?"

"Your grandfather loves you, Rachel, just as much as I do, but sometimes love makes us selfish. It shouldn't, but it can. The point is we all want what's best for you. Unfortunately we see that as something different."

"I'm almost sixteen. Maybe it was time you all started listening to me, and let me decide what's best for me." Her voice didn't have that usual sting of sarcasm.

Tom sat back in his seat. "You're right."

She looked up at him, her eyes wide. "I am?"

He smiled. "I am capable of compromise, you know. Maybe we've all been so busy trying to convince you of what we think is right, we haven't given you a chance to decide what you think for yourself. I never meant to put you in this situation, Rach. I'm starting to see that the harder I push, the worse that makes it for you."

She sat back, too, her shoulders sagging in obvious relief. "Yes, it does. Because just as hard as you're pushing, so is Grandpa. I feel like I'm the rope in your tug-of-war."

He had never looked at it that way. How had he missed it? "I'm sorry. I really am."

She sighed. "I know."

He'd made so many mistakes, but that wasn't all there was to him. His intention was to be a good father, and so Tom Murphy said the hardest thing imaginable. He wasn't sure if it was the right thing. But at least it was *something*. It was motion instead of stagnation.

"Rachel, the truth is, even when you are grown up and married, I will always, always want you to live with me because you're my girl. But more than anything else in this world, I want you to be happy. So if staying at your grandparents' house is what you want, I'm okay with it."

"You are?"

He plowed ahead, following his gut. "I am. But I want you to decide for yourself. Don't make your choice based on what Grandpa wants, or Grandma, or even me. There will always be a room for you at my house, but you can decide if you want to use it. And I do want to spend more time together. I want to have dinner, and watch movies and celebrate holidays, maybe go camping. And play backgammon. It's all that little stuff that I miss. And honestly, honey, I'm just tired of us being angry."

Rachel gazed around the restaurant, twirling her hair nervously and blinking fast. She finally looked back at him, her bright eyes sparkly with tears. "I'm pretty good at backgammon."

That vise squeezing his lungs loosened by a millimeter. "I know you *think* you are. I let you win before because you were a little kid. We play now, I'm taking the gloves off. It's game on."

Rachel giggled, and his heart, so full of dents and splices, felt a little better.

"I don't know what to say, Dad."

He shrugged. "Just say . . . say you're glad to be here with me now."

"You're glad to be here with me now." Her dimples showed just then, and she looked so much like Connie he had to clear his throat.

"Very funny. But listen, there's one other thing I'm going to ask. And it's a big thing. I need you to think about it."

"What is it?"

Jumping from a plane without a parachute must feel very much like this. "I'd like for you to forgive me. I can't forgive me until you do. It was an accident, Rachel, and I can't fix it. I can't undo it. So I need you to forgive me."

Those sparkly tears slipped out and she whisked them away. "I do forgive you, Dad. I just really miss Mom."

"I know, honey. So do I. We're supposed to. Just not so much that it squeezes out everything else. And certainly not so much that we can't remember to take care of each other. You have to know, deep down, that your mom would want you to be happy. So do I."

"I know." She picked up her spoon and paused. "Did you really let me win at backgammon?"

He could see her then, as she had been, with her hair in pigtails and braces on her teeth, bent over studying a game board. "Sometimes." He nodded.

"Why?"

"Because I'm your dad."

CHAPTER seventeen

"Watch your step, Dad Hamilton," Dante said as he helped Libby's father up to the porch of the ice-cream parlor.

The overcast November day was cool, but at least the rain held off as the Hamilton family walked from the tiny parking lot to the front door. Her dad had insisted they stop by his *beloved establishment* on their way home from the hospital. Against doctor's orders, naturally. But he'd assured them he could manage with his crutches.

"Peter, be careful," her mother warned. She held her hands out to catch him if he fell backward. He looked very much like he might.

"He's fine, Beverly. Stop hovering," said Nana, walking around all of them and going up the steps first.

"You can do it, Daddy." Marti wrapped an arm around his waist.

The only ones missing were Ginny and Ben, since they were home, undoubtedly staring at baby Teddy, waiting to take another photo of his next adorable yawn.

Libby watched from behind the cluster of her family, squinting as her father teetered sideways. Every single one of them reached out to catch him before he righted himself and moved up another step.

Just breathe. Her pulse was all over the place, but she knew it wasn't entirely concern over her dad that made her heart bouncy as a Ping-Pong ball. It was the thought of seeing Tom. It was late Sunday afternoon, so she hadn't expected him to be here, but his truck was parked in its usual spot, making her quake with a hundred different emotions. Anticipation, hope, lust, and worry. Worry that he'd retreat again.

Last night had been ooh-la-la incredible. Everything she'd wondered about Tom Murphy had turned out to be true. He'd been skilled and intense, but sweet and vulnerable, too. A sexy, potent combination that turned her limbs to water and her lungs into overinflated balloons.

One deliciously wicked moment flashed in Libby's mind and halted her feet.

"You okay?" Marti asked, looking over her shoulder at Libby.

Libby felt her cheeks go hot. "Yep."

Tom was over near a window as they entered. His eyebrows rose in surprise at the sight of them, her father with his crutches and enormous plastic boot protecting his broken ankle, her mother looking pinched with worry, and little Nana in her cherry red raincoat. Libby lingered in the back, but she could tell the moment he spotted her. His face flushed red, and a tiny smile dipped at his mouth.

He set down the hammer in his hand and came their way. "Peter! It's good to see you." Tom reached out an arm and clasped her father by the shoulder. "You look good. How are you feeling?"

"A damn sight better than I felt the day they wheeled me out of here on that metal gurney." He tried to shake Tom's hand, but the crutches made that difficult. "I can't thank you enough, Tom. What a blessing you've been to me and my family."

The color rose in Tom's face again. He pulled over a folding chair. "Here, sit down. I'm just grateful you're doing so well. I'm amazed you're up and walking."

"He's not supposed to be," Libby's mother said. "But he wanted to see his precious ice-cream parlor."

"I don't see any ice cream," said Nana, looking this way and that.

"It'll be along this wall here, Nana." Libby pointed. "Come on, I'll give you a little tour while Dad talks to Tom."

It wouldn't be much of a tour since there were only three rooms in the entire building. Plus the bell tower, but she didn't think she'd show them that. She pulled her mother by the hand, and Nana followed. Marti and Dante stayed with her dad.

"All the ice-cream cases will go here," she told them. "Tom's designed them to look like old-fashioned cabinets. They'll be gorgeous. Then over here is the cash register. I found an old one on eBay to sit here, but honestly, we probably won't use it. It just looks cool. And then over on this side will go all the little bistro tables."

Libby described to them all the details, the window seat Tom was building to go along the front, the vintage chairs she'd ordered, the porch swings they planned to hang out front, the window treatments, and the old-fashioned ice-cream dishes. Until that moment, she hadn't really considered how much of herself she'd poured into this building. She was doing it for her dad, but somewhere along the line, it had become Libby's vision, too. She was very proud of how she'd contributed, and she wanted to see it through all the way to the end.

She looked over at Tom on the other side of the room, sitting down next to her dad along with Dante and Marti. He wore his hat backward today, looking half his age, except for those big, broad shoulders that made him look every inch a full-grown man. He tipped his head and laughed at something her father said, and then he turned, as if he could feel her eyes on him. He held her gaze, not the least bit hesitant, and she stopped midsentence, forgetting everything she'd been about to say to her mother and Nana.

He smiled her way, relaxed and easy. He didn't regret their night. No walls had gone back up. She felt a blush stealing up over her own cheeks and a warmth down low at the thought of his kiss. She wanted to march over there and demand another one right now, but she felt Nana at her elbow and resisted.

"Well, you certainly have done a lot, it seems," Libby's mother said, her tone reluctantly impressed.

Libby turned back to them. "We *have* done a lot. Dad's been working really hard, Mom. I know you weren't thrilled about this place. And he should have told you before he bought it. But it's ours now, so I hope you can be excited."

Her mother shook her head and let her gaze travel around the circumference of the room. "This place does have a certain charm. I can see why you like it. But, yes, Peter should have told me. And he shouldn't have spent your wedding fund. That was unforgivable."

Libby chuckled. "I don't care about my wedding fund, Mom. I don't need it."

"You might," Nana whispered, tipping her head in Tom's direction, subtle as a brick through a window.

Libby smiled at her. "Anyway, let's finish the tour. Here's where we'll keep the extra supplies."

She showed them around for a few more minutes, sharing details until, at last, they rejoined Tom, her father, Marti, and Dante.

Tom stood up and gestured to Nana. "Please, sit here, Mrs. Hamilton."

Nana settled into the chair, her vinyl coat squeaking. "Thank you, young man. What nice manners you have. Did you enjoy the pie I made for you?"

Tom stole a glance Libby's way. She pressed her lips together, sealing off a smile as his cheeks flushed. He turned back to Nana.

"I can honestly say, Mrs. Hamilton, I don't think I've ever enjoyed a pie quite so much as I enjoyed that one."

Libby turned away and coughed into her hand.

Nana waved a hand at him. "Oh, listen to you. It's really all in the crust. If you make a decent crust, anything tastes good."

It wasn't the crust, or the filling, or the fact that it had arrived warm from the oven. It was the platter. He'd eaten a bite of that pie right off Libby's smooth belly, and in all his life he'd never imagined licking sweet, sticky peaches from a woman's body. His mouth watered, and his blood shot to his groin like a bottle rocket. He cleared his throat and tried to think of something hideously unsexy. But Libby was standing right there. It was no use.

He pulled up a wooden crate and sat down. He should've offered the seat to Beverly, but considering the hard-on taking root in his pants, it was really best for everyone if he sat down.

"So, Beverly, what do you think of this place now that you've seen it firsthand?" he asked.

She wrapped her coat around herself a little tighter. "I think you've done a very impressive job, Tom. My husband is lucky to have found you. I'm wondering what happens now, though, since he won't be able to lend a hand in the reconstruction."

Peter not helping could only improve Tom's pace. He'd be nearly finished by now if not for all the *assistance* he'd been getting. There was a lot that still needed doing to get this place ready for business, and Tom knew Peter was running low on funds. He'd do the best he could to speed the reconstruction along, although it might mean a financial hit on his end.

"Tom and I were just discussing that, Bev," Peter answered. "We have a couple of options. Either we postpone our grand opening until after the holidays, or we could hire a few subcontractors and get back on schedule."

Beverly turned to her husband and pressed her purse closer to her side. "Wouldn't subcontractors cost more money?"

"Just a little." Peter Hamilton would be no good at poker.

"I'm sure I can work a little faster," Tom added. "And Dante here says he's ready to lend a hand."

"Anything you need." Dante nodded. "As long as it doesn't interfere with my jousting lessons and the banquets."

Jousting. First a history teacher and a party planner, now a jouster. Tom smiled. Getting this place refurbished was taking quite an interesting assortment of unskilled labor.

Libby set her purse down on the floor and walked over toward the window. "Hey, it looks like it's going to rain. Maybe we should get Dad home."

Her hair was tied back in a low ponytail, but Tom knew what it looked like spread across his pillow. His pulse revved like a motorcycle about to jump a canyon. He wanted to see her that way again, with her arms reaching up to him and her skin pink with heat. He'd like that for tonight. And maybe the next night after that, too.

"We have to get Nana home, too," Beverly added. "Thank you again for all your help lately, Tom. Ginny appreciates it, and I just can't thank you enough for being there when Peter fell. I was wondering, in fact, if you had plans for Thanksgiving. We usually have just our family, but we'd be honored if you'd join us."

That invitation came from left field and plunked him on the head like a fly ball. Thanksgiving with the Hamiltons? He glanced over at Libby.

Her eyes were wide with surprise. She'd obviously not known about this invitation beforehand. But she smiled and tipped her head to one side.

"Unless of course you have other plans with your own family. But Rachel is more than welcome to join us, too," Beverly added.

"Um, I'm honored, really, Bev. I would hate to intrude on your family time."

"Oh, please," Marti said, getting up from her chair. "We have family time every frickin' Sunday. You should totally have Thanksgiving with us. My mom makes the best gravy on the planet."

"I make the best pies," murmured Nana.

Pie, and gravy, and time with Libby? That would be something to be thankful for. But being surrounded by all of them and trying to keep his feelings under wraps would be a tall order. He didn't know what she'd said to them about him. And it wasn't that he had regrets, because he didn't. But going public and sharing a holiday with a woman's family was a huge leap from tumbling between some blankets. Pie or no pie.

"I appreciate the invitation, Bev. I'd like to check with Rachel, first, if you don't mind. I need to know her plans first."

Libby turned back to the window.

"Of course. There's always plenty of food, so just let us know when you decide," Beverly said.

Rain started to pelt against the window. "Uh-oh, we're too late. Let's make a dash for it," Dante said.

Peter struggled up from his chair and adjusted his crutches with some help from Marti. "These things are going to get old very quickly."

"You're lucky you're not in a wheelchair," Beverly said.

They all moved to the door and clamored down the steps. Tom stopped in the doorway, watching. Libby moved past him without a word, and his chest went heavy, but halfway to the car she said, "Oh, I'll be right back. I forgot my purse."

She turned around and moved quickly back inside, pulling at his shirt. He let himself be maneuvered, and as soon as she had him behind the door, she wrapped her arms around his neck and kissed him with such swiftness that he bumped against the wall. His own arms circled her waist, and he pulled her closer.

It was a fast kiss. Too fast, because he wanted to hold her there for hours, but she stepped away as fast as she'd come at him.

"Sorry," she gasped. "I couldn't resist."

"I'm glad. Can I see you later?"

She shook her head and walked over to the chair to grab her purse. "I don't think so. I have to help my dad settle in at home. I don't really trust my mom around him. She's still really mad and keeps accidentally bumping into his broken ankle." Teasing was apparent by her tone, but she was sincere about not coming over. Disappointment thumped against his hope.

"Well, you'd better stand guard then."

She came back and pulled on his shirt once more. "I had a really good time last night."

Her smile was shy, but her eyes were full of mischief, plucking his breath away as neatly as her kiss.

"Me, too." He wanted to gather her close again, but her family was waiting, and the contact would just make it harder to send her on her way.

"Okay, well . . ." She sighed. "I'll see you . . . around."

He just nodded. What else could he say except "when?" It was the only word going through his mind.

CHAPTER *eighteen*

"Isn't it fabulous?" Marti's voice was breathy with excitement as she led Libby and Ginny into the private dining hall of the Medieval Times banquet facilities. "Doesn't it look just like a castle?"

"If you lived in a castle made of cardboard, maybe," Ginny murmured to Libby.

Libby was inclined to agree. This was definitely not the place she'd choose to have a wedding, but Marti seemed enthralled by the fake cinder-block walls and dark, distressed-wooden furniture. Dozens of black wrought-iron sconces lined the walls, the fake, flickering candles casting light and shadows over brightly colored pennants. Overhead were three enormous black chandeliers. At least they were made of metal and not antlers.

"We'll have the family table up here on this stage. So you guys will sit up here," Marti said, stepping up on the raised platform.

"This room is kind of small, isn't it?" Ginny asked.

"It's intimate. We've only invited about forty people."

"Is the ceremony going to be in here?" Ginny's lack of awe was patently obvious.

Marti rolled her eyes. "Of course not. That would be stupid. I'm riding up on a white horse, and they don't let horses in the dining area."

"Yeah, because *that* would be tacky," Libby whispered to Ginny.

Ginny sighed and looked at her watch. "How long is this going to take, Marti? I need to get home to feed the baby."

"Relax, we've only been gone for half an hour, and I need to check on a couple more things. Hey, maybe you should apply for a job here, Libby. They do all sorts of special events. You'd be awesome at that."

Libby smiled. "Sure. And lots of people feel like they work in a dungeon. I could come here and work in an actual dungeon."

"It's not a dungeon. It's a dining hall." Marti shook her head and rolled her eyes again. "Geez, you guys have zero sense of adventure."

Ginny pulled her phone out of her purse to check for messages.

"I'm sure Teddy is fine, Ginny," Libby said. "He's got three men and a little old lady looking after him, and Mom is looking after all of them."

Ginny put her phone back in her purse. "I know. He's fine, but I'm a wreck. I can't stand to be away from him, even for a second. I cried at the grocery store the other day because I had too many items to go through the express lane and Teddy was at home waiting."

Libby chuckled. Her normally composed sister had become a weepy marshmallow. "So I take it motherhood is everything you dreamed it would be?"

Ginny shook her head and laughed. "Oh, God, no. It's nothing at all like I expected it to be, but I still love it."

"What were you expecting?"

"Well, for starters, I thought I'd have all this spare time while the baby was sleeping." She made air quotes around the word *sleeping*. "I was going to read, clean my closets, try some new recipes, go out to lunch . . . but trust me, there is none of that. It's usually two o'clock in the afternoon before I even take a shower. I wear maternity pants half the time because they're comfortable, and all we ever eat is takeout. And Ben is already talking about having another baby."

"He is?" Libby couldn't disguise the surprise in her voice.

"Yes. I told him he could deliver the next one and I'd get drunk and pass out in the car."

"He's never going to live that one down, is he?"

Libby shook her head and chuckled at the memory of trying to fold her brother-in-law's long legs into the car after that night at the pub.

"Never." Ginny's tone was dry.

"But it's still good?"

Her sister's face split into a smile. "Yes. I just look at Teddy and I don't even care that I have spit-up all over my shirt or that I never get to sleep for more than three hours at a time." Ginny grabbed Libby's arm and gave it a gentle squeeze. "You should have a baby, Libby. Marry Tom and have a baby right away."

Libby nearly buckled at the knees from the chop of that comment.

Marti twirled around from examining some plastic battle shields hanging on the wall. "Yes, you should totally marry Tom and have a baby, Libby."

Libby looked from one sister to the other, her heart bouncing like a yo-yo. They were teasing, of course, but her throat squeezed shut anyway. "That's very funny. And a little premature, don't you think? I just met him."

"But you're crazy about him. You should have seen them yesterday at the ice-cream parlor, Ginny," Marti said, her voice coy. "It was practically slippery, there was so much drooling going on."

Libby gasped then, with laughter and embarrassment. "Are you high? There was no drooling. He didn't even say anything to me."

"I know, and it was so painfully obvious he was trying not to look at you. I think he pulled a muscle in his eye." She turned to Ginny. "I swear there was steam coming out of his clothes."

"That is ridiculous. There is nothing going on." Libby wasn't ready to talk about this. Everything with Tom was so new and so unexpected, she hadn't had a chance to process it for herself yet. Getting their opinions mixed up in her own would only make things more confusing.

"Can I have my condoms back?" Marti said, holding out one hand and tapping her foot.

"What?" Ginny burst out with an unladylike squawk of laughter.

Marti tapped her foot faster and looked at Libby. "Nana and I sent Libby over to Tom's house the other night loaded up with peach pie and condoms, and all she came home with was bed head and whisker burn."

Libby couldn't keep the heat from her cheeks or the smile from her face, though she fought them both. "How is this any of your business, Marti?"

"It's my business because I'm invested. I like Tom, and he has a truck. Do you know how handy it is to have a guy in the family with a truck?"

"You think I should marry Tom because he has a truck?"

"No, I think you should marry him because he's cool and looks fun to climb. The truck is just an extra perk."

Libby burst out laughing. "This is absurd. I'm not talking to you about this right now."

"I'm with Marti," Ginny blurted out. "You should absolutely marry him and have a baby. Fast, so our kids could play together." Practical, predictable Ginny must be on some sort of medication, and Libby was beginning to feel outnumbered.

"Aren't you the one who said Marti and Dante were rushing into things?"

"Yes, and I still think they are."

"Hey!" Marti frowned.

Ginny kept on talking. "But when I think back on it, I knew with Ben right away. We still dated for a long time before we got engaged, but we knew almost immediately."

"See!" Marti looked from Libby to Ginny and back again. "See what I told you, Libby? True love is spontaneous and powerful and impossible to ignore."

Libby's laughter faded, and the floor seemed to tilt. She wanted to believe Marti about that. She really did. Everything felt so right when she was with Tom. But that didn't mean it would work. Or that they should rush things.

"It's just not that simple, you guys. He's got . . . stuff on his mind. There's some history to him, you know. And he has a fifteen-year-old daughter."

"I saw you with her at the talent show. You two got along great," said Ginny, rummaging around in her purse for her phone again.

Libby walked away, staring at the rustic sconces but thinking about Rachel. And Tom. She turned back around to face her sisters. "I have to be honest, this thing with Tom is kind of a big deal."

Saying it out loud was the bravest thing she could imagine.

Marti and Ginny froze in place.

"It is?" Ginny dropped her phone back in her purse without looking at it.

It *was* a big deal. And not just because the sex had been good. Or even because the sex had been phenomenal. The truth was, Libby had never felt this way before about anyone, not even Seth, and they'd been together for more than three years.

"Yes, but it just doesn't make any sense to me. How could I like Tom this much, this fast?"

"Why does it have to make sense?" Marti scooted back to sit on a table.

"I'm not as spontaneous and daring as you are, Marti. Sometimes I like things to have an explanation."

Marti twirled her hair for a second, and then turned toward Ginny. "Why did you want to have a baby, Ginny?"

Ginny looked a little startled. "What? Why are we talking about me now?"

"Just answer the question. Why did you want to have a baby?"

"Um, I don't know. I just always wanted kids, and it seemed like the right time."

Marti held up her hands. "And there you go. No one can explain why we want to have kids. It's just a compulsion for most of us. Instinct. Just like being attracted to somebody. The only explanation you need is biology. Maybe this is nature's way of telling you to stop dating assholes and find yourself a nice carpenter."

Libby huffed with equal parts amusement and sting. "Wow. I'm not sure if that's scientific, or sentimental, or just plain stupid."

Ginny scratched her head. "I have to say it, Libby. Marti might be on to something here. I mean, first of all, you *have* dated a lot of assholes. Tom is the first really decent guy you've ever been involved with, so it makes sense you'd feel differently about him."

There was no point in defending the asshole comment, because it was true. She just hadn't realized it until Seth rode away into the San Diego sunset without so much as a postcard.

"You guys are ganging up on me."

"I don't mean to," Ginny said. "You probably should wait to get married, but I do think you finally have a keeper on your hands. And you know Tom will always be my hero. If it wasn't for him I might have had my baby in the back of a taxicab."

Tom's phone was in his pocket when he felt it vibrate. He pulled it out, optimistic since almost no one texted him.

RU HOME? Except Libby.

Ridiculous how such an abbreviated message could shift a practical man into a boyish mess. He texted back: *HEADING THERE NOW. WANT TO HAVE DINNER?*

I'LL BRING IT. MEET YOU AT YOUR HOUSE?

YEP.

Then he sent a second text. *HURRY.*

Libby stood at his door forty-five minutes later with a pizza box in one hand and a six-pack in the other.

"Wow. You may just be the perfect woman."

He wrapped his arms around her waist and pulled her into the house, the pizza and beer clunking against the doorframe.

"Wait, wait," she said, laughter making her quiver in his arms. "Let me set this down. There's more."

"More?" She was a vixen with pizza and beer. How could there be more? He loosened his hold, and she set the stuff down on the counter. Her eyes twinkled as she reached into her coat pocket and pulled out a little dark blue box. She tossed it with a flourish onto the counter next to the pizza.

Tom leaned over.

Condoms. The economy pack of twenty-four.

God bless her.

"Am I being presumptuous again?" she asked. Her hair was loose and fluffed up by the wind, and her eyes were bright.

"You're being awesome." He pulled her close and kissed her with all the longing he'd saved up over the last two days. She was warm and eager, wrapping her arms around his shoulders and lifting up on her toes to press against him.

Every time. Every time he kissed her he was amazed by the sheer thrill of it, the push and pull between them.

"Do you know the best thing about pizza?" she murmured against his cheek.

"What?"

"You can eat it cold."

His desire reflected in her eyes. He grabbed the edge of her jacket and pushed it off her, letting it fall to the floor, and then he reached behind her for the little box.

"Let's go." He turned and dragged her down the hall toward his bedroom. She followed, hopping intermittently to kick off one shoe, and then the other.

Blood pounded in his veins as they fell on the bed and she started tugging on his clothes. The world fell away until it was just the two of them in an ocean of blankets. He kissed her up and down, reveling in her touch and taste and the sounds of her pleasure. Libby Hamilton was a treasure he'd never thought to discover. And when he sank into the depths of her, and she breathed his name so softly against his ear, Tom knew there was no going back, and no standing still. There was only moving forward.

"So, what do you think about Thanksgiving with my family?" Libby asked as they snuggled together under the covers. "Sorry my mother put you on the spot like that."

Tom adjusted his pillow and twined a lock of Libby's gold hair around his index finger. "You looked a little surprised by her invitation, too. Sorry she put *you* on the spot."

The idea of dinner with the Hamilton family had been on his mind ever since Beverly had made the offer. Last year Rachel had celebrated with her grandparents and he'd stayed home, watching old home movies and getting drunk by himself, just like he'd done on Christmas and New Year's Eve. It was not a tradition he planned on keeping. One year of that was enough.

"I'm good with it," Libby said, moving a little closer. "I mean, I'd be glad to have you there. Or I would, if . . . if you'd be glad. I'm just not sure where you are with all of this." She gestured toward the bed, but he knew what she meant. Whatever was between them had yet to be defined, as if he were unfolding a map but didn't know at what county he was looking.

A little crease formed between her eyebrows. "And like I said before, I don't want to be anybody's quicksand and drag you into where you don't want to be. I know my family can be a little overwhelming."

Remorse tapped him on the shoulder. "I told you I didn't mean that the way it sounded."

She smiled then, but the question was still evident in her eyes. "Yes, you did, but I can hardly blame you. Why do you think I moved to Chicago in the first place? My family can be very needy. I guess I can be, too."

That was laughable. All she'd done was give and give and give. "I don't see you as needy at all."

"Really? You don't think showing up here to seduce you with pizza and beer isn't needy?"

Tom's laughter rolled from deep inside. "Uh, I thought it was incredibly generous, so I guess it's all in how you look at it. But you're right. This is sort of uncharted territory for me, and I'll be honest, I'm not sure how I feel about spending the day with your family. Please don't think I'm saying I have regrets, because I don't. I'm just not sure how all the pieces fit together. Especially with Rachel."

"Or where I fit in? I can understand that." She traced a finger over his shoulder.

"You do?" His relief was cool rain on a hot day.

"Yes. This has all been kind of unexpected for me, too, you know. Not that long ago I was living with someone in Chicago and thinking my life was right on track. I didn't realize then how wrong I was. Or how different things could be."

He'd never asked Libby specific questions about her life before coming back to Monroe. It never seemed necessary, since she was prone to sharing details most people save for their doctor or their priest. Aside from the volume of things she volunteered about her career, he'd also gleaned quite a bit from the fragments of conversations he'd overheard between her and her sister, or Libby's chats with Peter.

One thing he knew for certain, though. That old boyfriend sounded like a grade-A asshole. Thinking of Libby in that guy's bed, or in any other guy's bed, made Tom want to put his fist through a wall.

He gave her hip a squeeze instead. "It's different for me, too. But I guess we should take this day by day. Don't you think?" His heart sped up as he waited for her answer. Her blue eyes were dark in the dim light of the bedroom.

"I think that's a pretty good plan."

More relief.

"But I want you to know, Libby, I am glad—about all of this." He lifted his hand from her hip and circled it over them.

Her smile was sweet. "Me, too."

He kissed her then, but his stomach growled, and pizza beckoned. It was about the only thing that would make him get out of that bed.

He and Libby dressed and relocated to the pine table in the kitchen to eat. He opened two slightly warm beers and handed one to her before taking a sip of his own.

"How is your dad feeling about the ice-cream parlor these days? He seemed pretty reluctant to say much in front of your mom." He pulled a piece of pizza onto a plate and passed it to Libby.

"He's worried about the money. He wants to make sure you get paid, of course. I think he's concerned he'll run out of cash before you have time to finish."

"I'm not going to leave him in a lurch. We're only a little behind schedule because of his accident. And his help." Tom smiled at her, and Libby chuckled.

He took a bite of pizza. It was room temperature and soggy, but he didn't care because Libby hadn't buttoned her blouse up all the way, or put on her bra, and the shadowy crease of her cleavage was right in his sight line.

"But he's spent more on supplies than he budgeted for," she said. "He was actually hoping it would be done faster than you guys had originally talked about so he could open for business sooner. He just hadn't said anything to you yet. But now with his leg, I'm just not sure what's going to happen."

"Well, I'll do my best. The detail work with restoration can be time-consuming, but you know I'll work it fast as I can."

He was already working as quickly as possible. That was just his nature, but this project had taken on a personal aspect he'd never expected. He didn't want to disappoint Peter Hamilton, and he especially didn't want to disappoint Libby. He'd figure something out.

"You know I'll help in any way I can, too," Libby added. "Or do I slow you down as much as my dad does?" She took a bite, and a droplet of marinara landed on her chin before she wiped it away.

"You slow me down in a completely different way." He took a long drink from his bottle, and she smiled.

"In what way?"

"You bring me to an absolute standstill every time you climb up on a ladder and wiggle your ass at me."

Libby burst out with laughter and set down her pizza. "I have never done that."

"I swear to God, you do it every day."

CHAPTER *nineteen*

Tom arrived at Rachel's grandparents' place at six thirty sharp, and as usual she was standing outside. This time she was even waiting at the end of the driveway, her nose pink from the cold.

"Hi there," he said as she pulled open the door and scrambled in.

She shivered, and buckled her seat belt. "Hey, thanks for being on time. It's freezing out."

He glanced at his watch. "I am on time, aren't I?"

"Yes. I wasn't being sarcastic." Rachel smiled, her dimples deepening. "God, Dad, can't you even tell when I'm being nice?"

Her teasing warmed him. It had been such a long time. "I guess I'm just not used to it."

She shook her head and rolled her eyes, but playfully, with none of the past drama, and he was struck by the difference in her since they'd started seeing Dr. Brandt. And even more so since he'd said he didn't expect her to move in with him. She'd dug in like a mule over that, and now that the decision was up to her, she'd relaxed. He'd made the right choice, even though he still missed her like crazy.

"How's school going?" he asked as he put the truck in gear and started to drive. He hoped to approach the topic of Thanksgiving with the Hamiltons, but this was a far safer subject to start with.

"Not bad. How's the ice-cream parlor coming along?"

"Pretty good. Should be finished by Christmas."

It felt good that Rachel had even asked. It was the first bit of interest she'd shown in him in ages. "Mr. Hamilton is doing pretty well, hobbling around on those crutches. He and his daughter stop by a few times a day to check on the progress and help with what they can manage. Hey, speaking of the Hamiltons, I wanted to talk to you about Thanksgiving."

"What about it?" Something shifted in her tone, a hesitation, the guard rising.

He glanced her way, but she was staring straight ahead instead of at him. He turned his eyes back toward the road. "Well, since I've been doing so much work for them, and since I was there to help out when Mr. Hamilton fell and everything, they've invited me to have Thanksgiving dinner with them. But what I was really hoping was that you and I could spend the day together, or even just part of the day. I'm not sure what your grandparents have planned, though."

He ended up almost stammering, and it frustrated him down deep. He shouldn't have to ask Anne and George's permission to spend a holiday with his daughter. That wasn't Rachel's fault, of course, but it was something he needed to fix. Soon.

Rachel fidgeted with her gloves. "Well, it's kind of funny that you should mention that, because I wanted to talk to you about Thanksgiving, too."

His heart lifted. "You did?"

Rachel nodded. "Yeah, see, I've been invited to go skiing that weekend in Colorado with . . . with a friend. And I wondered how you'd feel about that."

And down it came again. That was hardly the response he'd been hoping for. "Colorado? That's pretty far away for a weekend trip." That wasn't the only issue he had with that idea, but he'd tackle them one at a time.

"I'd have to miss a couple of days of school. I'd leave next Monday and come home the Sunday after Thanksgiving."

"So you'd be gone almost a week? Who's the friend?" Not that it mattered. He wasn't about to let his fifteen-year-old daughter travel halfway across the country over a holiday weekend.

"Um, it's the Robertsons. Do you know them?"

He shook his head and tried to remember anyone from town with that name and a daughter Rachel's age. The only Robertsons he knew were . . . Shit. "You're not talking about Don and Lindsay Robertson, are you?"

He glanced at his daughter. She bit her lip. Don and Lindsay Robertson only had sons. Big, lanky, hormonal sons.

"Um, yeah, actually, that is who I'm talking about. So you do know them, huh? Excellent." She tried to make her voice all singsongy and breezy, as if she wasn't asking him if she could go away for a week with a boy. A boy who had to be about seventeen years old.

"So, this friend of yours, is it a boyfriend?" Tom felt a little nauseated and couldn't keep the edge from his tone.

Rachel tapped her fingers on her legs. "Sort of, well, yes. But it's not like it'll be just Jake and me. I mean, his parents are going, too. And his brothers. We'll be supervised the entire time. And they're all really good skiers, too."

"Didn't that kid get arrested?" Bits of a story were working forward in his mind. A group of sixteen-year-old boys. A pasture. Farm animals.

Rachel sighed, and her expression turned from optimism to exasperation. "He tried to tip a cow and got arrested for trespassing. That hardly counts." She was looking at him now like she was ready to rumble about it.

Tom scoffed. "It counts as stupid."

"Oh, and you never did anything stupid?" There it was, the old snark to her tone.

But she did have a point.

He took a big, deep breath, just like Dr. Brandt had taught him to do.

"Yes, Rachel. I have done many stupid things in my life, and I would hope you'd learn from my mistakes rather than repeat them." That sounded pretty logical, but in his head, what he really meant to say was *No fucking way are you going somewhere with this kid.*

Rachel took her own deep breath and huffed it back out. "I *have* learned from your mistakes, Dad, which is exactly why I'm perfectly safe going away with a boy and his parents for a week of skiing. Honestly, there is zero percent chance of me getting pregnant."

His stomach felt like a water balloon about to hit the pavement. That was exactly what he'd been thinking, of course, but to have her throw it out there so bluntly, and in such a superior way, was enough to knock the air from his lungs. "Well, I'm glad to hear that."

He rolled the window down, the heat in the truck suddenly stifling. He unzipped his coat a bit. Is this how George had felt every time Connie snuck out of the basement window to go for a late-night joyride with him?

God, no wonder George hated him so much. All Tom had ever heard was Connie's side, that her father was overbearing and overprotective. That may have been true, but now Tom understood the reasons behind that better than ever. The drive to protect his daughter was at the root of it.

"It's not just that, Rachel," Tom said, although that was most of it. "It's the travel and the missing school. I'm not sure I'm comfortable with that."

"I've already asked my teachers, and they're fine with me missing. It's only two days anyway because we get Wednesday, Thursday, and Friday off for Thanksgiving. Half the kids are going to be gone that week. I'll be the only one in class if I go to school."

He suspected she was scowling but chose not to look.

"What do your grandparents say? Did you ask them?"

Her shrug was noncommittal. "I wanted to talk to you about it."

That pleased him, that she'd come to him first. It made him feel like her father again. They really were making good progress.

"Even if I wanted to say yes, Rachel, I don't have the money right now to buy your plane ticket and your ski passes. Colorado is expensive, and I certainly couldn't expect the Robertsons to pay your way."

"The Robertsons are paying for the condo, and I have some money saved up from babysitting."

"Probably not enough."

"Grandma would give me some money, too. Dad, I really want to go on this trip. I haven't been anywhere in ages. Not since we went on vacation with Mom before we moved."

That tugged at him. They'd gone to Gatlinburg and stayed in a little log cabin. They'd panned for gold at a touristy amusement park and ridden an old-fashioned steam train. Somewhere in a shoebox, stuffed away in a closet, were pictures from that trip. Nostalgia for that vacation threatened to overwhelm him. Rachel had been a child then, a child who adored him. If he could get a little of that back, his life would be so much better.

"How long have you been seeing this kid? What did you say his name was?"

"His name is Jake, Dad, and he's very nice. And other than that silly cow thing, he's actually very responsible. I think you'd like him."

No, he wouldn't. He'd hate him. On principle alone, he was obligated to detest this kid who probably felt about Rachel the way Tom felt about Libby. The notion of it made him shudder to the marrow of his bones.

"I have to think about this trip, Rachel. I'm not for it, but I'll give it some thought." He'd try to, at least. But he wouldn't like it. "And honestly, with you living at your grandparents' house, you should probably ask them, too. Grandma might have plans for you for Thanksgiving."

Her sigh came from her toes. "I already asked them. Grandpa said no."

"You already asked them?" That was a kick in the gut he wasn't expecting. Tom gripped the steering wheel more tightly, and that water balloon in his gut dropped another inch. "And now you're asking me? So, if Grandpa had said yes, would you have even told me? Or would you have waited until you'd gotten back?"

She stared straight ahead. "Of course I would have told you."

"Told me or asked me?" Now it was getting really hot inside the truck. Tom adjusted the vents to blow on his face.

"What's the difference?" she asked.

"Uh, there is a significant difference. I'm still your father, Rachel, no matter where you live, and you can't just leave the state without getting my permission."

"I wasn't going to. You're getting mad at me for something I didn't do. You're reacting with emotion instead of logic."

Tom bit back his retort. Her comment was straight from the Dr. Brandt handbook. At least Rachel had been listening. But he still felt like he'd very nearly been played.

"Okay, using logic, Rachel, if I'd said yes, were you going to go back and tell George you had my permission and therefore you could go? You can't pit us against each other, because that's not okay."

"I wasn't trying to do that. Honestly. But why do I have to get two sets of permission? That's not fair. If I only get to do things that both you and Grandpa agree on, I may as well lock myself in my room right now because I'll never get to do anything, or go anywhere, ever."

His anger faded a notch. After all, what kid wouldn't try to work the system to his or her advantage? And if Dr. Brandt had taught him anything, it was that Rachel's behavior wasn't personal. His daughter wasn't doing this to mess with him. She just wanted to go skiing. Still, he couldn't resist saying, "Isn't that a little melodramatic?"

She huffed and crossed her arms. "No more melodramatic than you being so certain that I'll get knocked up on this ski trip."

"Rachel."

"Well, seriously, Dad, isn't that what this is about? You and Grandpa both being worried that I'll be just like Mom? If I was going to Colorado with a girlfriend and her parents, I bet you both would've said fine."

He wasn't certain about that. But her point was annoyingly plausible. And effectively ruined most of his arguments about her going.

"Look, I know you're smart and reasonably cautious," he said. "But it's my job to keep you out of situations you're not ready for. Trust me, Rachel. Things can get out of hand pretty quickly when you're faced with the opportunity."

She turned toward him. "Dad, seriously? Do you have any idea how easy it is to create the opportunity? I don't need to go to Colorado for that."

Splat went the water balloon. "I don't think that point is really helping your case here, Rach. It just makes me want to pull you out of high school and lock you in a shed."

She took a big, exaggerated breath and exhaled, loud and slow. "Dad, I'm going to try really hard here to look at your intentions instead of your actual words, okay?" Another Brandt-ism. "And what I hear you saying is that you want me to be safe, right?"

"Right."

"Well, I want me to be safe, too. I don't drink or do drugs. I do all my homework. I never miss my curfew. And my boyfriend's parents want to take me skiing and stay in a condo with, like, nine other people. Trust me. If Jake and I were going to hook up, it would not be there. So is it really such a big deal for me to go?"

Sullen, silent Rachel was a lot easier to maneuver around. This new kid was too smart for him.

"I can't wrap my head around all this right now, Rachel." He pulled into the parking lot of the restaurant and turned off the truck. "You have to let me think about it, okay? I do hear what you're saying, but that doesn't mean I'm going to agree. And I'm not crazy about undermining George's opinion. Frankly, you should have asked me first, but it's not going to smooth things over with me and your grandparents if he says one thing and I say another."

She stared at him for the space of a heartbeat. "If I lived with you, we wouldn't need Grandpa's opinion." Her voice was quiet but deliberate.

Tom's heart sped up, and tripped and fell, and got back up.

"Rachel, don't use that as a bargaining chip to make me change my mind about this trip." His voice was just as quiet. "I couldn't take that."

She looked at him, her eyes big and serious. "I have been thinking about it a little bit, is all. I haven't made any decisions, but I'll be able to drive next summer, and then I could live with you but still go to the same school. Assuming I had a car." A tiny smile crooked at the corner of her mouth.

Tom felt the pull of her teasing. Another tactic from the good doctor. Lighten the mood with humor. His daughter just might have a career in psychology. "So, a skiing adventure in Colorado and a new car? That's what it'll take to make you move back in with me?"

She giggled and tipped her head back against the seat. "No, of course not. It's just Grandma and Grandpa have been really nice to me, but they're also really old, and I think they kind of want to move to Florida. All their friends go down there for the winter, and they're stuck up here taking care of me. I don't know. Maybe it's time."

He couldn't breathe. He wanted her to come home so badly. He'd tried and tried to convince himself it was okay if she stayed with Anne and George, that he could manage by himself, if it's what she wanted. But here she was saying maybe, just maybe, she'd come home.

"I haven't decided anything yet. Please don't get that look on your face," she said.

"What look?"

"The one you get when you're really excited about something. I just wanted you to know I was considering it. And I really need you to start talking to Grandpa." She reached out a hand and touched his sleeve. "Because if I try to tell him this on my own, he'll talk me out of it."

"Has that happened before?" His joy turned sour.

She shrugged and pulled her hand back. "Sort of. Anytime I suggest moving back in with you, he gives me ten reasons why I should stay with them. He's pretty convincing. And then there are the piano lessons, and the new clothes, and the laptop. I have to admit it, Dad. I have a pretty good setup over there."

At least she was being honest. Now there were two ways he could take this. The selfish, domineering path that shot down all those perks and made her feel guilty for staying so long, or the loving path that gave her some autonomy.

"You do have a good setup there, and they do love you, even if that makes George come down so hard on you. I don't blame you for staying. And I won't blame you if you decide to stay longer because I can't offer you all of that. But I'll say it again, Rachel. I'm your dad, and I love you. There is a room for you at home, and it's always ready for you. I will talk to Grandpa. I should have done that sooner, and I'm sorry. But I'll make sure he understands this is your decision."

Her sigh was light with relief. "Good. Can we eat now? Because I'm starving."

CHAPTER *twenty*

Tom pulled up in front of the ice-cream parlor at seven thirty the next morning to find a brand-new green pickup parked outside. The windows were a little foggy, and the sun was just starting to rise, so it was hard to see into the cab. He got out of his truck, his feet crunching on the gravel as he walked closer to it.

The truck's door opened, work-booted feet came out, and suddenly Tom was face to face with his old friend Steve.

"Tom Murphy! You keeping banker's hours? I've been waiting here for fifteen minutes."

Steve's beefy hand rose up and grabbed Tom's, giving him a bear-quality shake.

"Steve, good to see you, man. I haven't seen you in ages." He hadn't seen any of his friends in ages, come to think of it.

"Too long, for damn sure. How the hell are you?" Steve smiled wide.

"I'm all right. How are you? And Abby and the kids?"

"Fat. Everybody at my house is fat. Including me. But we're good. Steve Junior started his senior year at Monroe High, Bonnie is a sophomore, and Grace is in eighth grade. Can you beat that? Where does the time go, huh? How's Rachel?"

"She's good. So, what brings you over here at this time of day?" His curiosity was burning.

Steve took off his hat and scratched his balding head before putting the hat back on. "Well, here's the thing, Tom. My daughter is on that, whatcha call it? Facebook. And she sees this story about how old Hot Air Hamilton fell out of the bell tower and broke his neck."

"His ankle."

"What?"

"He broke his ankle, but it was still pretty serious. He's supposed to stay off his feet for two months. And he knocked his head pretty good. Got some staples in it."

"Okay, yeah, that's probably what my daughter said. You know how girls are. I only listened to about half of her story. So anyway, a few of us guys were down at the bar, and we start talking about Pete Hamilton and his ice-cream place, and Joe says to me, 'Isn't Tom Murphy working over there?' And a couple of other guys said, 'Yeah, and it's just the two of them.'"

Steve belched and thumped a fist against his chest. "Excuse me. Breakfast burrito. So anyway, we decided you could probably use some help."

A lump lodged in Tom's chest. A lump that had nothing to do with his own breakfast. Steve had always been a good guy, the kind to help an old friend. Even one he hadn't seen in almost a year.

"Wow, Steve, I'm not sure what to say. That's really generous of you. I could certainly use an extra set of hands for a couple of hours."

Steve's ruddy cheeks got ruddier still. "I hope you need a whole lot more than that, because I've got about sixteen guys coming over the course of the next two weeks."

"What?" The lump in his chest increased, like a snowball rolling downhill. Only this one filled him with warmth.

"Yep," Steve said. "Once we all started talking, it didn't take long to figure out you'd done stuff to help just about every single one of us at one time or another. Remember that time my water heater busted while I was out hunting, and Abby called you to come and fix it?"

Tom waved that away. "That wasn't a big deal. I could hardly leave her for four days with three kids and no hot water."

"Well, it meant a lot to her. And it meant a lot to me. And then you helped Ed replace that plate-glass window his idiot son broke. And you fixed Conner Maxwell's leaky roof, and helped Joe Martin install that basketball hoop. And what's more, not a single one of us could think of a time you'd asked for help back. So, we're here to pay up."

"Sixteen guys?" It may as well have been a platoon of marines. Sixteen sets of hands on a project this size and he'd be done in record time.

"Yep, sixteen, give or take. Couple of them had other guys they were going to call, too. Lot of us had old man Hamilton as a history teacher, not that I ever learned anything. Except crazy animal facts. He was full of those things."

Tom smiled. "He still is. But man, Steve, this really means a lot to me. You just have no idea. This project is a little behind schedule, and I am anxious to get it done. But I can't pay anybody."

Steve waved his hand, dismissing the comment. "You've already paid us, remember? With all the help you've doled out. This is payback time. Although I'm sure some of the guys might like some beer."

Libby arrived at the ice-cream parlor at noon ready to hammer, or sand, or do whatever task she was able to help with, but the tiny parking lot was full of trucks. She parked in the street and started walking. The sounds of voices and laughter and power tools got louder, growing along with her curiosity as she got closer.

She pushed open the door to find a room full of flannel-shirted workmen with tool belts slung from their waists. Tom was off to one side with two other men, looking at some type of diagram, but he lifted his head and smiled brightly as she entered. He crossed the room, dodging around cords and random boards, until he reached her side. He nudged her back through the door until they stood out on the front porch.

"What is all this? Why didn't you tell me?" she asked.

He shook his head, a look of pleased disbelief on his face. "I didn't know. I showed up this morning, and an old friend of mine was here waiting. The next thing I knew, I had a full crew. They do carpentry, Libby. There are builders and plumbers and electricians working in there right now." His voice was gruff with joy. "This is going to save us a ton of time."

"But how is my dad supposed to pay for this?" Marti's nonexistent wedding fund was next on the chopping block, but surely that little bit of money had already been promised to the Medieval Times banquet hall.

"It's free," he said.

"Free? Why?"

Tom shook his head again, solemnity washing over his features. "Because I did a few favors for a couple of friends, and now they're here paying me back."

Tom's head dropped with his voice and his shoulders, humility and gratitude hitting all the angles. This obviously meant a great deal to him.

Tears prickled at her eyes, and she wanted to hug him, but not with so many eyes watching them through an open door.

Tom rubbed a hand across his jaw and looked at her. "I just don't know why they'd do this for me, Libby. I didn't do anything special. Not enough to make them take time away from their own jobs to be here. I haven't even talked to half of these guys since before the accident."

He didn't know why, but she did. "I guess they see the whole elephant."

A smile tilted the corners of his lips, and he nodded with understanding.

"Yeah, maybe. But it's for your dad, too. A lot of these guys had him for a teacher, and everybody liked him."

A blossom of appreciation bloomed inside Libby's chest. She pressed her hand against it. "That's so incredibly sweet, it makes me want to cry. Do you think I should bring my dad down here? It might really cheer him up, because he's feeling very blue today. And maybe I could even have Dante come to take some video? Do you think that would be okay?"

Tom nodded. "Yeah, of course. The guys would get a big kick out of that, being movie stars."

"Dante will be all over it." Her excitement bubbled over.

"Hey, do you know what I would get a big kick out of?" He lowered his voice and stepped closer.

"What?"

"I was thinking I'd like for you to come over again tonight."

His words sent a sizzle to all the right places. "It might cost you." She'd been wondering how to bring this up. Here was just the chance.

"I'll pay it. Any amount."

She laughed out loud at his eagerness. "Not money."

He tilted his head up. "Not money? Hmm, now I'm intrigued. What's your price?"

"I know you're still not sure about Thanksgiving, which is totally fine, but will you come to Marti's wedding with me?"

His mouth opened, but no sound came out for a few seconds. "The dungeon-themed wedding? With the costumes and the horses and the big turkey legs?"

"Yep. I'll be wearing a corset."

"A corset?" He ran a hand across his jaw again. "Well, that certainly sways me."

CHAPTER *twenty-one*

Tom drove up to Connie's parents' house just as the sun was dipping behind the tree line, casting gold streamers and elongated shadows across a lawn scattered with autumn leaves. His daughter wasn't outside in the driveway. This time he was going in. Rachel had arranged it with her grandparents.

It was foolish, really, his avoidance of this house. It wasn't as if the memory of Connie could wound him any more here than it did anywhere else.

He glanced up at the house now, his hands shaking a little as he took the keys from the ignition. This meeting was long overdue, and he was ready to put it behind him. A fleeting ray of sunshine skimmed over his left arm, halting on his hand where his wedding band had once been, warming the spot. He'd taken it off only a few months ago. It was one of the hardest things he'd ever done. But that little ray cheered him. Tom wasn't the type to believe in signs, but if he were, he might think that was Connie waving.

What had happened in the past was no less tragic today than it had been a year and a half ago. But it was time to put that moment where it belonged. In the past.

He got out of the truck and strode to the front door, knocking with no hesitation.

Anne opened it, looking smaller and more frail than he remembered. Rachel was right. They were getting older.

"Hello, Anne," he said, wishing that encouraging little ray of light might follow him into the foyer.

Rachel came into view just then, smiling. "Hi, Dad. Come on in."

Anne opened the door wider. "I'm glad you called, Tom. It's good to see you."

Was it? Or were her manners that impeccable? Anne was gracious to a fault. It used to drive Connie crazy that her mother never said anything that hinted at a real opinion. Probably because George was so full of them there wasn't any room in this house for anyone else's.

"Please, come into the study. Would you like a drink?"

"No, thank you." He followed her into the next room and looked around. Little had changed inside this place. Big flowers on the wallpaper, stiff, striped furniture that looked about as inviting as his old father-in-law was sure to be. Everything here had a sharp-edged formality, elegant and refined. Just as Connie had been before she'd fallen for him in the backseat of his beat-up old Chevy Cavalier.

George came in from the kitchen, carrying a drink that looked like bourbon, the ice clinking against the glass. Tom's mouth went a little dry. A good stiff drink would surely help his nerves, but he never drank the hard stuff anymore.

"Won't you sit down?" Anne murmured, gesturing to the least comfortable chair in a room full of uncomfortable chairs.

"Thank you. You're looking well, Anne." He settled into the stiff little seat. Rachel sat on the love seat closest to him while Anne and George found spots in the two chairs across from him.

"What brings you here, Tom?" George interrupted before Anne could reply. This was going to be a smack-down if Connie's father had his way. Skip the pleasantries.

Tom had thought long and hard about just what to say. He recalled every bit of advice he'd heard from Dr. Brandt and tried to roll it up into one tidy package. He'd done everything except rehearse it in the mirror.

"First of all, I wanted to thank you for taking such good care of Rachel. She's thrived here, and I know that's because of your love and support."

George took a sip of the drink. "We don't need your thanks for that. Someone had to be responsible."

The implication was clear. Tom was irresponsible. He couldn't fault George for thinking that, but he was here today to prove him wrong.

Anne pressed a subtle hand against her husband's leg. "Tom, it's our privilege to have Rachel here with us."

George turned his head. "Rachel, honey, why don't you go on in the kitchen and find yourself a snack? Let the grown-ups talk for a minute."

Tom looked her way and saw the color rise in her cheeks.

"I'd like to stay, Grandpa, if you don't mind."

George's brows pinched together, his jaw jutted forward. "But you don't need to be here for this."

"I'd like Rachel to stay, George. This concerns her, so she has every right to be a part of it."

George opened his mouth, but it was Anne who said, "Yes, of course she can stay."

The tides were turning. It seemed Anne was at least partially on his side and willing to show it. Suddenly Tom wished he had done this much, much sooner.

But maybe if he had, Rachel wouldn't have been ready. Hell, maybe he wouldn't have been ready before today either. He had needed time to forgive himself.

Rachel folded her legs up under her bottom just like she always did at Dr. Brandt's office. The familiar gesture relaxed Tom, even though it may have been her subconscious way of showing how stubborn she could be.

"As I was saying, I appreciate all you've done for my daughter. This has been an extremely difficult period for each of us, and I know we all want what's best for her. I also think she's old enough to make certain decisions for herself. That's why I haven't insisted she come home to live with me. But if Rachel chooses to move home, I'm asking you to respect her wishes and not try to change her mind."

"*If* she chooses?" George's brows rose in surprise then just as quickly dove into a frown.

"Yes, Grandpa," Rachel spoke up. "Dad and I have been talking about this, and he agrees it makes sense for me to stay here and keep riding the bus to Monroe High until the end of the school year. But once I can drive, it might be time to move back in with him. I haven't completely decided yet."

Relief washed over Anne's face, giving her a less pinched expression. It was obvious to Tom that they'd both expected him to toss Rachel over his shoulder and steal her away from them that very night.

"That's ridiculous," George said, turning his glare toward Tom. "You can't expect a child to understand the ramifications of that kind of decision. She's far better off here where both Anne and I can keep an eye on her, not out there in that farmhouse all alone while you're off doing God knows what."

Tom leaned forward in his chair, resting elbows on his knees and clasping his hands together. Staying calm was the best way to handle this. If he got defensive or angry, George would only do the same, and they'd get nowhere.

"Look, I know what you think of me. And I know I haven't handled every aspect of this situation in the most constructive manner. In hindsight, I should have brought Rachel home as soon as I got out of the hospital, but at the time, I thought I was making the best choice for her. I didn't want her going through the upheaval of switching schools. And I should have kept in closer contact with the two of you and not put Rachel in the center. Now I know better."

George's ruddy complexion deepened to crimson. "Now you know better? What good is that to us? You should've known better than to take my daughter out joyriding when she was seventeen years old. And you sure as hell should've known better than to drive so recklessly on an icy road. Your poor judgment has cost me enough already." He tossed his drink back, and then slammed the empty glass down on the table.

"It wasn't his fault, Grandpa." Rachel sat up and put her feet back on the floor. "It was an accident."

They all turned to her, and Tom's heart vaulted upward.

He'd never heard her defend him. Not once. Not in the counselor's office or even when it was just the two of them together. Her support meant as much to Tom as if she'd promised to come home with him that very minute.

George glowered at his granddaughter. "Accidents happen when people are careless, Rachel. And I'm not so careless that I'd let you live where no one can look out for you."

"I'm not a little girl, Grandpa. I'm nearly sixteen years old, and being stuck in the middle of this feud between you and my dad is exhausting.

If I decide to move, you have to let me." Her cheeks turned bright pink, and her voice rose an octave.

"George," Tom said, "I understand your determination to protect Rachel. But mine is equal to that. I'm ready and absolutely capable of taking care of her. I know you doubt that. But I don't."

Tom's lungs burned from the effort of keeping his breath steady, but he'd say what he needed to.

The moment hung suspended. It was Anne who spoke up first. "Rachel, darling. You are welcome to stay here for as long as you like, or move when you're ready. I support your decision."

"Now wait a minute," George finally sputtered. "This isn't some lark, Anne. We're talking about her safety and her future."

"Yes, George. I know that." Anne stared back at her husband, her spine ramrod straight, until he grumbled and stood up. He walked over to the window, stuffing his hands into his trouser pockets.

Anne reached out to Rachel. "Maybe we should let your father have a minute with Grandpa."

Rachel glanced at Tom. He nodded, pleased she'd looked to him for guidance. Once she and Anne had left the room, he joined George at the window. It was dark out now. No sign of that encouraging little beam of sunlight. These next words were harder than the others but needed saying even more.

"George, until recently I never fully appreciated how it must have felt to you, knowing Connie was sneaking out to be with me. Or what you must have thought when she got pregnant. Now that Rachel is nearly that age, it makes me a little crazy thinking she might do the same thing. And I'd hate that kid just as much as you hate me."

Tom took a breath, searching for the best words. "None of us expected things to play out the way they have. God knows I regret my mistakes. Every single one of them. But demanding Rachel live here doesn't fix what you've already lost. It just puts her in the middle. Let my daughter come home with a clear conscience. Don't guilt her into staying just because you want to punish me."

George turned hostile eyes Tom's way. Tension coiled taut inside the quiet of his voice. "My daughter was a good, respectable girl until you came along. You didn't deserve her then, and you don't deserve Rachel now. You've been nothing but bad luck since the first time you walked in that door. Now I want you to leave my house and never come back."

The sides of Tom's heart twisted against each other. "Don't leave it this way, George. Don't force her to choose between us."

"Or what? Is that a threat?" George's voice lowered into a growl. "I could take you to court, you know."

"For what? Custody? You'd lose. Are you so selfish you'd put her through that?"

Perspiration trickled from George's temple. "You're nothing but a punk, Tom Murphy. You might try to pretend otherwise, but you and I both know, you're still a punk."

Tom felt like one for the blink of an eye. George could make him feel that way. But it wasn't true. Tom was through with being defined by his past mistakes.

"What I know, George, is that in spite of how we started off, Connie and I were happy. I was a good husband. And I'm a good father, too. Now I'm going to go in the kitchen and talk to my daughter. You can stand out here and call me names if you want, but it doesn't change anything. My daughter is coming home as soon as she chooses."

He turned and walked away, leaving George by the window. Tom's limbs quaked. David facing Goliath.

But the victory was hollow, because deep down he was a father, and he understood George was just a man trying to hold on to something he loved.

Tom found Rachel and Anne sitting at a table in the kitchen sipping tea from china cups. He didn't have any china at his house. If Rachel liked that sort of thing, he'd have to buy some. And he'd have to get a room ready for her. Right now it was nothing but bare walls and a bed.

"Well, how did it go?" Rachel asked quietly. She pulled out a chair for him, and he sat down.

Tom crossed his arms and leaned back. He looked into Rachel's hopeful eyes. She wanted them all to be happy. She wanted to come home but keep her grandfather's love, too. No one should be put in that situation.

"He wants what's best for you, Rachel. His heart is in the right place."

"Hogwash," said Anne. "I know him better than that. He's stubborn and narrow-minded. I love him, but I still know this about him. So Rachel, if and when you decide you want to move home, you tell me, and we'll make it happen. And if your grandfather tries to cause a ruckus? Well, I'll handle that on my own."

She lifted her teacup and took a sip, calm as if they'd just arranged a lunch date at the club.

Rachel gave her a tremulous smile. "Thanks, Grandma."

Rachel turned back to Tom. "I do appreciate you letting me choose. And I kind of hate to bring this up, but I promised Jake I'd ask one more time. Can I go skiing with them on Monday? Grandma said she'd give me the money if you said yes."

Tom looked over at his mother-in-law. Sweet, quiet little Anne must be drinking straight whiskey from that little tiny teacup of hers tonight to make such an offer. George always had been a pompous prick. He probably always would be. But Anne was kind, and Tom saw an ally to his cause.

"Have you met this Jake kid?" he asked Anne.

Anne nodded. "He's a very nice young man, and his family goes to our church."

"Dad, I told you, you can trust me," Rachel said.

It would be so easy to give in, to let her have this and be the good guy for a change. And what she'd said before made sense. She was far less apt to find an opportunity in a condo full of brothers and their parents than she was on any given evening after dark, a thought that both mollified and terrified him.

He looked at her face, her eyes shining with expectation.

"Okay," he said.

"Okay? Okay as in yes I can go?"

He nodded and was instantly smothered by her arms hugging him around the neck. His heart went *boom* like a cannon inside his chest, and he heard Rachel's squeak of delight.

"Thank you, thank you, thank you! I promise I'll be super-careful, Dad. Oh, my God, I have to go call Jake."

She kissed Tom on the cheek and was gone, a flurry of rushing legs and giggles.

Stunned, he paused to wonder: When was the last time his daughter had kissed his cheek? Or hugged him? The morning before the accident. That had to be the last time. He gazed over at Anne and found her smiling back.

CHAPTER *twenty-two*

"Why, Beverly, this stuffing looks delicious," said Nana. "I'm sure all it needs is a little touch of sage. What do you think, Libby?"

She held out a fork with a bite of stuffing, and Libby dutifully ate it. It tasted just right to her, but then again, she was no judge. She liked the dry stuff right from the box.

"It doesn't need more sage, Nana. Leave my stuffing alone." Libby's mother opened the oven to baste the Thanksgiving Day turkey.

Nana took a quick peek over one shoulder, and as soon as Libby's mother was distracted, she sprinkled in more sage. Libby shook a silent, reprimanding finger at her.

Marti wandered into the kitchen from the family room. "Ginny won't let me hold the baby until I wash my hands. She's going to give that kid a phobia if she doesn't stop making such a fuss about germs. Mom, where's a screwdriver?"

"In the same spot it's been for twenty years. Why?" Beverly pointed to the drawer on her left.

"Daddy and Dante are trying to put together the bassinet, but they're as clueless as Ben. Hey, Libby, when is Tom getting here? They could use some of his handymanliness."

Libby glanced at the wood-framed clock on the kitchen wall.

He was late. Not by much but enough to make her wonder if he was having second thoughts. Rachel was off on an impromptu ski trip, so he wasn't delayed by her. But he'd expressed some valid reservations about coming here. She'd been a little surprised when he'd said yes.

"He should be along any time," Libby answered. "And don't forget, you guys, please do not badger him with a bunch of tacky, invasive questions, okay? That goes double for you, Nana." She shook a finger at her again.

"I am the soul of discretion, Liberty. If you want to give away the milk for free it's none of my business," Nana answered.

"See? That's exactly the kind of comment I'm talking about. Tom is kind of shy, and if you say stuff like that, you'll embarrass him. So don't." She turned around and pointed at Marti. "And you either. I like him, so please don't scare him away."

Marti held her hands up. "Hey, I'm not looking for trouble. I'm just looking for a screwdriver."

"It's right here." Libby's mother tugged open the drawer with her oven mitt and pulled it out, handing it to Marti. "And maybe you could take Nana out into the other room to see the baby."

"Oh, I can't leave you in here all alone to fix this meal yourself, Beverly," Nana answered.

Libby's mother took Nana by the shoulders and steered her toward the door. "Yes, really, you can. Put your feet up and relax and let me get the rest of dinner taken care of."

Marti took the hint and scooped Nana's narrow shoulders away from her mother. "Come on, Nana. I think Ginny would really like some advice on how to make baby Teddy sleep through the night. What was that you said the other day about giving him a dropper full of whiskey?"

"That's for teething," Nana answered, her voice fading as they moved from the kitchen to the living room.

Libby's mother let loose an exaggerated sigh and wiped the back of her hand across her brow. "That woman, God bless her, is an enormous pain in the ass."

"I think she means well," Libby said, but her laughter negated her statement.

"Well, I'm not sure that's true, but either way we're stuck with her. And with your father around, it's like having puppies. Two demanding, opinionated puppies." Beverly smiled and wiped her hands on her apron. "But it's Thanksgiving Day and I'm supposed to count my blessings, aren't I?"

Libby nodded and plucked an olive off the relish tray on the counter. "I believe that is the custom, yes." She popped the olive into her mouth.

"Well, in that case, I sure am grateful that your father is all right. He's going to give me a heart attack one of these days, but I sure do love that man. It's the only thing that stops me from killing him. And I'm also very grateful that you're home."

Libby looked up, surprised as her typically nondemonstrative mother came around the corner of the kitchen island and hugged her.

She leaned back and looked Libby in the eye, smiling.

"I'm so grateful you've decided to stay in Monroe. It's what I've wanted all along, but I didn't want to be too pushy. You have to follow your own path. I'm just happy it's led you back home. You've been so magnificent at helping your father. He never could have managed that ice-cream parlor without you, even with Tom's help. Oh, and speaking of Tom, there he is."

Her mother stepped back and gestured to the window. Libby watched Tom's truck pull into the driveway.

She opened the kitchen door and waved as he climbed down from the cab. It was cold and windy, with a misty rain in the air, but to her it felt ridiculously like tropical sunshine.

Libby had it bad for Tom Murphy.

The carve your initials in a tree, doodle his name, can hardly breathe without him kind of bad.

It was scary. In a good way.

But scary in a scary way, too.

Libby had all this emotion, wound up so tight inside of her, it was bound to pop out at the worst possible moment. She'd promised Tom to take things day by day. That was the practical, logical, mature thing to do, after all.

But here he was, about to have Thanksgiving dinner with her family. That was pretty bold on his part, all things considered. Even if it was her mother who'd invited him.

"Hey," he said, coming up the two steps into the kitchen. His smile was crooked and earnest, his gaze a little sheepish as he moved closer.

She didn't kiss him. She wanted to, but he glanced over her shoulder at her mother instead. "Hello, Beverly."

Libby moved over so he could come inside.

"Hello, Tom. How nice to see you. I'm so glad you decided to join us. Libby, take Tom's coat."

Libby blinked up at him and smiled. "Can I take your coat?"

He shrugged out of it and handed it over. "Thanks. Sorry I'm late."

"No problem. Everything okay?"

He nodded. "Yep. You?"

She nodded back. She loved these little chats. "Can I get you a drink?"

He shook his head. "No, I'm good. Thanks." He turned to her mother. "Everything smells delicious, Beverly."

She smiled and retied her apron strings. "Thank you. I'm sure Nana will claim all the credit."

Tom chuckled, and Libby tugged on his sleeve. "Come on. Everybody is in the living room." She hung up his coat on a hook near the kitchen door.

Tom hesitated, taking in a big, deep breath and exhaling slowly.

Libby smiled. "Don't be nervous. Just ask my dad a question, and you won't have to talk for the rest of the day."

Dinner was served an hour late, which was technically a family tradition since Nana and her mother got into some sort of snarl each year. Today was about how much sage was in the stuffing. Libby was Switzerland on that one. She knew better than to get between her mom, Nana, and sharp kitchen knives.

"We're actually right on schedule," Libby said to Tom as they finally gathered around the table and took their seats. "Last year the fight was about yams."

Marti leaned forward from the other side of Tom. "No, it was about the green bean casserole. The yam fight was two years ago."

"They remember I don't eat turkey, right?" Dante murmured to Marti, who nodded in response.

"I thought last year it was about the butter in the mashed potatoes," Ben said.

"Stop that, all of you, or this year will be remembered as the time I threw the turkey in the trash." Beverly smiled a big, fake smile and held up her wineglass. "Now sit down."

She might have been kidding, but no one could be certain, so they shut up and settled into their chairs instead. Libby's parents sat at either end. Nana, Ben, and Ginny with baby Teddy in her arms were on one side, with Libby, Tom, Dante, and Marti on the other. The checked tablecloth was covered with platters of food, enough to feed twice as many people, while the walls of the dining room could barely contain them all.

Libby glanced at Tom. He seemed to be holding up remarkably well, and so far no one in her family had asked an out-of-bounds question. She had Dante to thank for that, because once he'd mentioned how a cow lets off hundreds of liters of methane gas each day, and that veganism could end global warming, her dad was off and running. No one had to participate in the conversation much after that.

"Are you going to hold that baby all through dinner?" Nana asked Ginny. "You should put him down once in a while or you'll spoil him." She spread a green napkin across her lap.

"He's six weeks old, Nana. You can't spoil a six-week-old baby," Ginny replied.

"Of course you can. He's smart. He'll figure out you pick him up every time he cries, and then he'll just cry more."

"The first Teddy Roosevelt had a photographic memory. Did anyone know that?" Libby's father said to no one in particular.

"I bet his mother didn't carry him around all day," Nana muttered.

"She can hold him if she wants to, Nana. Peter, would you please say grace so we can get this meal started?" Beverly's cheeks were flushed a bright, splotchy red. It might have been from the heat in the kitchen. Or her annoyance with Nana. She gulped down half the glass of Pinot Grigio.

Or it might have been from that.

Libby bowed her head along with the rest of them, and stole a peek at Tom. He had his eyes closed and his hands folded reverently in his lap, but a smirk played around his mouth. He tapped his leg against hers. She tapped back.

At the head of the table, Libby's father cleared his throat. "Look out, teeth, look out, gums—"

"No, Peter. Not that one. It's Thanksgiving." Libby looked up to see her mother take another swallow of wine.

Her dad looked only slightly chagrined by her scolding and lifted his glass, clinking his fork against it. "How about a toast, instead? Forgive me for not standing." He cleared his throat again. "This year, as in so many years past, I am grateful for the love, and tolerance, of my family." He tipped his head at Libby's mother, who arched a single brow in response.

He continued, "I'm grateful for the arrival of my most perfect grandson, and his good health. I'm grateful for the new friends we have at our table this year." He smiled at Tom.

"And me, too, right, Dad Hamilton?" Dante leaned forward and put his tattooed arm out to clasp her father's wrist. "You're thankful for me, aren't you? A little bit?" His smile was broad, his teasing apparent.

Dante and her father had come to discover quite a lot in common, and Libby suspected her father didn't mind him nearly so much as he had that first night they met.

Her father nodded. "Dante, in the spirit of the holiday, I say yes. I am grateful for you in much the same way that the Native Americans were grateful for the warm, woolen blankets given to them by the first Europeans."

Dante chuckled. "Ah, that's very clever. I get it. Smallpox."

"Daddy, that's not very nice," Marti said.

Her father winked at Dante. "That was a test, kid, to see if you know your history. But few people realize that story about the blankets is a myth. The smallpox was true enough, but they've never found evidence—"

"Peter! Grace. Or the toast, or whichever, but this turkey is getting colder by the minute."

"Sorry, Bev." He lifted his glass again, and spoke fast. "I'm thankful for being right here, right now in this moment, and sharing it with each of you. Amen, and let's eat."

Harp music began trilling, and everyone looked around. Dante reached into his pocket and pulled out his phone. "Sorry, that's me." He glanced at the screen and frowned. "It's my boss. I'm sorry, but I should answer this. Please go on and eat."

Dante rose and left the table, walking into the family room.

"We may as well go for it. The kid doesn't eat any of the hot food anyway," Ben said. "And I'm starving."

The room filled with clinks of platters being passed and spoons clinking against the side of serving bowls. Conversations started in between requests of "please pass me that," and plates were piled high with food. Libby's hand brushed against Tom's as he handed her the basket of rolls, and he gave her such a look of longing she nearly laughed out loud.

"The turkey is perfect, Mom. And it's hot. I haven't had hot food since the baby was born. Maybe I will put him down."

Ginny took a bite of turkey and stood up to take Teddy into the other room where a pristine bassinet was now waiting. But before she could wind her way behind the chairs and out of the dining room, Dante was back.

His forehead was creased with a frown, his lips pressed into a thin line. He was even a little pale.

"Baby, what's the matter?" Marti gasped.

Forks clanked as they were dropped against the china plates.

Dante looked at Marti. "There was a water main break at the banquet hall. My boss says the entire place is flooded and there's mud everywhere. He said it's going to take weeks to clean it up."

Marti's eyes widened. Her mouth went slack, until she whispered, "But it can't take weeks. We're getting married there in nine days."

This was just the type of thing to happen around the Hamilton family. Tom should have known the day couldn't go by without some sort of mishap. Their luck was nearly as bad as his. If there was an abandoned well around, one of them was bound to fall in. But at least he'd be far removed from this dilemma. Marti's dungeon-themed wedding was way outside of his jurisdiction. Of course, so was Ginny's baby, and he'd been vaulted into that pretty tidily.

And in that instant, he knew.

He'd land intimately in the middle of this one, too. But a funny thing happened on the way to that thought. He realized he didn't mind. For a guy who fancied himself a loner, he couldn't seem to stop helping people. It made him feel good. Especially helping this family. Especially helping Libby.

He'd finally figured it out.

She wasn't the quicksand. She was the vine he needed to pull free from the past.

The meal seemed to be forgotten as everyone huddled around the forlorn bride and her dazed groom. Even Peter tried to move from his chair, but ended up just turning it and sitting on the edge.

"What did your boss say, exactly?" Marti asked, sniffling.

"He said he went into the stables tonight to feed the horses and he heard water running. And when he went into the jousting yard, part of it was muddy. He kept looking around and finally he found the water pipe in the men's room had come right through the wall into the banquet room, and water was spraying everywhere. He said it looked like it had been going for hours."

"What are we going to do?" Marti leaned against his arm. She was a pitiful sight, and Tom felt for her. She reminded him of Rachel, her emotions so raw and intense.

"I don't know. But we'll figure out something." Dante set his jaw, looking determined.

"We just need a place, I guess. I mean, I don't really have to ride up on a white horse. But we've already bought the dresses."

"I'd be willing to not wear mine," Ginny said, which earned her a glare from Dante and another sniffle from Marti.

"Maybe you could just wait a few more weeks," Peter suggested. "Then I'd be back on my feet and the banquet hall could be repaired."

"I'm not waiting, Daddy. Stop asking me that." Marti turned toward Dante's chest and burst into tears.

"Ivan is going to New Zealand for a few months right after the wedding, Dad Hamilton. If we wait, then he can't be the one to marry us. And he went to all that trouble getting certified online. It would be rude to not use him."

"Ah, yes. Rude." Peter nodded.

"How big of a place?" Tom heard himself asking.

Everyone in the room turned to him as if he'd shot off a flare gun.

Marti sniffled and lifted her head from Dante's chest. "Not that big. We only have forty-four people coming. Why?"

"No reason. I just wondered."

That wasn't entirely true. In fact, it wasn't remotely true, but he wasn't going to toss out his idea without a second opinion. He looked down at Libby, who was pressed against his side.

She looked up, and it took only seconds before she guessed his intent.

"The ice-cream parlor," Libby said loud and clear. "You guys could have your wedding at the ice-cream parlor."

"I can totally pull this together, Marti," Libby said as her sister sniffled and wiped a tear off her cheek. "I've organized corporate events for six hundred people in a month. I can certainly coordinate a wedding for forty-four people in nine days."

Libby felt a rush of adrenaline, the excitement of having something to plan. She'd missed that part of her job. She was good at this, and she could prove it. She would scout out the best deal, coordinate all the details, and bring it together with precision. And have fun doing it.

Marti sniffed again, looked up at Dante, and then over at her father. "What do you think, Daddy? It's your building."

Her father stared back for a long moment, his brows furrowed, and Libby thought for certain he was looking for some way to shoot down the idea. Then he twisted in his chair to face Tom. "What do *you* think? That's the bigger question. Is the place ready? Ready enough for something like this?"

"It can be ready in a week. With my buddies stopping by to lend a hand, it's all come together lately. And if we don't install the ice-cream freezers until after the wedding, there will be plenty of room."

Libby felt a swell of anticipation, as if she'd become part of a grand, ridiculous scheme.

"Couldn't you just have it at a regular banquet room?" Ginny said, swaying back and forth as she rocked the baby. "I mean, like a place with an actual kitchen. How are you going to deal with the food?"

Marti shook her head. "We can't afford a restaurant or anything like that. We were getting the food, and the decorations, and everything from Dante's boss at a huge discount. Well, not a discount really, because Dante was working extra shifts to cover the difference."

"You were working for that discount?" Libby's dad asked. He leaned forward in his chair.

Dante shrugged. "Of course."

"I thought it was an employee benefit. Why didn't you kids ask Beverly and me for some money?" He looked from Dante to Marti.

"Because, Daddy, you needed that money for the ice-cream parlor. And we wanted to show you that Dante and I can take care of ourselves."

Libby's father leaned back in his chair. "Well, I'll be damned. And I guess you can, too. I'm very proud of you, Martha. And you, too, Dante. That shows real initiative. Real pluck. And that's a fine quality."

He looked back over to Tom. "You say the place can be ready in a week?"

"Yes, sir."

"And Liberty, if Bev and I made a contribution toward this endeavor, do you really think you can set it all up?"

"Daddy, we don't need—" Marti said, but he cut her off.

"Martha Washington Hamilton, what kind of a father would I be if I didn't help pay for your wedding? It's not because I think you can't. It's because I want to. And so does your mother, right, Beverly?"

Libby's mother looked frazzled and dazed, that hot pink flush still staining her cheeks. She lifted her wineglass in resigned agreement. "Of course we do."

CHAPTER *twenty-three*

"All right, I admit it," Ginny whispered to Libby. "These dresses are as uncomfortable as hell, but I feel kind of sexy, in a wenchy sort of way."

Libby giggled behind her bouquet of posies. "Kind of makes you want to get swashbuckled, doesn't it?"

They stood together next to the makeshift altar inside the ice-cream parlor. Friends and family, some even wearing medieval costumes, including her parents, sat on fabric-covered folding chairs. Lute music wafted through the room, courtesy of a very modern iPod and some good speakers, and the heavy, sweet scent of roses clung to the air.

"I think you have a pretty good chance of getting yourself swashbuckled," Ginny whispered back. "Tom hasn't stopped staring at you since we walked in."

Libby caught his eye and smiled. She'd seen him quite a bit over the past week and a half, and each time she did, she fell for him a little harder.

At last, Marti and their father came through the door and began their progression. It was slow going with him on crutches, but he was determined to do it. Marti looked every inch the gorgeous bride in her velvet dress, with her auburn hair spun in ringlets down her back. Happiness glowed all around her.

Arriving at the altar, Marti kissed their dad's cheek. "I love you, Daddy," she murmured.

"I love you, too, Martha." His voice was thick. He shook hands with Dante before hobbling over to his seat, the feather in his jaunty hat fluttering a bit. Libby saw him dash away a sentimental tear, and her mother handed him a handkerchief that was knotted up and probably already damp. Nana sat on the other side of her in a sparkly, pink chiffon dress.

Dante took Marti by the arm and smiled at her as if she were an oasis in the desert. He was charming in his medieval garb. Two of his brothers stood at his side, dressed as he was. Even Ivan had joined in and wore a brown monk's robe. And in spite of being a tattoo artist/minister of dubious origins, he did a commendable job leading the bride and groom through their vows.

Libby felt her emotions swell, and she nearly erupted into tears when Dante promised to love and cherish her little sister. She wanted to look at Tom just then but didn't dare. He'd read every emotion on her face if she did. It was bad enough to have fallen so stupidly in love with someone she'd known for only three months, and quite another thing to let him know it.

Libby's father stood at one end of the long table set up in the middle of the ice-cream parlor, with Marti and Dante on either side of him, beaming at each other.

Everyone had taken a seat, but the conversation stopped as soon as Dante clinked his fork against the goblet he was holding.

The forks had been a concession by the bride and groom. They'd wanted to use their hands in true medieval fashion, but that was where Libby drew the line. She wasn't going to set up any event that didn't include utensils.

Libby reached over and squeezed Tom's hand as all the guests quieted around them. He squeezed back.

Her father cleared his throat. "As I'm sure everyone here knows, the term *honeymoon* comes from the old tradition of a bride and groom drinking honeyed mead for one month after the nuptials to ensure good fortune."

"I didn't know that. Did you know that?" Tom whispered in her ear, his breath warm and enticing.

She squeezed his hand again.

"In that spirit, my lovely daughter Liberty has procured several bottles for us to toast with this evening. Therefore, please indulge me while I say a few words about my daughter and her new husband."

Everyone seemed to shift and find a more comfortable position in their chairs. Word about her father and his long-windedness must have spread.

"When I first met Dante, I'll admit, I didn't quite know what to make of him."

A murmur of laughter rippled around the table, mainly from Dante's relatives.

"But over these last few weeks I've come to recognize him as dependable, industrious, inquisitive, and quite honestly, a little eccentric. A man not unlike myself."

More ripples of laughter.

"Dante is a good man, and he loves my daughter, and so it is with much joy that I welcome him into our family."

Libby's father turned toward Marti. "Martha, you have been my little girl, my constant cheerleader, and my biggest challenge."

Marti smiled, her cheeks flushed with pink.

"I'm very proud of the young woman you've become. Your happiness is tantamount to mine, and so I send you off on this matrimonial journey with an Irish blessing: May the saddest day of your future be no worse than the happiest day of your past. May your hands be forever clasped in friendship, and your hearts joined forever in love. To the bride and groom."

Glasses went *plink* and *clink* as they were raised from the table and everyone toasted. Libby tapped her glass against Tom's and nearly melted into a puddle at the sentimental look in his eyes.

Dinner went on, more toasts were offered, and quite a few jokes were made at Dante's expense. The bride and groom laughed and kissed . . . and kissed again. And Libby felt a wonderful certainty that her sister was going to be happy. She looked down the table at Ginny. Ben was next to her, holding Teddy in the crook of his arm like a football, a comfortable, cuddly football. Still the picture-perfect couple. Even her mother and Nana were chatting together with smiles on their faces. It must be something in the mead, a magical ingredient. Good fortune, her dad had said. She took a gulp from her glass and smiled at Tom.

It was late in the evening when Libby's mother came to Libby's side and said, "Your father and I need to get Nana home, Libby. She's a little loopy from the mead. And quite frankly, I need to get out of this dress. I can't believe I agreed to wear it."

Libby kissed her mother on the cheek. "You look like a queen, though, Mom. Dad looks more like a jester."

"That's no coincidence." Her mom smiled. "Listen, I hate to even ask you this, but would you mind making sure everything is locked up once everyone is gone? I told Marti, but she's not listening, and Ginny needs to get home to feed the baby."

"Sure. That's no problem. Is it?" Libby turned to Tom. He was her ride and her official date, after all. And she'd come here in Ginny's car.

Tom shook his head. "No, of course not."

Libby's mother patted her shoulder. "You did so much to pull this all together. Both of you. And I'm amazed at how lovely everything looks. You outdid yourself, Libby."

Libby warmed from the compliment. "It was fun. This used to be my job, you know."

"I know. I was actually thinking about that. Maybe you could do this for other people in Monroe."

"Host dungeon-themed, ice-cream parlor weddings?"

Her mother chuckled. "No, not exactly. But you could plan events just like you did in Chicago, couldn't you? I know you're used to great big venues, but you've got a real knack for this. Just a few days ago this was an empty room, but now it's all so pretty. I wish we could keep it like this."

Libby looked around. Her mother was right. It *was* pretty in here, and Libby had made that happen. She'd promised a pretty significant number of free ice-cream cones to the vendors around town, too, but in the end, they'd all come through with low prices, and some had even donated flowers and tulle. And in the process, she'd made some good connections. She'd forgotten how interwoven everyone was in Monroe, how much people were willing to lend a hand. And how much fun it was to assemble all the pieces of an event. Like putting together a real-life puzzle and watching as it turned into a picture. Her mother's idea had some merit.

"I'll have to give that some thought, Mom. Give Nana a kiss for me, okay?"

"I will. I'll see you later. Your father says good night. He can't be up on that foot anymore."

Her father was waiting by the door, his medieval tunic hanging down past his hips, his cap now askew. He raised his hand to wave good-bye.

"Maybe we should help your dad and Nana get to the car," Tom said.

Libby shook her head and tugged on his plain white dress shirt instead. No amount of cajoling could convince him to dress the medieval part tonight, but he looked damn fine in a regular old suit. His jacket was hung over a chair somewhere now, and he'd rolled up his sleeves and loosened his tie.

She pulled him under a trellis of flowers just as soon as her mother turned her back.

"No, they're fine," Libby whispered. "And we haven't had much time together tonight. I'm sorry I've been so busy."

His hands came to rest on her waist. "You do put on a nice party, Miss Hamilton. And might I add, that is some dress. It's got me quite distracted." He peered down at her well-displayed cleavage. The corset was uncomfortable, but it did serve a useful purpose if it made him look at her like that.

"What, this old thing?" She laughed, and then she kissed him, not caring who saw or what they thought. Not her sisters or her parents or her grandmother. She just needed to kiss him.

He wrapped his arms around her waist and hugged her tight, kissing back as if they were alone in the world.

"Hey!" Marti called. "It's my wedding night, not yours."

Libby felt another giggle welling up and pulled away. His eyes were dark and full of promise, and she wanted nothing more than to explore that.

But it was another hour before the last of the guests left. Libby tried to shoo them out faster, even turning off most of the lights, hoping they'd get the hint, but Marti and Dante were full of euphoria and love for every single person, dragging out the good-byes way too long.

"Are you sure we can't stay and help you clean up?" Marti offered. "I feel bad leaving you here to do this yourself."

"No, we got it. Honestly, you go on." Libby waved them away with both hands. "Go play married couple now."

Marti giggled. "Oh, that's right. We're married, aren't we? How cool is that?"

Dante slid his arm around her waist and swung her toward the door. "Very cool. Let's go." He reached out with his other arm and shook Tom's hand. "Thanks—you guys are the bomb. We couldn't have done this without you."

"You're welcome. Now get out so we can clean up." Libby pushed him by the shoulder, out the door into the dark, and shut it tight behind them.

She turned around and leaned against it, exhausted. But Tom was standing there in his nice pants and his dress shirt, and she suddenly felt reenergized. Or at least bits of her did.

"Hi," she said, a flutter starting in the center of her and spreading out in every direction.

"Hi." His voice was husky and rich.

"We're alone."

In two strides he was pressed up against her, his body hard and hot.

Relief and desire stirred all her senses wide awake. She hadn't been to his house in the last three days, and it felt like three months.

It must've felt like that for him, too, because he kissed her with a welcome urgency and pushed her back against the door. She tried to move her leg, but the heavy fabric of her skirt trapped her.

Tom trailed his mouth down the side of her neck and ran his hands up the stiff corset, stopping near the top. He lifted his head and stared down.

"I like this dress," he told her breasts, and Libby laughed as he kissed the tops of them. She loved this playful side, the one he'd kept hidden down deep.

The ice-cream parlor was bathed in a faint glow from just a few borrowed lamps tucked away in the corners. Roses still scented the air, giving the whole place an oddly otherworldly feel. But tables cluttered with cups and plates were all around.

She looked over his shoulder and gave a little sigh. "This place is kind of a mess."

"I'm kind of a mess. Let's go to my house and get you out of that dress." His words sizzled against her skin. A deliciously wicked notion filled her thoughts. A hungry, wicked idea.

"Uh-uh." She ran her fingers around the back of his neck as he lifted his head again.

"Uh-uh?" he repeated, looking dismayed.

"This dress is a labyrinth to get out of. I can't wait that long. We'll have to work around it." She grabbed him by the shoulders and kissed his mouth, maneuvering him backward toward a chair. "Sit down."

He smiled. "Really? Here?"

"Yep."

"You are quite the event coordinator, aren't you?" He chuckled, and tested the sturdiness of the chair, jostling it a little against the floor. "This should work." He sat down and peered up at her. "What now?"

She was bold and brazen. It must be the dress. Or the magical mead. She reached for his belt, a sense of adventure frolicking along her nerves. Tom Murphy was about to get swashbuckled.

His hands slid up her arms and he looked down the front of her dress. "I like the view from this chair."

"Less talk, more action, Murlan." The belt thwacked against her hand as she unhooked it from the clasp and reached for his zipper. He gasped in surprise, but moved forward on the seat to give her better access.

She wanted to touch him, right now, and his body sprang forth, eager to comply. He tipped his head back, his breath fast and shallow as she teased him with her fingers. He was already rock solid in her grasp. She squeezed and ran her hand along the length of him.

"Goddamn, Libby. What's gotten into you?" The laughter down low in his throat turned into more of a groan. "Whatever it is, I like it."

She didn't know what had gotten into her, exactly. She only knew she wanted him. Forget the complications or the hesitations. Forget guarding her emotions. This moment was about the two of them and nothing else.

She kissed him, breathy and unsteady, loving the taste and texture of his mouth, the heat of his kiss.

His hand moved to reach up under her skirt. His fingers skimmed upward, along her legs, scorching a trail over sensitized skin until he reached her lacy underpants. She chuckled as he hooked them with his thumbs, and slowly, slowly tugged them down until they were a lacy heap between her feet. Her knees nearly gave up, but she stayed where she was, anticipation a bubble ready to pop.

He tilted his head back and their eyes met. The teasing stopped. Only craving remained. Tom reached up again and gripped her bare hips.

She caught up the fabric of her skirt and let him guide her forward, over his lap. And without another thought, she settled down on him, giving in to that hot, sweet stretch.

She wrapped her arms around his neck, and he groaned into her kiss.

"Libby." His voice was a rasp. He caught her lip between his teeth and bit, but the sting of it was glorious. She pressed her feet against the floor and rocked against him.

"God. Too reckless," he murmured.

"I know. But we should be fine."

"It's not fine."

"We'll be fine."

He kissed her then, deep, breaths catching between them. She tugged at his hair, folding her arms around his head, tilting her own so he could drag kisses across her shoulder. He wrapped his arms around her waist, and when she might have slowed the pace, he gripped her hips and urged her on. She smelled the roses and tasted his skin, sweet and salty. Delicious.

Her heart stood at the cliff's edge, peering over, until there was no more thought, no poetry, or rationalizations. Just motion and need until, at last, her body gave in to that familiar quiver. It swelled and unfurled from her center, pouring out and over in every direction until she shattered from the strength of it. She pressed her face into the curve of Tom's neck, her arms still locked around his shoulders. She felt him hesitate, but she squeezed him with her legs and with her body, moving again until he gave in to his own need and let loose into her, pulling her tight against him and breathing endearments into her ear.

His body shuddered in the aftermath, and she held him tight, their breaths rapid and mingling. He pressed his face against the curve of her neck until he tipped back and his eyes met hers.

She saw the question on his face, heard it without his even asking.

"We'll be fine," she said.

CHAPTER *twenty-four*

What the hell had he just done? Sixteen years had passed and still the same impetuous mistake.

But it didn't feel like one. It felt like home. It felt like hope.

Tom caught Libby's face in his hands and kissed her mouth, slow and tender. Maybe he hadn't learned anything at all. Maybe his heart fell too hard, too fast, but it was the only way he knew how to live. And somehow he'd make all the pieces fit together.

He gazed at her. Her eyes were big and dark in the dim light, her lips plumped up from his kiss. His heart beat once, twice, then paused like a hummingbird, fluttering madly but not going anywhere.

"I love you, Libby. I know it's crazy, and I know it's fast, and God knows it's complicated. But there it is. I love you."

She stared back at him for such a long time he very nearly wished he could take the words back—except he wouldn't. Because he meant them. And no matter what happened next, he wanted her to know.

A smile started at the corners of her mouth, moving slow like sunrise over the lake. She laced her fingers around the back of his neck.

"It is crazy, and it is fast, and it doesn't make any sense at all, but"—she shrugged her shoulders—"I love you, too. A lot."

She leaned forward and kissed him, hard. So hard she bumped against his nose, the sudden pain an odd contrast to all the pleasure still reverberating through the rest of him. Tom started to laugh.

Liberty Belle Hamilton was a hazard, but she was the right woman for him, at the right time. He was certain of that. He could fill all of his tomorrows with her laughter and her touch. Sorrow was behind him.

He squeezed her waist. "I don't want to clean this place up right now. I just want to take you back to my house and work on that corset. How does that sound?"

"Perfect."

They gathered up a few things, her purse, their coats. Her panties. And walked arm in arm to the truck. He helped her gather up that enormous skirt and climb into the cab.

"I'll be right back. I want to make sure the door is locked."

He climbed up on the front porch and checked the handle of the ice-cream parlor, and smiled to himself. He'd never imagined all those weeks ago that when he walked through that door, he was walking into a brand-new day. Libby Hamilton had crashed into his life and turned everything right-side up again.

Libby snuggled down under the bedding, feeling thoroughly adored and satisfied. "I bet even the bride and groom aren't having as good a night as we are." She reached out to ruffle his hair. They were lying in his bed, face to face, the afterglow of another dizzying romp fading slowly.

His hand rested on her naked hip, and he gave it a squeeze. "I don't imagine they are. We're lucky." He pressed a kiss against her shoulder.

Something in his tone hinted there was a *but* to that sentence.

"But?" she prompted when he said nothing more.

He lifted his head from the pillow and rested it on his fist, elbow bent against the mattress. "But we were stupid earlier. What happened at the ice-cream parlor—we can't make a habit of that." He shook his head. "I'm crazy for you, Libby. Obviously, but no matter how I feel, I'm not ready for another baby."

Remorse plunked her in the ribs, rattling her breath. Not because she was worried. She knew her cycle and was certain they were in the clear, but because Tom was worried. She shouldn't have put him in that situation.

"I know. I'm sorry. I just got carried away because you're so sexy." She ruffled his hair again, to tease him, but his smile had faded. She wanted it back. "Please don't start feeling guilty now, okay? Because that escapade at the ice-cream parlor was entirely my fault. I seduced you."

His forehead creased. "Yes, you did. Quite effectively. But I had a choice. And I'm the one who should know better."

"Tom, we should both know better. But I'm certain we're fine. I learned everything there is to know about ovulation cycles when Ginny was trying to get pregnant. Anyway, we can always blame it on the mead." She smiled, determined to lighten this moment back up.

He pulled her closer. "I could blame it on that corset."

Libby laughed and slid her calf up his leg. "Let's blame it on my sisters. It was kind of their fault."

Tom's eyes crinkled up with his smile. "How do you figure that?"

"Because they said I should marry you and have a baby right away."

The laughter splashed away from his face. He flipped to his back as if kicked in the chest and stared up at the ceiling. "Wow."

Cart. Horse. Damn it.

She hadn't meant to say that. She had no self-control at all tonight, it seemed. Remorse kicked her again. Wearing cleats.

Libby rolled to her stomach and rose up on her elbows. "I'm just kidding, Tom. That was a joke."

He looked back at her. "It's not really a joke if you end up pregnant."

"No, of course it isn't, but we only did it that one time."

"It only takes one time, Libby. The effects of sex aren't cumulative."

Frustration was unraveling at the fringe of her good mood. "Listen to me, Tom. Ten thousand dollars says I'll get my period tomorrow. I am like clockwork."

He sighed and looked back at the ceiling. "You don't have ten thousand dollars."

"It doesn't matter, because I won't lose this bet."

A smile tilted at the corners of his mouth. "I don't have ten thousand dollars either."

The pain in her ribs receded. She held out her hand. "Six bucks, then? Deal?"

He stared at that hand for a moment while Libby's heart crumbled like a cookie. But then he turned his face toward her. "Six bucks and a blow job, and you've got yourself a deal."

Libby smiled. "Nice."

"It's getting pretty late. Maybe you should take me home." Libby's voice was soft, her gentle tapping on his shoulder rousing him. He'd fallen asleep with her in his arms, and he never wanted to leave this bed.

"Home? I was kind of hoping you'd stay." The bed without her would be too empty.

"Until morning?" She sounded surprised.

He opened one eye and stared at her. "Don't you want to?"

She'd never spent the night at his house, always leaving before midnight with the excuse her parents might be worried. He really hadn't come very far at all, had he? Still dating a girl with a curfew. "I'm sure your parents know where you are."

Laughter curled the edges of her voice. "I'm sure they do. I just don't want to overstay my welcome."

He opened his other eye. A glow of light came from the hallway and cast a ray over her bare shoulder. Libby liked to have some lights on whenever they made love, and he adored that about her. And a dozen other things, too. "Libby, in case you haven't figured this part out, I'm pretty happy that you're here."

She smiled and traced her hand over his chest. "Careful about sweet talk like that. I might start showing up here all the time. And then I'd bother you."

He brushed the hair back from her face. "It never bothers me when you're here. It bothers me when you leave."

She lifted her head off the pillow and stared at him. "That's a pretty romantic thing to say, Mr. Murphy."

"Maybe you're turning me into a romantic guy." He laughed at himself. "Probably not, though. It's just the truth. These last few weeks with you have changed everything."

He'd already admitted he loved her. He may as well throw it all out on the table. Being alone and sad had become a habit for him, just like getting dressed or drinking coffee. But Libby had shattered all that monotony. She'd lifted the fog, and he could finally see the sun again.

She traced her thumb over his lip. "I know what you mean. For me, too, but it's a little overwhelming. I never planned on you. I didn't even particularly like you at first."

He laughed at this. The moonlight was bringing out the honesty from both of them.

"You didn't like me? You sure flirted a lot for a woman who didn't like me."

"I wasn't flirting. I was just trying to be nice. Plus you were cute. But oh, my God, you were such a grouch." Libby pulled the blanket up and tucked it under her arm. "And arrogant. *You can't run around here in those floppy shoes, Miss Hamilton.*" She lowered her voice, trying to sound gruff, and he laughed even harder.

"You were wearing flip-flops at an industrial work site!"

Libby chuckled, and her breasts jiggled against him. His body stirred, but exhaustion chased his arousal away. For the moment.

"I'm not saying you were wrong," Libby said. "I'm just saying you were kind of a dick about it."

He'd been called worse. "Well, I'm sorry. I just didn't want you to get hurt."

"I know."

"I still don't." His meaning had shifted, and when her gaze turned solemn he knew she understood him.

She leaned over and kissed his mouth, warm and soft and tender. "That goes both ways, you know. I don't want you to get hurt either. You've had enough of that." She kissed him again, and his heart thumped hard against the wall of his chest.

He'd spent so much energy trying to protect other people, and failing miserably, but at last, here was Libby wanting to shelter him.

"Will you stay until morning?"

"I don't have much choice. You're my ride, remember? But it's going to be a little awkward strolling into my parents' house in my wench dress."

"You can borrow something of mine, but I hope Nana's there to give you a hard time." Even the mental image was enjoyable, and laughter rumbled deep down in his belly. "Maybe you can sneak in through the back door. Anyway, I'm picking Rachel up at eleven thirty, so I'll take you home in the morning."

"Rachel." Libby said her name softly, and let it dangle out there between them. "We haven't talked about her lately. And you know, we've kind of skipped past the whole taking-it-day-by-day thing. I think you could say we are officially dating."

They had skipped forward. But that didn't mean he knew where Rachel fit into the equation. Dr. Brandt had said he had every right to a private life, and he understood that now. He'd even come to terms with moving on from Connie. But if Rachel moved back home, things would change again. For all of them.

He'd talk to her about it tomorrow at brunch. Nothing formal, just a casual mention to ease her into the idea of him seeing someone. Rachel liked Libby, after all. This shouldn't be a big problem.

A wave of fatigue swept over him.

"No, we haven't talked about her lately. But let's do that tomorrow. You've tapped me like a maple tree, and I'm very, very sleepy."

Libby chuckled, and he pressed his lips against her temple. Life was good again.

CHAPTER *twenty-five*

Rain pelted against the window, and branches scraped along the siding of the house as Libby walked into Tom's kitchen. He was making coffee wearing nothing but boxers and a T-shirt.

"I don't think these pants are going to work." She let go of the waistband, and his jeans slid down her legs and into a heap at her feet.

She hadn't wanted to nose around in his closet too much that morning. It felt like a slight invasion of his privacy, so she'd just grabbed the first pair of pants she'd seen on top of a pile, along with a faded flannel shirt. She had that on now and knew it was one of his favorites. He wore it all the time.

He turned round in time to watch the pants land on the floor.

"Oh, I don't know about that. Looks like they're working just right to me."

He set the coffeepot back in place, pushed the brew button, and walked over to her, looking adorably scruffy with his pillow head and whiskers.

Tom scooped one arm around her waist and clasped the other as if they were dancing.

She warmed straight through from her toes to her smile. "Oh, that's right. You're a morning person, aren't you?" She'd learned that at the ice-cream parlor. She'd stumble in at nine thirty with a double-shot espresso, while Tom was already halfway into his day.

He started spinning her around slowly. "Don't worry. I've got your coffee started."

"Ah, thank you. Just one more thing to love about you."

The pants around her feet were cumbersome, but his body was warm and inviting. She lifted one foot and then the other, effectively kicking the denim out of their way. They shuffled in a tiny circle. The storm raged outside, but in the little kitchen it was sunny.

"I didn't expect you to be a dancer, Mr. Murphy."

His laugh was rich and warm against her ear. "This is about the extent of it, Miss Hamilton. Don't get your hopes up."

"This is all I need."

She meant to be flip and funny, but the words came from somewhere deep, and he paused. Tom lifted his head from the crook of her neck and gazed down at her.

"You could do better, you know."

She lifted up on her toes and kissed the corner of his mouth. "On the contrary, I think you're quite the catch. Marti says so, too."

He started shuffling them again. "Does she now?"

"Yes, because you have a truck, among other admirable attributes." She hadn't shared the best with Marti, but there had been some guessing.

"If it's all the same to you, I'd rather you didn't discuss any of my attributes with your sister. It's likely to end up in Dante's documentary."

She breathed in, catching a hint of yesterday's cologne. "That would make it a whole different kind of movie now, wouldn't it?"

Tom's arm around her middle tightened.

"Yep. But it could certainly start the same. A woman walks into a room and drops her pants."

Libby laughed. "Technically those were your pants."

"Whatever. All I know is that right now neither one of us is wearing pants. And that seems like a terrible opportunity to squander."

He pressed his lips against hers as if it had been weeks instead of moments since their last kiss, hungry and thorough. He scooped her up and set her bottom on the counter. She wrapped her legs around his waist and twined her arms around his shoulders. Even through the fabric of his shirt she could feel his muscles bunching. The thrill of that would never get old.

"Aren't you supposed to pick up Rachel?" she asked as he started on a button of the flannel shirt.

"Not until eleven thirty. We've got time."

He popped the first button and kissed her neck again as the windows shook against the storm. It was exotic, feeling his warm mouth and his whiskers scrape across her skin while the thunder rumbled outside. Libby gave over to her senses.

A muffled *bang* sounded off in the distance, familiar but unrecognizable as Tom's kiss clouded her awareness.

Then she heard it again, and she opened her eyes.

Time stopped.

Libby saw it all from a distance. Everything in slow motion.

Rachel pushing open the door, bursting in from the rain in a bright red coat, like a stop sign in the middle of the road where you least expect it. Her smile fading and turning to astonishment. The sound of a backpack hitting the floor.

An older woman coming in just behind her, with pale blond hair and Rachel's features.

Tom lifting his head and twisting his upper body toward the sound, even as he pulled the edges of Libby's shirt back together.

Her legs around his waist went slack, and her head bumped back against the kitchen cabinet.

"Rachel?" Tom gasped.

His daughter stood frozen, nothing moving but her eyes. She looked to him and then to Libby, and Libby had never felt so small.

"Dad? Miss Hamilton? God, what the hell?" Rachel turned away then, toward her grandmother's outstretched arms, for certainly that's who the other woman was. She glared at Tom with such contempt, Libby felt him wince.

"Jesus, Rachel," Tom said. "What are you doing here?" He tugged on the edge of his shirt, but it didn't help. He was still standing there in his underwear.

Rachel looked up at the ceiling. "You told me I was always welcome, remember? It never occurred to me you might be busy screwing someone in Mom's kitchen."

"Honestly, Tom. How disgraceful," Anne said, a frown cutting deep into her skin.

Libby wanted to disappear. She worked to close the buttons of her borrowed flannel shirt, but her fingers were shaking and clumsy.

"This is why you stopped pushing me to move home, isn't it?" Rachel said, still not looking at him, her voice stretching thin. "Because of her. Because you're up to this kind of shit. God, Dad, you are so gross."

Tom reached over and grabbed the jeans that Libby had left on the floor. He struggled to put them on as Libby slid down from the counter like a reptile, wishing she could slither into the other room and not be any part of this.

"Clearly I wasn't expecting you, Rachel. I was supposed to pick you up at eleven thirty. So what are you doing here?"

His daughter turned back around, her eyes flashing, her cheeks stained red. She sneered at her father as he zipped up his pants. "I asked Grandma to drop me off here after church. I wanted to surprise you. But I guess the surprise is on me, huh?"

"Surprise me?" His voice was flat and hollow.

Libby's heart felt hollow, too. As if it might pop like a bubble and disappear forever.

"Yeah, I was thinking I'd stay here for a few weeks," Rachel said. "Give us kind of a trial run, you know? Glad I didn't bother bringing my suitcase in from the car." She picked up the backpack and jerked open the door. "Take me home, would you please, Grandma? I'm not staying here now. I'm not staying here ever."

Rachel walked out into the storm.

"Rachel!" Tom tried to follow, but Anne stepped in his way, blocking his path with her palm to his chest.

"You haven't changed a bit, have you? I kept telling George you'd finally grown up. But now I see I was wrong. I gave you too much credit. Connie would be so ashamed of you."

Tom wouldn't talk to Libby at all on the drive to her parents' house, and she struggled with every breath to hold it together. She just didn't know what to say. The venom in Anne's voice had poisoned her, too.

She and Tom hadn't done anything wrong. They were adults, and she loved him. But that didn't matter. For Rachel to learn about them that way, to discover them in that situation, was unbearable, even to Libby.

Tom was in flames on the inside. She could feel it. But he wouldn't say a word. With every mile he retreated, away from her, away from all the goodness they'd found.

Because now it was tarnished. Even she could see that. No matter how much he might care for her, no matter how much love they might have built between them, she'd just cost him his chance to get Rachel back.

She was still wearing his flannel shirt, and a pair of drawstring exercise pants he'd pulled from the closet after Anne and Rachel had driven away. Her glorious wench dress was stuffed into a black plastic garbage bag.

He pulled up in front of her house and didn't even shift the truck out of drive. He just pushed his foot against the brake with all his might.

"I'm sorry, Libby." His voice was scratchy as sandpaper.

She turned his way, clutching the plastic bag. "I wish you'd talk to me about this."

"There's nothing to talk about. It's a total clusterfuck. All of it. I forgot my priorities. I'm sorry you got caught up in that, but this isn't going to work."

"That's not true. Rachel will come around. She was surprised, that's all."

He looked at her as if he wasn't sure why she was still there. "She's not your daughter. It's really none of your business."

His words were brutal and raw, and she wanted to fight him. She wanted to remind him that what they had was good. And it was real. He'd let her inside his life, and he'd made Rachel her business the moment he asked for help with that goddamned collage.

But she knew he wouldn't hear her, so she got out of the truck and slammed the door. He drove away and left her standing in the rain.

CHAPTER *twenty-six*

There wasn't enough booze in his house to get him as drunk as he needed to be. It took a lot. He remembered that from the months after Connie's accident. But he drank what he had in the house. Four beers and a shot of Jack Daniel's. Not a bad buzz for four o'clock on a Sunday afternoon. He kept waiting for George to show up and throw gasoline on this fire. But he didn't.

Evening came. It got dark, and somewhere around midnight Tom must have slept because he woke up at six in the morning with a neck stiff from lying on the couch, and a head splitting from alcohol and self-loathing.

He'd been here before, in this ugly place. The misery was comforting in its familiarity. He knew how to behave in this space. Knew what to expect. Nothing but more of the same.

Tom ate leftovers from his refrigerator, took a shower, and thought about going to get more food. He thought about watching television, or raking some leaves, or calling Dr. Brandt. But he did none of that. He wasn't really sure what he did, but suddenly it was dark again, so he got undressed and climbed into bed.

Lying in the quiet darkness, with the scent of Libby's perfume wafting up from the sheets, all those thoughts he had blockaded from his mind for the last day and a half broke through. The numbness gave way like an avalanche, and the pain grew chisel sharp. But he understood this kind of pain better now. He knew he simply had to feel it, ride it out, or suffocate from it.

The truth was, he loved Libby Hamilton. With all his heart. And in a long line of mistakes, letting her go would be the biggest of his life.

Losing Connie had been an accident. A tragic, unavoidable twist of fate, but this thing with Libby, and what had happened with Rachel—that was stuff he could fix. Hurt feelings and misunderstandings could be talked through. Dr. Brandt had taught him that.

He and Rachel were learning how to do that together. She was old enough to understand what his feelings for Libby meant. In fact, the worst thing he could do would be to behave as if his relationship with her was less than it was. Libby had shaken him back into his own life. And while what happened yesterday morning in his kitchen had been regrettable, it wasn't a tragedy. It didn't have to devastate anyone. It was an obstacle to overcome, not a life-defining moment.

Anne was wrong.

He *had* grown up. He wasn't a coward, and he wouldn't hide behind misdirected guilt or self-inflicted shame. Connie would never have let him do that. He owed it to her memory, and he owed it to Rachel, to push past this.

And he owed it to himself to make things right with Libby.

Tom was up before dawn the next morning, not that he'd slept much. He'd spent most of his night chasing visions, and an hour or more just pacing around the bedroom wondering if Libby was asleep, or if she was thinking of him. He'd nearly sent her a text, but it seemed too juvenile. He'd sent one to Rachel, though, at one in the morning.

We need to talk.

She'd answered immediately.

I know. I can meet you at the coffee shop next to the high school at 7 a.m. Good?

She was willing to meet him, anxious to talk. That had to be a good sign. But he was nearly sick to his stomach as he drove there the next morning.

He walked in and saw her sitting with a tall, dark-haired boy. She was wearing a beret and looked far too grown up. They both stood up when Tom came near.

"Um, hi, Dad. This is Jake." She gestured to the boy.

They sized each other up, and Tom wasn't sure who this was more awkward for, because certainly Rachel must have filled this kid in.

After a slight pause, Jake held out his hand. "Mr. Murphy. It's nice to meet you."

Tom shook it. "You, too."

Rachel blushed. "Um, thanks for waiting with me, Jake. I'll see you later, okay?"

"Sure." He gave Tom a nod and loped away.

"Nice kid," Tom said.

"Yeah, he is. You want to sit down?"

They slid into a booth.

"Rachel, about Sunday, I—"

"No, Dad, let me go first. Please?"

He was relieved by her insistence, since he had no idea where to start.

Rachel picked up a sugar packet from the tabletop and twisted it in her hands. "I think I owe you an apology."

If she had tasered him, he could not have been more shocked.

"I should have called you first to let you know I was coming. And I shouldn't have freaked out like that. It's just that, well, you freaked me out."

"You freaked me out a little bit, too. I had intended to say something to you about Libby sooner. I just didn't know how to get it out there."

"Well, it was certainly all out there in the kitchen. I think my retinas are scorched for life."

Rachel had Connie's sense of humor. He wasn't sure that was such a good thing for him at the moment.

"It was unfortunate for you to see . . . that. But I want you to understand, my relationship with Libby has nothing to do with why I let you make your own choice about moving back. I've been very clear about wanting you home."

"I know. That's what Dr. Brandt said."

Tasered again. "When did you talk to her?"

"Yesterday. I asked Grandma to take me to see her." She picked up the paper coffee cup from the table and took a sip.

When did she get old enough to drink coffee?

"What else did Dr. Brandt say?" Waiting on that response was like waiting for test results. He wanted to know, and yet, he didn't.

But Rachel shrugged. "Oh, you know her. She just kept asking me how I felt about things."

If he wasn't so wired and nervous right now, Tom might have laughed at that. As it was, all he could do was ask, "And? How do you feel about . . . things?"

Rachel gave a big, ponderous sigh. "I've thought a lot about all of this, and I guess I have to understand that you're not really that old."

"Old?" Fly ball, left field.

"Yeah. I mean, so it kind of makes sense that you'd want to be with somebody that you like. Part of me was really mad the other morning because it felt like you were cheating on Mom, or that you'd forgotten her, but I don't think Mom would want you to be all by yourself forever."

Grown men didn't cry. And if they did, they sure as hell wouldn't do it in a coffee shop.

Rachel took another sip of coffee. "And I guess if I had to pick somebody, Miss Ham—um, Libby is kind of cool."

Tom would have fought her on Libby if he'd had to, would have worked to help Rachel understand there was a place for both of them in his life. But now he didn't have to. Gratitude flooded through his limbs, filling him with a long-absent contentment. He was going to have to send that Dr. Brandt a very nice fruit basket come Christmastime.

"I don't know what to say, Rachel. I'm so proud of you for being grown up about this." He wished he could claim some credit for what a wonderful young lady she was turning out to be.

"I'm kind of proud of you, too, Dad."

Yet another jolt to his system. He was going to have heart failure any minute now. "Proud of me?"

Rachel nodded, her blond waves bouncing slightly. "You've come a long way in the last few months. I like you again, now that you're not being a big, bossy jerk."

Just like her mother. Compliment him with an insult so that he couldn't feel too good about it. But he did feel good. Because she was proud of him.

"I don't really appreciate you calling me that, young lady." He probably should have sounded stern, but he was so goddamned relieved, he couldn't help but smile.

She sipped her coffee. "I'll make a note of that. But one thing you should know. If it's all the same to you, I think I might stick to that other plan of moving home after I have my license. Not because of any of this, but, well, I don't want to be that far away from Jake."

This would probably be a good time for a paternal lecture about responsible behavior and good judgment, but given his track record, it seemed a little hypocritical. And the only part of that statement he cared about was the bit about moving home. "That would be fine, Rachel. Come home whenever you're ready."

She nodded, and a little smirk tilted at the corner of her mouth. "I'll call first."

CHAPTER *twenty-seven*

Libby stood at the doorway of the ice-cream parlor surveying the remnants of Marti and Dante's wedding. Like every other aspect of her life, this now seemed an insurmountable mess for her to clean up.

The roses had wilted and turned brown with no water, a sink full of dirty dishes smelled funky and sour, and the cloudy December day outside painted everything in a sad, gray palette. Everything about this place had lost its luster. Or maybe that was just her. Every place she'd looked since Sunday morning seemed to be missing color and warmth and invitation.

She'd waited all day yesterday for Tom to call, or send a text, or even a smoke signal. Anything to let her know where things stood between him and Rachel.

And between him and Libby.

He'd left her standing in the rain without a backward glance. At least Seth had the decency to *pretend* he was coming back. But Tom Murphy was not one to give encouragement where none was intended.

She'd played the scene out in her head, over and over. Rachel walking in, the look of shock on her face, and Tom's complete emotional shut-down afterward. She'd never felt so useless or so helpless as she had that morning.

If there was any way to fix this, she sure didn't know what it was. Her heart was broken down and rusted on the side of the road.

She set the bucket of cleaning supplies on the floor and walked over to the chair sitting in the middle of the room. The very chair on which she'd seduced Tom Murphy. It was nothing special to look at now. Just an ordinary folding chair. Practically disposable.

Like the time they'd spent together.

At least she knew she wasn't pregnant. Her dependable cycle had made its presence known that morning. No loose ends to worry about.

Libby folded the chair and leaned it against the wall. Then she stacked all the others, mixing them up so she couldn't even be certain which chair it had been.

It didn't help.

She couldn't stop thinking about him, wondering, reassessing. It left her raw and tense. Her dad would say she was as nervous as a porcupine in a roomful of balloons. And he'd be right. She thought about Tom so intensely, she could practically hear the sound of his truck rumbling into the parking lot.

Or maybe . . .

She looked out the window, and there he was, climbing down from the cab. Her stomach flipped and flopped as he made his way closer and came through the door.

He looked good in his old jeans and his brown jacket. But then again, he always looked good.

He stood for a minute, just gazing at her with his hands in his pockets. He didn't smile. Neither did she.

"Hi," he finally said.

"Hi." Question after question tumbled through her mind, but she'd be damned if she'd ask. It was his turn to talk.

It took a lifetime before he finally did. "I'm sorry, Libby."

It wasn't enough. His words were as gray as the sky outside. "About which thing?"

"All of it. For every mistake. But for starters, I'm sorry for leaving you standing out there in the rain. No good man would've done a thing like that to a woman he loves."

Woman he loves? That had a little color to it. But still not enough. "You're right. That was pretty shitty," she said.

Everything inside her leaned toward him, but she stayed put.

He took a step closer. "And no good man would've left you dangling for so long with no phone call, either."

"Yeah, that was shitty, too." It was, and she should be furious. But right now he was moving closer, and she just wanted to understand what he was building up to. Was he here to apologize, or to say good-bye? He never *had* been very articulate.

Where was a collage when you needed one?

He took another few steps until he was standing right in front of her, close enough that she could see those pale little freckles on his cheek.

"But hopefully a good man knows that when he makes a mistake, it's up to him to fix it." He spoke softly, his voice rich and tender.

Her heart sped up as time slowed down.

"Hopefully," she whispered.

He looked at her mouth, and then back to her eyes.

He took his hands out of his pockets and slid them down her arms until their fingers intertwined.

"I've made a mess of things again. I know that. One thing I've learned this past year is that I can power through just about anything. But the one mistake I could never get over would be losing you. You've got a hold on my heart, Libby Hamilton. I don't want to be without you."

That didn't sound like good-bye at all. It sounded like forever.

"I don't want to be without you either," she said.

"Are you sure? I'm a work in progress, you know." He squeezed her hands in his own.

"I know. And I'm sure." And she was.

He smiled at last. "You could do better than me. There are other guys out there with nicer trucks."

"Yeah, but there's just something about yours."

All the tension and worry left her body, replaced by certainty and hope. He kissed her then, at last, and colors filled the room.

Tom breathed against her cheek. "God, Libby. I'm so sorry about the other day. I just didn't know what to do."

"I know. Me neither." She wrapped her arms tightly around his waist. "But talk to me next time. You can't shut me out. You have to let me help."

"Let's hope there's never a next time. Not for something like that." He kissed her again, as if his life depended on it.

Then she captured his face in her hands and looked into his big brown eyes. "I love you, Tom. You know I do. But I don't want to be the cause of friction between you and Rachel."

He nodded. "I know. I had coffee with her this morning, though. We're good. She says you're kind of cool."

"Really?" Her heart lifted, joy rising.

"Really." His smile was earnest and pleased. She blinked back happy tears.

"So . . . there is nothing to keep us apart?"

Tom smiled. "Nothing at all."

She shook her head in blissful bewilderment. "Who knew my little sister was so smart?"

"Marti?" His head tilted.

Libby nodded, and smiled. "Yes. She's been telling me all along that true love is spontaneous and powerful and impossible to ignore."

Tom laughed and pulled her closer still. "Yes, it is. Speaking of spontaneous, where's that chair?"

Her senses thrummed at the thought but she shook her head. "Uh-uh. Sorry. I'm out of commission today. By the way, you owe me six bucks. I told you my body is like clockwork."

He looked back at her, realization dawning over his face. "Are you certain?"

"Positive."

He kissed one cheek, then the other. "That's for the best, I guess." He smiled down at her. "But just for the record, I'm planning to marry you anyway."

ACKNOWLEDGMENTS

First and foremost, thank you to my family, for taking care of life without any help from me while I wrote this book. Your support and enthusiasm makes all the difference in the world. Without you, none of the rest matters.

Thank you to my writing posse, for making this job fun, even when it's not. Thank you for the good advice, the encouraging cards, the phone calls from the ledge, and the shared celebrations. A special shout-out to McQ for sending me a Kip Moore video just when I needed a little inspiration. Turns out there really *is* somethin' 'bout a truck. . . .

Thank you to Nalini Akolekar, Kelli Martin, Melody Guy, and the entire Montlake team for doing the million and twelve little things it takes to create one big, beautiful book. Working with you is the best, and I am grateful for everything you do.

And finally, a heartfelt thank-you to the readers who enjoy my work, send lovely notes, and recommend my books to friends. You bring me joy. I hope to do the same for you.

ABOUT THE AUTHOR

ALLIE GADZIEMSKI

Past or present, Tracy Brogan loves romance. She spends half of her time writing funny contemporary stories about ordinary people finding extraordinary love and the other half of her time writing sexy historical novels full of political intrigue, damsels causing distress, and the occasional man in a kilt. She is a two-time Romance Writers of America® Golden Heart finalist, and she has won several RWA awards.

During rare moments when she's not writing, or thinking about writing, Tracy enjoys time with her family, traveling, and spoiling her dogs. She loves to hear from readers, so please visit her website at tracybrogan.com, or find her at facebook.com/author-tracybrogan or twitter.com/@tracybrogan.